IF HE DIES
BEFORE HE WAKES . . .

The huge front door was just a crack open, and Jean rang the bell, waited for a moment, then stepped in. The long paneled hall was in the Scottish baronial style, with elaborate carvings on the heavy oak staircase. She peered into the vast living room on the right. Then there was a sound in the hall. Stella appeared at the door of the downstairs bedroom. The look on her face made Jean gasp. In a second she ran up to her.

"Stella, what's the matter. Why. . . ?"

Stella drew a long, rattling breath. She couldn't speak, but took Jean's arm and almost pushed her into the bedroom. It was very quiet in there, and Stella started to shake and made a low noise like some animal in dreadful pain. Jean leapt toward the cot. Stella's son was lying at a strange position . . .

A NASTY
BIT OF MURDER

A NASTY BIT OF MURDER

A Dr. Jean Montrose Mystery

C. F. Roe

A SIGNET BOOK

SIGNET
Published by the Penguin Group
Penguin Books USA Inc., 375 Hudson Street,
New York, New York 10014, U.S.A.
Penguin Books Ltd, 27 Wrights Lane,
London W8 5TZ, England
Penguin Books Australia Ltd, Ringwood
Victoria, Australia
Penguin Books Canada Ltd, 10 Alcorn Avenue,
Toronto, Ontario, Canada M4V 3B2
Penguin Books (N.Z.) Ltd, 182–190 Wairau Road,
Auckland 10, New Zealand

Penguin Books Ltd, Registered Offices:
Harmondsworth, Middlesex, England

First published in the United States by Signet, an imprint of New American
Library, a division of Penguin Books USA Inc. Previously published in Great
Britain by Headline Book Publishing PLC under the title *The Lumsden Baby*.

First Signet Printing, December, 1992
10 9 8 7 6 5 4 3 2 1

Chapter One

"Come on, Fiona, get up!" It was the third time Jean Montrose had called her daughter, and her voice was beginning to get an edge on it. Still in her faded blue terry-cloth dressing gown, Jean padded from the basement door back to the kitchen and filled up the electric kettle. Through the small window, she could see Mr. Forrest's prize border sheep standing in a white clump in the middle of the last remaining green field within the city of Perth. Out there it looked like a typical cold September morning, and Jean shivered, retied the belt of her dressing gown and patted her tummy. It was a pity she was so short; whenever she ate too much it showed up instantly at her waist. Last month they'd taken the caravan to France for ten days and eaten too much and too well.

Fiona appeared at the top of the basement steps, wordless, her black hair sticking up all over the place, her pyjama front unbuttoned. She came past her mother and headed for the stairs, looking like the morning after Hogmanay. Her friends, the ones she'd gone out with last night, would not have recognized the pretty, carefully turned-out trainee manager who'd kept them laughing all evening with her stories.

"When did you get home, dear?" Jean spoke in

a motherly, uncritical tone, putting two pieces of bread in the toaster. With her other hand she swirled some hot water in the bottom of the teapot.

"About three." Fiona went up the stairs toward the bathroom as if every step hurt. Jean shook her head. Those kids! Jean's own mother, God bless her, wouldn't have spoken to her for a week if she'd ever come home that late, even at the age of twenty-one . . . Well, times certainly had changed, but thank heaven both Fiona and Lisbie were good girls, she didn't have to worry about that.

Jean looked at the old, square-faced clock on the kitchen wall. A quarter to eight; she set out a little gold-colored metal tray with a plate, a cup, sugar and filled the little milk jug from the bottle on the counter. The toaster popped like a jack-in-the-box, and then she was on her way slowly upstairs, carefully balancing the tray. She could feel the belt on her dressing gown loosening again, but there was nothing she could do about it. By the time she reached the landing she was holding herself together with the tray against her tummy.

She pushed the door of their bedroom open with her hip.

"Steven? Here's your breakfast." Steven answered with a grunt, then in a muffled, annoyed voice. "Leave it on the table, I'll get it in a minute."

"It's time you were up, Steven, it's almost eight." Her voice was affectionate and firm. She pulled the curtains open; the clouds were low and scudding, and Jean could almost smell the rain waiting to fall from them. Her husband had been late at a sales meeting and hadn't got home until after eleven, so no wonder he was tired. It didn't occur to Jean that she herself had gone out on a call at one in the morning and hadn't got home until two.

She trotted back down the stairs, putting an extra twist in her belt. She must have looked really silly a minute ago, she thought, with her dressing gown hanging open . . .

Just as she was thinking that Lisbie would be late too if she didn't hurry up, her second daughter emerged from her room, looking awake enough, although Jean knew that both girls had come home at the same time. Lisbie kissed her mother on the cheek. She looked like a younger version of her mother, plump, pretty and rounded, unlike her older sister who was slim and darker. Like Jean, she had understanding brown eyes, always ready to break into a smile. Unlike her mother, Lisbie had a little gap between her front teeth, which made her a bit shy with new people, but she soon forgot about it, as did they. Lisbie was more affectionate and gentler than her older sister Fiona, and would rather just leave if an argument threatened. The two girls, however, got along well most of the time, sharing friends and frequently going out together.

Jean had the cutting board out, and was chopping up some leeks for the lunchtime soup.

"You'd better get moving, Lisbie. Your sister's in the bathroom, so you're going to have to wait a minute. Do you want a buttery or some toast?"

Lisbie made a face. "Just tea, thanks. I'm in a hurry . . . Why does Fiona always take so long? Gordon's going to yell at me again if I'm late."

Jean poured Lisbie's tea, then opened her appointment book on the table. Her pen hovered over the list of half a dozen names. Mrs. Cattanach; she had to go and see if the cortisone cream had helped the eczema between her buttocks. The poor old thing, and to have it there, of all places. Dod Grant; he couldn't sleep for the pain in his hip and the hospital said it would be almost two years before he could have a replacement . . .

Maybe she could get him a bed in Dundee, or Glasgow, except they were probably just as booked-up there. Anyway she had to go and see how he was doing. Why was it that the people she had to visit always lived at the opposite ends of the town?

The phone rang. Jean ran to pick it up, hoping it wouldn't wake her husband again, but he'd already picked up the bedside phone, and sounded really grumpy. "It's for you!" he snapped, and Jean could hear the phone being slammed down. Poor Steven, it wasn't easy for him, being married to a general practitioner.

It was Eleanor, the secretary she shared with her partner.

"Just a second, Eleanor, till I get my pen . . . Okay . . . Right, I know about them, any new ones?" Jean wrote the names of the patients she had to visit. "The Lumsden baby? Did she say if it was urgent? Okay, if there's no rush I'll see her after the surgery. Phone Stella back, tell her I'll be there be-tween eleven and twelve . . . I know the address, we were there for dinner a couple of weeks ago."

Fiona came down, transformed. Her black hair was in a short, fashionable cut, and she wore a smart gray skirt with a dark green lambswool jumper which showed off her small, pert figure. Her normal com-plexion was so fresh and clear, Jean wondered why she bothered with makeup; even so, she could never understand how Fiona could go from bedraggled to beautiful so quickly.

Twenty minutes later, Jean had packed Fiona off, and Lisbie was desperately trying to find her car keys. She worked as a secretary for a lawyer in a small firm in town, and if the traffic was at all slow, she was going to be late. Jean helped her to look for the keys, and finally found them inside a glove on the table.

"Off you go now," said Jean distractedly, handing her the keys.

"Could you lend me ten pounds until Friday?" asked Lisbie. "I spent all I had last night."

Jean rummaged in her bag and came out with a ten-pound note. "Here, don't forget to give it back." She tried to look stern.

The house was quiet with the girls gone. It was now eight-thirty, and Steven really had to get up, and she had to get dressed and out of the house. Jean bustled up the stairs, thinking about the Lumsden baby. Poor little creature!

Steven had gone back to sleep, the breakfast tray sat by the bed, untouched. Jean never wasted any time thinking about what she was going to wear; her dark blue suit and a white silk blouse, that would do, although she had to pull her tummy in to fasten the waistband of her skirt. She turned sideways to sneak a look at herself in the mirror. Not terrific. She was going to have to do some serious dieting. Actually, if she'd just eat at mealtimes and not nibble, maybe that would be enough. She put some cream on her face and puckered up her lips for the lipstick. Maybe she should make more of an effort with her appearance—Steven had been making comments again recently—her hair was graying a bit at the sides, but with a little pat she covered it up with a dark curl so she could barely see the gray . . .

The wrinkles around her eyes really showed now, especially when she was tired, but at her age, she thought, you can't reasonably expect to have the complexion of a nineteen-year-old. Thank God she didn't have arthritis, or anything else that would slow her down.

Steven had to get to work, but if she shook him awake he was quite liable to say something nasty. She wound up the extra-loud alarm with the two bells on the top, set it to ring in five minutes, put it on the little shelf just above his head and crept out. She didn't want to be around when it went off.

Jean's little Renault was her pride and joy; the only thing it needed was power steering; wrestling that wheel around all day, with all the parking she had to do, really tired her sometimes. Steven's Rover had power steering, but it was a bigger car anyway, in keeping with his status as manager of the Scone Glassworks. He'd let Jean use it a couple of times, and it was really easy, for such a big car.

Jean drove her Renault slowly down the hill, her foot resting on the brake, past the other quiet, red-gray sandstone semidetached houses in Argyll Crescent. At the bottom she waited briefly for a gap in the traffic on Alford Street; she could see the low clouds shrouding Kinnoull hill, and the air felt chilly and damp. It would rain before the morning was out, Jean was sure of it. She wound up the window and switched on the heater, although it always took a while to warm up, and she would be at the surgery first. Her partner Helen was going to be seeing patients too, this morning, and Jean enjoyed working with her. Helen Inkster was clever, with a good knowledge of rare syndromes and esoteric diseases, and Jean was always glad to have her around when something unusual came up. In the same way, Helen valued Jean's robust common sense and surprisingly accurate insights; the two of them made a good team.

Jean parked in Williams Street, just past the corner, opposite the surgery. It had begun to rain, and the drops were beading on the windscreen. Jean had forgotten to bring her raincoat, so she hurried up the few steps to the door of the surgery and pushed the door open with her bag.

Eleanor was sitting behind her desk opposite the door. There wasn't much room, and she felt the draught every time the door opened. "You're going to have quite a crowd this morning," she said. Eleanor was large, comfortable and competent, and seemed to know every single person in the county, let alone the practice. "Would you like a quick cuppa afore you start?"

"It's starting to rain, and that'll keep a good few of them home," replied Jean. "Yes, I will, please, and a biscuit too, if there is one. I didn't have much breakfast."

There was the usual collection of coughs and colds and sore throats, and Jean dispatched them all with brisk efficiency.

A boy came in to the examining room; Jean had heard him coughing in the waiting room. He looked about eighteen, thin, with bad acne. Jean knew his mother, who had been in several times because of depression. The boy didn't look well, and admitted he'd been getting quite breathless over the last week. When Jean listened to his chest, there wasn't much air getting into the left lung, and when she tapped his chest with her fingers it didn't have the normal hollow resonance.

"Did your mother come with you?" she asked,

reaching for the phone. "You've got pleurisy, and you'll have to go to the hospital."

He shook his head, but Jean was already through to the admitting houseman at the Infirmary, a Dr. Ramasandra. She explained about the boy, and immediately ran into the usual problem.

"I'm very sorry, Dr. Montrose, very sorry indeed, but there is a very great shortage of beds and we do not have any vacant right now," he told her firmly in a quick, singsong voice. "Maybe if you try again in the next week . . ."

"Finding a bed is your problem," replied Jean tartly. "What I'm telling you is that this boy needs to be in the hospital. I'm sending him over in a wee while, as soon as we have the forms done. It'll give you time to find a bed for him. And he's going to need the fluid drawn off his chest this morning, of course."

The houseman sighed. There was never any point arguing with Dr. Montrose.

"Right then, doctor, I will try to find a bed somewhere. Would you kindly tell me the boy's name?"

"Jimmy Castle, eighteen years old, no previous hospital admissions," replied Jean. She smiled at the boy, who was beginning to look apprehensive, and put the phone down. "That's Dr. Ramasandra, you'll like him, he'll take good care of you. Now, where can we find your mother to take you there?"

Jimmy's mother was at work, and his father wasn't home, so Jean finished up taking the boy to the hospital herself when she'd finished her surgery. It was no trouble, because the hospital was on the way to the Lumsdens' house.

"Now, this is where you get your form to fill in," said Jean, heading for the admissions desk. "You sit down and tell the nurse everything she wants to know.'' She smiled at the nurse. ''He'll be going up to Medical,'' she said. ''Dr. Ramasandra knows all about him.''

Just to be sure, Jean helped him to fill out the hospital admission form, and finally delivered him personally to Dr. Ramasandra up on the medical floor before going back to her car. It had stopped raining, and the low clouds had passed on, leaving the air with that clarity which always made her happy to be living in Perth, and not in some smog-infested industrial town. Standing in the hospital car park, searching for her car keys in her handbag, she could see a tree-lined bend of the river Tay, and beyond that the iron-gray hills of the Trossachs to the west, some still with occasional purple streaks of heather, surmounted by Ben Chonzie, almost twenty miles away, its peak already covered with snow.

Jean drove carefully out of the car park. Only last week some fool driver had come hurtling out between the parked cars and almost hit her . . . She pointed her car downhill, past where she could see the high wall of the prison, and swung onto the Dunkeld road. There wasn't much traffic and she buzzed along, making good time. She put a tape in the player; the music always soothed her, helped her to think, and calmed her down during hectic times.

The Lumsden baby, little Magnus—it was really a sad story. Born six months before, he had developed epilepsy soon after birth; it wasn't very severe, and controlled pretty well with small doses of phenobarbitone, but still . . . Dempster, his father, the future Lord Aviemore, whose bouts of alcoholism were getting worse and more frequent, seemed to be having great difficulty accepting the fact that he had a flawed son and heir. Only a couple of weeks ago, when Steven and Jean had gone there for dinner, Dempster was already half-drunk when they arrived. Jean quivered with embarrassment when she remembered what he'd said to his wife, Stella, referring to Magnus, who was being shown off to the guests: ''Let's throw the little bugger down the drain and start all over again.'' Stella had handled the situation well, laughing the whole thing off, but it had not been a comfortable evening.

From time to time Magnus would get a cold, and invariably it would develop into bronchitis or even, on one occasion, into pneumonia. Poor Stella, it was really a shame, living in that huge house, with only a woman coming in twice a week to help her keep the place clean. She had to take care of just about everything herself. Her sister Amanda probably helped when she was there, but she didn't visit that often. Stella came from a county family near Inverness, where Dempster's father lived in the ancestral castle and still managed the estates. And she was so beautiful, it had taken Jean's breath away the first time she saw her. Stella was tall, willowy, with classical dark looks and a perfect, oval face with the kind of complexion women would kill for. She had married Dempster in Inverness about a year and a half ago, and he'd brought her back home to Perth. Although many of their friends were landed gentry, the Lumsdens included people like Steven and Jean and some of their neighbors in their social activities. Stella had stunned the local people with her kindness and civic-mindedness as well as her beauty, and most of the men in their circle had openly fallen in love with her. But she was a quiet, self-possessed woman, untouched by any breath of scandal, in spite of her husband's increasingly frequent absences on drinking sprees.

With these thoughts in mind, Jean turned off the main road a couple of miles further on to a quiet street, past a grocery, an outdoor fruit and vegetable market with wooden trestles loaded with great baskets of tomatoes, avocados, grapes and flowers. She slowed as she passed a launderette, and just beyond that she turned into a small, secluded road with three sizeable houses, two on the left, one on the right. All three were about the same size, set back from the street by well-kept front gardens. The Honorable Dempster Lumsden had built them on part of his estate, just over a year before, keeping the big house and a few acres of farmland for himself. The gossip at the time was that they needed the money, and Jean knew that Dempster was a big spender and had made some dubious investments. Still, with the kind of money his father had, Jean couldn't feel too sorry for them.

She knew all the people on the street; the first house on the left was empty; Graham Ross, the manager of the National Bank, and his wife Evelyn lived in the one next to it. Graham's old Jaguar was parked outside, sleek and well cared for, with his wife's small Austin behind it. Graham must have come home for an early lunch. Jean wondered if any of her own brood were coming home, and if they would remember to put the soup on to heat. Opposite the Rosses lived the Armstrongs: Keith, Danielle, and their two children. Keith had taken over a hand-weaving workshop and studio on Commerce Quay near the harbor.

Past the three houses, the road narrowed into a short rhododendron-lined drive, which swung round

in front of the house under a portico large enough
to take a coach and four. Jean parked under the huge
cast-iron lantern over the entrance, behind Stella
Lumsden's Volvo, and wondered again how on earth
Stella managed to keep up that big house. Surely
they could afford to have more help, but maybe that
was how Stella wanted it. She was a pretty indepen-
dent person.

The huge front door was just a crack open, and
Jean rang the bell, waited for a moment, then
stepped in. The long panelled hall was in the classic
Scottish baronial style, with elaborate carvings on
the heavy oak staircase, which curved upwards to the
left. There should be a butler here, Jean thought, and
maids and cooks scurrying about . . . She paused in
the hall, and peered into the vast living room on the
right, with its carved cross-beams and tall, diamond-
paned windows. A tiny fire crackled insignificantly
in a fireplace that could have comfortably accom-
modated an ox. There was nobody in the dark old
leather armchairs or at the table at the far end of the
room. Jean thought Stella might be in the kitchen,
but there she found only four full grocery bags on
the kitchen table; Stella must have just come in. Before Jean could wonder why she'd been out shopping
with a sick baby at home, there was a sound in the
hall. Jean looked out, and Stella appeared at the door
of the downstairs bedroom, down at the end of the
hall. The look on her face made Jean gasp. In a
second she ran up to her.

"Stella, what's the matter? Why . . . ?"

Stella drew a long, rattling breath. She couldn't
speak, but took Jean's arm and almost pushed her
into the bedroom. It was very quiet in there; the
baby was in its cot with the bar down, the Mickey

Mouse pillow in the corner. Stella started to shake, and made a low noise like some animal in dreadful pain. Jean leapt toward the cot. The baby's head was at a strange angle . . . It had been smashed in, one crooked eye gazing sightlessly out in a grotesque stare. Jean's eyes were drawn irresistibly to a round, reddish stain about the size of a small melon on the wall next to the window. There were bits of pink matter stuck to the wallpaper, and two little zigzag runnels of blood went halfway down to the floor.

Jean stood there, appalled, unable to move. At that moment, the doorbell sounded with a strident, urgent ring.

Chapter Two

The two women looked at each other, and Stella couldn't prevent herself letting out a quiet sob of fear.

"You stay here," said Jean quickly. "I'll answer the door." She went back into the hall. Evelyn Ross, Stella's neighbor, had stepped in; Jean hadn't shut the door behind her.

"It's the Wee Doc herself!" said Evelyn cheerfully. "I thought that was your car outside. I was just bringing Stella some trifle I've made . . ." She stopped suddenly, noticing Jean's shocked face. "What's the matter?" Stella came slowly out of the bedroom and looked dully at her.

"Magnus . . . Magnus . . ." She couldn't say anymore, and Evelyn quickly put down the bowl with the trifle in it, and held out her arms. Stella almost fell forward, burying her head in Evelyn's shoulder. Evelyn looked questioningly at Jean, stroking Stella's long hair.

"Magnus is dead," said Jean, recovering her voice. "There's been a dreadful accident." She shook her head, as if she couldn't believe what she'd just said. Pull yourself together, she told herself, you have a lot of things to do. She reached for the hall phone, dialed the number of the main police station and asked for Detective Inspector Niven. "Yes, Inspector *Douglas* Niven," she said sharply. "How many Inspector Nivens do you have?" There was a delay. Jean looked through the window. It was threatening rain again.

"Doug? Jean Montrose here . . . You know the Lumsdens' house, part of the Lossie Estate, down the Dunkeld road? Well, you'd better come out here. Yes, it's a homicide, a baby . . . Right, we won't touch anything."

She put the phone down, turned quickly to Stella and spoke in a low, urgent tone. "Is there anybody else here in the house that you know of?"

Stella put her hand up to her throat, and her eyes dilated. She shook her head, unable to speak. Evelyn looked back fearfully at the open door. Jean suppressed a shiver of apprehension and went into the living room, returning with a large iron poker. She felt better with that in her hand. If she got the chance, she'd make mincemeat out of the man cowardly enough to kill a baby in cold blood.

Jean made a big effort to appear calm; she knew that Stella and Evelyn depended on her and would follow her lead, but she had trouble keeping her voice steady.

"Evelyn, would you like to make some tea? I think we'll need a big pot; we're going to have a lot of company in a few minutes."

Stella sat down suddenly on the big sofa in the hall, and started to weep silently into her hands, her fingers in her hair, twisting and grasping the dark strands.

"You stay here, Stella," said Jean softly, but she wasn't sure if Stella heard her. Slowly she went back into the bedroom. It seemed even stiller than before, but now there was an aura of pure evil that had invaded every corner of the room. She forced herself to approach the cot. The baby was wearing a blue jacket with buttons down the front, but no nappy. He looked as if he'd been swung against the wall, then put back in the cot. Jean looked around; she took care not to disturb anything, but she knew that at some point the coroner would be asking her questions, and she wanted to fix the scene exactly in her mind.

It was a big room, the only downstairs bedroom in the house. Jean knew that at night Magnus slept upstairs with his parents, and downstairs during the day, so Stella didn't have to run upstairs all the time. And with Magnus being epileptic and often ill with one thing or another, he needed a lot of attention. Gently she moved his arm; it offered no resistance; rigor mortis hadn't set in yet; the murder had been recent. Jean got a crawling feeling under her skin. The killer might still be here, hiding in a cupboard, or even upstairs, waiting . . . She went back into the hall. Evelyn was sitting silently next to Stella, her hand on her arm.

"What happened, Stella?" asked Jean quietly. "Do you know who . . . did this?"

Stella raised her head. Her beautiful eyes were red and glistening with tears. "I just got in from shopping, just before you came in . . . There was . . . nobody here . . . I went to see if Magnus was . . . all right, then I came up to the cot . . ." Stella got up, and her voice rose. "Oh God, Magnus, who could have done this? Who? Who?"

"Where's Dempster?" asked Jean suddenly. "We'll have to tell him . . ."

"I don't know," replied Stella, sitting down again

in the restlessness of her anguish. "He hasn't been home for three days . . . I suppose he's in Glasgow, that's where he always goes when he has a bout . . ."

"Well, Douglas Niven's people'll know where to find him," said Jean.

"Is there anything I can do?" Evelyn said quietly. "Should I go home?"

"I think you'd better stay here," said Jean. "The police'll want to know if you saw anybody suspicious wandering around, stuff like that, and anyway you're in charge of the tea." Evelyn was being very calm, Jean thought. Lucky for Stella to have such a good friend for a neighbor.

Suddenly there was a noise from the kitchen, and Evelyn screamed, but it was only the kettle starting to whistle. Evelyn went through to take care of it.

They only heard the siren for a few seconds when the ambulance came round the corner, its final decrescendo howl almost drowning the scrunch of tires and the squeal of brakes as it pulled up outside, followed by a police car. The three women remained fixed, almost petrified, as the ambulance men came running up to the front door. They had been alerted by radio, and came in with their stretcher, running right into the house, but the Wee Doc stopped them in their tracks.

"You'd better just wait," she said, the inertia suddenly lifting from her shoulders. "There's nothing you can do now . . ."

The ambulance driver, a lanky, long-jawed man, looked disappointed, and the light died in his eye. He hesitated, but his helper took one look at Jean and tugged at his sleeve.

"We'll wait outside, ma'am," he told her, and turned back toward the door. "We'll be sitting in the ambulance until you need us,'' he went on over his shoulder, pushing his driver out by the elbow.

Detective Inspector Douglas Niven came in as they went out, and stood still, almost rigid in the doorway for a moment, taking in the scene. He was wearing a plain gray overcoat, no hat, and seemed more like a young professor than a policeman, with his smooth, triangular academic face and short, almost bristly hair, graying at the temples. He looked through round glasses at the world, which he seemed to survey with a mixture of alarm and distrust.

''Dr. Montrose, Mrs. Lumsden, Mrs. Ross,'' he murmured, coming into the hall. Constable Jamieson followed him in. Jean had come across him before; tall, earnest and none too bright. Douglas Niven knew all the people there; his wife Cathie occasionally played bridge with both Evelyn Ross and Stella Lumsden.

Jean got up, leaving the other two on the sofa. ''You might want to check if there's anybody in the house,'' she said softly. ''None of us has been upstairs.''

Douglas nodded to Constable Jamieson, who unhesitatingly moved toward the staircase, pulling the truncheon out of his pocket.

''In here, Inspector.'' Jean led the way into the bedroom. Usually she called him Doug, but somehow the horror of this occasion made her address him more formally.

Another car came racing up, no siren this time, the footsteps again clattering up to the door. This was the forensic team, a photographer, a fingerprint man, Dr. Malcolm Anderson the police surgeon, and a young woman with straight blond hair whom Jean had not seen previously. They came in carrying the boxes, tripods, lamps, and other paraphernalia of their various trades.

Inspector Niven sent all of them, except Dr. Anderson and Jean, to wait in the living room until he finished his examination of the bedroom and its gruesome contents. Dr. Anderson worked quickly, with no wasted movements. He obviously knew his job well. While he was looking at the baby's injuries and estimating the time of death, Douglas Niven prowled around the room, looking at the cot, spending time at the ghastly stain on the wall, checking the windows, the carpet, touching nothing. Jean stood there, feeling totally unnecessary and saddened beyond measure. Poor Stella, she thought. She'd gone through so much with that baby, and now all for nothing. He had been difficult even before he was born; Stella had suffered from swelling, fluid retention, and her blood pressure was going up alarmingly. Pre-eclampsia, said the obstetrician grimly, and decided to cut the pregnancy short. Almost a month before her due date, he induced labor and the baby didn't do too well for a week or so, with breathing problems which had him on a respirator for two days. And then the poor little devil developed epilepsy the day they got home from the hospital, and when she saw him convulsing Stella almost died of weakness and fright.

"Time of death?" asked Niven when Dr. Anderson straightened up.

"Within the last two hours," he replied. "The blood's clotted firmly, but there's no rigor yet." He looked curiously at Niven and then at Jean. "What's the story?"

"I got a call to come and see the baby because he was coughing a lot, and wheezing," said Jean. "He's been epileptic almost since birth, so I wasn't about to take any chances.''

"Who did it? His mother?" Anderson interrupted, ignoring Jean, addressing the inspector.

"I don't know," replied Niven curtly. "That's what I'm here to find out." He glanced covertly at Jean. Maybe she knew. But all he could tell from her expression was that she was saddened and hurting.

"We'd better let the team in now," said Niven, heading for the door. "I'll talk to the two ladies separately," he told Jean. "Is there anything you need to tell me? Otherwise, I won't keep you, I know how busy you are."

Jean hesitated, then said, "No, I don't think so . . . I'll call you if I think of anything. And you know where to reach me." She went into the living room, now full of people. Emboldened by the presence of all the others, the ambulance men had come back in and were waiting by the door, their stretcher at the ready. Stella and Evelyn were where Jean had left them, sitting numbly on the sofa.

"The inspector needs to talk with you," she told them. "I'll come back later this afternoon to see you're okay, Stella. I'll be at the surgery if you need anything. I'll see you in a wee while."

At that moment the front door opened and a young woman came in. Jean looked around and recognized Stella's sister Amanda; she'd met the two of them in Marks and Spencer the week before, and they'd all gone across the street to have a quick coffee together at Strathdee's. Amanda looked around the crowded room with scared eyes.

"What's happening here?" she asked loudly. Jean heard the sharp edge of hysteria in her voice. "What are all these people doing in the house?'' Stella ran to her, sobbing suddenly.

Jean slid unobtrusively out and went down the path, feeling as though she should be tiptoeing. She passed through the open gate and went to her car. As she drove back to town, a thought kept on coming into her head. Who was supposed to have been looking after the baby while Jean was out doing the shopping? And where was Dempster Lumsden? Oh my God, she said out loud as another thought hit her, right in the stomach. I don't care if he's in some dive, drunk out of his mind, just as long as that dive's not anywhere near here . . .

When Jean got back to the Lumsdens' house later that afternoon, all was quiet again, as if nothing had happened. Inside, however, she found a young constable who had been left to guard the women. When Jean came in, he mumbled something, looked embarrassed, and got up from his chair in the living room and went off in the direction of the kitchen.

The front door closed and Jean heard Stella's hurried footsteps coming downstairs.

''Doug Niven said one of his men was to stay here,'' explained Stella. She was looking better, but was still very shaken, and her lower lip trembled as if she might start crying again any minute. ''He thinks maybe . . . whoever it was might come back. It was so violent, he said, it must have been somebody deranged . . .''

''How did Amanda react? She seemed to be taking it very badly when I left this morning.''

''She's very upset. She went upstairs, she's trying to sleep. I think she has second sight, you know.

She seemed to know something awful had happened, almost before she came inside the house."

"Well, there were police cars and an ambulance outside," said Jean reasonably, but a seed of doubt germinated in her mind. There *had* been something strange about Amanda's reaction, but she couldn't pin down what it was. "Anyway, how are *you* feeling? Do you need anything?" Jean watched Stella as she spoke, looking for signs of delayed shock.

"I'm just numb," she said. "I don't believe it really happened. I'm listening, waiting for the baby to start crying, he must be hungry by now . . ." The tears came into her eyes. "And where's Dempster? Why is he never here when I need him?"

"Has anybody contacted his family? Maybe they've heard from him, they might even know where he is . . ." Jean's voice faded away. She knew Dempster never told anybody where he was going when he went off on a binge. "How about *your* folk?"

"My parents are both in Australia," replied Stella. "And Dempster's mother's dead, and his father is old. He has a brother, Alexis. I haven't talked to him for a while. Maybe I should call him, what do you think?"

At this point Stella seemed unable to make any kind of decision for herself, and looked helplessly at Jean for instructions.

"Yes, I think you should. Where is he?"

"In Inverness . . . I couldn't . . . I can't face talking to him . . . Jean, would you phone him? His name's Alexis . . . and tell him what's happened?"

Jean put a sympathetic hand on Stella's arm. It was shaking. "Of course I will. Do you have the number?"

Stella gave it to her, and Jean dialed. After a few rings, a pleasant young male voice answered. Jean told him briefly what had happened, and Jean could hear the disbelief in his voice. He demanded to speak to Dempster, and when Jean told him he wasn't at home, he asked to speak to Stella. Jean passed the phone to her. She kept her eyes on Jean as she spoke, as if she were her only hope of salvation.

"Yes, it's true," she said dully. "I don't know. He went off on Friday . . . Okay. How long will it take you? Drive carefully, Alexis, don't rush. I couldn't bear another accident."

She put the phone down, her hand still shaking. "He's coming right away," she said. "He should get here sometime late tonight."

Amanda poked her head round the door.

"I heard the two of you talking . . ." Her eyes were red and staring, and she moved jerkily, like a crazy woman. Her voice was loud and strange, almost accusing.

The doorbell rang and Evelyn Ross came in, looking very subdued and shaken. She was carrying a shopping bag from which she took two foil-covered dishes.

"I didn't think either of you would want to do much cooking," she said. "There's a leg of lamb in one, potatoes and brussels sprouts in the other. I'll just go and put them in the kitchen."

While Evelyn was out of the room, Jean looked at Stella and her sister, hesitated, then made up her mind. "The two of you, you need to get some rest. You'll both be quite safe now the policeman's here." She fished around in her bag and pulled out two blister-packs each with six oval green pills visible through the clear plastic. "You're both going to need something quite strong. Take one of these before you go to bed, both of you, and don't take any alcohol within six hours, okay? You may need to take them for the next few days, but don't take more than one at a time.''

Amanda and Stella looked at each other, and suddenly Jean felt the tension between them. Stella nodded wearily. "She's quite right, Amanda. There's nothing we can do except sit here and drive each other mad. Thanks, Jean. You're a real friend and we appreciate it.'' She gave Jean a quick hug.

For some reason Amanda didn't look at Jean when she got up to go; her eyes moved restlessly around the room, but she didn't seem to be looking at anything in particular.

Jean drove back into Perth faster than usual; she didn't want to impose on Helen's good will more than she had to, although everything had been quiet at the surgery when she left. Almost automatically, Jean pushed a cassette into the player, and soon Mozart's "Magic Flute" was filling the car, but she barely heard it. She was thinking about the first time she'd met Douglas Niven, about four years before, soon after his promotion and arrival from Glasgow, and when he was still the new boy in town. There had been a drug scandal at the local school, and nobody could find out where the stuff was coming from. Jean, whose work took her not only in and out of the prison but also into the less savory parts of the town, knew exactly what was going on and gave him some broad hints. Douglas took them, cleaned the situation up, and never forgot who had helped him. Doug was a good man, clever and capable, but with a sinking heart Jean could already see that there were some very strange aspects to this case, and she had a dreadful premonition that the horrors might only be starting.

After Jean left Lossie House, Stella and Amanda sat silently looking at the flames of the small fire. The constable had not reappeared; they could hear him walking around upstairs, checking each room.

Amanda started to say something, but her voice cracked. Stella's lips compressed and she stared straight in front of her as if she didn't want to hear whatever it was Amanda had to say. Suddenly, Amanda jumped up and rushed from the room. Stella still didn't move, and remained staring at the fire. She heard Amanda run up the stairs and into her room. There was a pause before she heard the sound of her sister turning the big, old-fashioned lock. The dying flames added flickering highlights to Stella's high cheekbones, but there was a flush of hatred there already; she had never loathed her sister as much as at that very moment.

Chapter Three

When Jean had left Lossie House in the hands of Doug Niven and his troops that morning, the first thing he did, after making sure that no killer was lurking in the house, was to separate the three women. He set up his headquarters in the living room, using the big desk at the far end; Stella, Evelyn and Amanda sat outside on the big leather sofa in the hall, like patients in the dentist's waiting room. To his own annoyance, Doug had two voices, his normal rather plebeian Glaswegian twang and a more cultured-sounding, learned voice. He couldn't help assuming this second voice when he was talking to better-educated people or those who belonged to a more elevated social class than his. He decided to interview Stella in the living room and send Evelyn to the kitchen and Amanda up to her room, with instructions to stay there until she was summoned.

As he spoke to the three women, he watched their reactions carefully. This was the time that he'd be most likely to see and hear what they really felt and thought, before they had a chance to put their defenses in order. Stella looked numb and vacant, her red eyes occasionally going over to her sister with a strange expression he couldn't quite fathom. Amanda, on the other hand, seemed so shattered she couldn't stay still, twisting her hands, getting up, taking a few steps and coming back, making quiet sobbing noises. Evelyn seemed to be the calmest of the three; after Jean left, she appeared to have taken charge, making sure there was enough tea for everyone, and talking gently and comfortingly to Stella and Amanda. Doug asked her to stay in the kitchen, as it was apparent that was where she was most useful and it also kept her out of the way.

Doug took Stella's arm and led her gently into the living room and up to the desk.

"Tell me what happened, Mrs. Lumsden," he said simply. He sat very stiff and upright in the desk chair, trying not to look too much at home. Even in her grief, Stella managed to remain elegant and regal. Only the whiteness of her knuckles showed the stress she was enduring.

"I came home from doing the shopping," she said, her big eyes steady on his. "I went straight to Magnus's room . . ."

"With the groceries?" asked Doug gently.

"No, I put them down on the kitchen table," she replied. "It's almost on the way to his room."

"Did you hear or see anybody, or notice anything unusual? Like a car in the drive, or going down Lossie Street?"

"No . . . There was a strange kind of silence when I got in the house. I suppose that's why I hurried to his room . . ."

"Mrs. Lumsden," said Doug, watching her carefully, "you called Dr. Montrose earlier to say the baby wasn't well. Who was supposed to be looking after him? I mean, while you were away doing your shopping?"

Stella's lip trembled. "I was only gone a short

time, down the road to the shops . . . He was asleep, and he wasn't coughing anymore. I thought it would be all right, just for a couple of minutes . . .''

Stella started to cry silently, and Doug's heart went out to her. Normally, it *would* have been all right; she'd have done her shopping, come home and nobody would have been any the wiser.

"Did it occur to you to take the baby with you?" he asked, rather lamely.

"I'd have had to wake him up, dress him for outdoors and risk him getting a chill . . . No, it didn't. But if I had, he'd still be alive now . . .'' Stella turned her head away from him.

"Which shops did you go to?" he went on. He took a pen from his breast pocket.

"First the greengrocer, then Mrs. MacIntyre's for bread and rolls, then Patel's for eggs and milk."

Doug made her give him a list of everything she'd bought, the time she spent in each of the different shops, the people she'd seen there, and what she'd said to them.

"How long were you out of the house? Try to be as exact as you can.''

"Not more than half an hour . . .'' Stella looked at her watch. "Well, maybe forty minutes at the outside. There was a long queue at the grocer's."

"Do you happen to know where your husband might be, Mrs. Lumsden?" Douglas Niven knew about Dempster's absences.

"No, but he usually goes to Glasgow, sometimes Dundee. He never tells me when he's leaving. I usually know, because he gets very restless for a few days, then he vanishes.''

"When was he last home?"

"Last Friday. He went off after lunch. I knew he

would be going soon, because he was getting snappier, more unreasonable, the way he always does.''

"Has he been home at all since that time?"

"No. At least I don't think so. Sometimes he comes back for money or fresh clothes, but not this time. Not so far, anyway.''

Doug decided to try another tack. There wouldn't be much trouble finding Dempster; they'd pick him up within a few days, he felt pretty confident of that, unless he turned himself in first.

"Your sister Amanda, Mrs. Lumsden . . .'' Doug stopped. Sometimes it was better to give only a topic to someone who was being questioned; the responses tended to be more wide-ranging and sometimes resulted in unexpectedly useful information. But Stella waited for him to formulate a question she could answer.

"Amanda, that is her name, isn't it?"

"Yes. Amanda Delincourt. She's been divorced from Ivor about two years now.''

"Would you spell his name for me, please?'' Doug knew well enough how to spell it, but he had a sudden feeling that Amanda's name had triggered something in Stella's mind, and he wanted more. Stella calmly spelled the name out, but Doug's tiny lead seemed to have evaporated, and he was back where he started.

"Do you have any idea, any suspicion about who might have done this terrible thing?'' he asked. Stella shook her head.

"Who in the world would want to kill a little baby?'' she asked, a tone of stunned wonder coming into her voice. It was a question Doug was unable to answer.

A few minutes later he got up and thanked Stella.

He told her they would do everything in their power to find the person or persons who had committed this dreadful murder. Oh, by the way, he added, almost as an afterthought, had Dempster ever hit his son? Even a bit? Maybe when he'd had too much to drink?

"No," said Stella. She hesitated and her eyes wavered. "No," she repeated, with almost too much emphasis. "Never."

Doug followed her with his eyes as she walked back toward the door. She was quite a lady, Stella Lumsden. He turned and asked Constable Jamieson, who had been standing discreetly behind Stella's chair, to go upstairs and ask Amanda Delincourt to come down to the living room.

While Jamieson was off on his errand, Doug got up and went to see what the forensic people were doing in the downstairs bedroom. The photographers were still there, and in the middle of the floor was a growing pile of labeled bags of clear plastic containing everything from clothing to scrapings from the wall. A high-powered vacuum cleaner started its whine; Doug knew that the aspirated material would be tested for different fibers which could pinpoint the clothing and possibly the identity of the killer.

Dr. Anderson was buttoning up his coat. He had done all he could do here—the remaining questions would be answered in the laboratory and the autopsy room. That is, thought Doug grimly, if they were to be answered at all. Anderson nodded briskly at Doug, but was obviously in a hurry and didn't have anything new to tell him.

Doug heard Amanda, or rather the ponderous footsteps of Jamieson clumping down the stairs behind her. He returned to the desk he had commandeered and watched the young woman come hesitantly across the room toward him. The desk was a good vantage point; Doug was skilled in evaluating a person just from seeing him or her walk across a room.

"Sit down, please, Mrs. Delincourt," he said. "My name is Douglas Niven, I'm a Detective Inspector and I'm in charge of this case. Now I'd like to start with your full name and address, please."

He wrote the answers to his questions in a slow, methodical hand, partly because that was the way he normally wrote, but also because of the effect it had on his interviewees. The guilty ones got a sense of doom, of inevitability, a knowledge that he would follow them relentlessly to the ends of the earth if necessary. The effect on the others was often one of irritation at his slowness, and that itself sometimes had unexpected and useful results.

After finding out that Amanda lived in her own house near Rosyth, that she was two years older than her sister Stella, that she didn't have a job and didn't need one, that she came up to spend a week or two with the Lumsdens every couple of months, Douglas paused and looked at her thoughtfully. There was something odd about her answers, or rather the way she gave them. There was an undercurrent of unbearable tension, an almost neurotic quickness about her responses and the sudden violent way she had of throwing her head back to get the hair out her face, and the direct, wide-eyed way she stared at Douglas while he asked his questions. Amanda was attractive in an intense, clean-limbed kind of way, but did not have Stella's classic beauty.

"Where had you been when you came in this

morning?'' he asked, pen poised above the official note-pad.

Amanda stared as if she didn't understand.

"Just now," he said. "Before you came in. Where were you?''

"Oh," she said. "I just went out.''

Douglas showed no signs of impatience, but his pen seemed to bear down just a little more heavily on the paper.

"Tell me exactly the time you left the house, where you went, who you saw and who you talked to.''

It turned out that she'd left just after Stella had gone to do her shopping, and had gone for a walk around the property, just for some exercise. She was used to swimming every day, and the lack of facilities here made her feel restless, even claustrophobic. She hadn't seen anybody and hadn't talked to anybody.

"Must have been pretty muddy out there, with the rain and everything,'' commented Doug, writing.

"Not too bad,'' said Amanda. "I know which bits to avoid.''

"Do you have an extra pair of shoes?'' asked Doug, looking up.

"Yes, of course, upstairs . . .''

Doug motioned to Jamieson to approach.

"Would you give the shoes you walked in to Constable Jamieson, please? Or do you have any objection?'' He gave her a stern look.

"No, as long as I get them back,'' said Amanda. "They're in my bedroom at the foot of the bed. They're walking shoes, Veldtschoens, and they're wet. I stuffed them with newspaper to get them dry.''

Doug got up. The interview was over. Just as

Amanda turned away, Doug snapped, "You were supposed to be looking after the baby while Stella was out, weren't you?"

Amanda's mouth opened, and her lips started to tremble. Doug thought she was going to fall, and he came quickly round the desk to catch her, but she pulled herself together and went off quickly without a word, followed by Constable Jamieson who hadn't noticed anything unusual.

While he wrote up his notes, Doug tried to avoid coming to any conclusions or even making a hypothesis about the baby's murder. Gather data, he told himself, that's all you can do right now. You don't know enough yet to make even a guess. But still, in his mind, he could see the large, drunken figure of Dempster Lumsden holding the baby by the legs and swinging him furiously against the wall.

Jamieson reappeared with a pair of sturdy walking shoes. He was holding them by the laces.

"Take them to the forensic people in the bedroom," said Doug. "Here, let me see them first . . ." The shoes were caked with still-wet mud.

"Get Mrs. Delincourt to take you exactly where she went walking this morning," he said. "Get some plastic bags and take five or six samples of the earth on your way round. And make sure you label them and mark where the samples come from."

Doug got up and went to find Evelyn Ross. She was in the kitchen, and had been joined there by the ambulance men and the photographers. He led her back to his desk. There was no need for introductions, as he knew both the Rosses and they knew him. Evelyn looked very self-possessed, and seemed to relish the fact that she had stayed calm and hadn't broken down with grief at the baby's death.

Doug put his hands on the desk. Evelyn was sitting down, completely at ease. It was quite extraordinary, thought Doug, how many really attractive women there were in this neighborhood; and Evelyn was no exception. She was taller than the two others, with a striking face, a perfect complexion, a majestic figure and beautiful clothes. It suddenly occurred to Doug that her gray silk dress with long slits at the sides and the Celtic silver brooch below the shoulder were more appropriate for a cocktail party or an evening on the town than for a visit to a neighbor's house to deliver a trifle.

"I'm surprised to see you here," said Doug bluntly. "I thought you and the Lumsdens weren't exactly the best of friends."

"That's old news," said Evelyn easily. She crossed her legs and Doug involuntarily caught his breath at the glimpse of her long and exquisite thigh. "We're good friends now—have been for months."

"How did you just happen to arrive at that moment?" he asked. "That was quite a coincidence, wasn't it?"

"Yes," said Evelyn, shrugging. "I suppose it was."

"Do you normally walk from home through the rain, bringing food to needy families like that?" Doug was beginning to feel sarcastic; there was something about Evelyn's quiet confidence that really irritated him.

"First," said Evelyn calmly, "it had stopped raining, and it only takes a minute to get over here from my house. Secondly, Stella brought over a pheasant last week and I was just reciprocating."

"When did you last see Dempster Lumsden?"

Douglas's tone was sharp, and Evelyn raised an eye-brow.

"I don't know, last week sometime, I suppose . . ."

"Think," insisted Doug. "When was it?"

"Wednesday, maybe Thursday," she said, tapping her fingernail on her strong, white teeth. "I saw him go by in his car. Why?"

"Wednesday or Thursday?"

"Probably Wednesday. I'm out most of the day on Thursdays, so yes, it was probably Wednesday, but if I have to repeat it in court, I'll swear you made me say it under torture."

Doug didn't smile. He felt an increasing sense of unease with her, in spite of her carefully nonchalant attitude.

Doug stood up. This time his parting shot was different.

"Do you always put on a silk dress to come over to visit your neighbors?"

"I really don't know why you're being so unpleasant to me, Douglas Niven." Evelyn's eyes flashed, but Doug could see she wasn't a bit put out. "The reason I wore this dress was because I was going out to lunch in Perth. With my husband," she continued when she saw the next question in Doug's eyes. "And now I'll wish you a good day, sir."

Evelyn looked just as good from behind as from the front.

Doug tapped his pencil on the desk, thinking. Although he didn't for one moment think any of the three women he'd seen were murder suspects, he could tell already that there was a great deal more going on under the surface of this apparently quiet little upper-class enclave than met the eye. He'd have to talk to Jean Montrose about all these people, their background, who were friends and who were not. Although he had been stationed in Perth for just over four years now, and had got to know a lot of the people in the city, he didn't mix socially with people like the Lumsdens or even the Rosses. That kind of class and wealth made him uncomfortable, although his wife Cathie didn't have any problems with them. Coming from Skye, Cathie had a lovely lilting soft brogue, much more acceptable than his common Glasgow accent. And in any case, why would they, the nobility, the bankers and landowners, why would they want to have anything to do with him, a humble policeman?

Doug shrugged off his mild case of self-induced paranoia and went to use the telephone in the hall.

Find Dempster Lumsden, he told them, but be careful; he could be violent. He gave a few suggestions where they might start to look for him. Dundee, possibly, or more likely around Glasgow, maybe down in some dockside pub on Clydeside. "Be discreet," he said, "really discreet. Just find him and tell me where he is. There are no charges pending as of this moment. Right, he's the son of Lord Aviemore. Doesn't that tell you everything you want to know?"

Chapter Four

One of Jean's few iron rules was that the whole family had to sit down together for the evening meal, and for other meals too at weekends. Otherwise, she said, they would all pass like ships in the night and lose touch with each other.

The front door slammed and Lisbie came in.

"God, what a day!" she said, dropping her coat at the foot of the stairs, and joining her mother in the kitchen. "That damn Gordon! Some days I could just kill him!"

"Don't swear, dear." Jean went on peeling the potatoes. "What did he do this time?"

"You know the postage meter? Well, I was getting all the post ready, and somehow it got a one in front of everything, so all the stamps were for one pound and nineteen pence, and he said he'd take it out of my pay."

"He was just joking, dear. He's a lawyer, and knows he can't do that. Now you go and set the table, we'll be eating in half an hour."

Lisbie went into the dining room, opened the sideboard, pulled out a bottle of vodka and took a big swig. She kept it in her mouth as she pulled out a handful of cutlery and started to set the table.

"Lisbie?" Lisbie swallowed the vodka, choked,

and coughed. "Lisbie, are you all right?" A vision
of Jimmy Castle, the boy with pleurisy, came to Jean,
and she put down her potato peeler and came through
to the dining room. Lisbie was sitting on a chair,
red in the face and wheezing.

"I'm okay . . ." she got out finally. "I just swallowed the wrong way, or something . . ."

Jean's brown eyes looked at her worriedly. "All
right. But if you're doing a lot of coughing I want
to know about it." Distractedly she put the vodka
bottle back in the sideboard and finished setting the
table. She had it done by the time Lisbie got her
breath back.

Fiona came in from her day in the department
store, looking as fresh as when she had set out that
morning. Jean looked at her with a kind of perplex-
ity, but Fiona had always been like that. Even when
she was little, she used to come in immaculate from
playing in the garden, whereas Lisbie would look as
if she'd been rooting around in a pigsty.

"Mum, did you hear about the baby? It was on
the radio coming home."

"Let's keep that topic for after dinner, if you don't
mind," said Jean firmly.

"But Mum, they said . . ."

"After dinner."

A little later, Jean heard Steven's car pull into the
drive, and that was the signal to put the fish under
the grill. Steven just had time for a quick drink before they all sat down. Jean placed the plate with the
fish on a trivet in front of him.

"Be careful, the plate's very hot," she said. They
all passed their plates and Steven dished out.

"Can we have some wine?" asked Lisbie. Steven
went to the fridge and brought a bottle about two-

thirds full of white wine to the table. They all had a glass except for Jean, who was on call.

Fiona burst out. "Dad, they said on the radio that a baby'd been killed, and it was Magnus, Stella Lumsden's baby." She looked at Jean for confirmation, but Jean kept her eyes on her haddock fillet.

"I heard that too," said Steven unexpectedly. "Your mother probably knows all about it."

They all looked at Jean. There was no way she could avoid saying something.

"It's quite true, unfortunately. Stella's very upset . . . ."

"Did she do it?" asked Lisbie, shocked. She had stopped eating her dinner. They all knew the Lumsdens and had seen Magnus several times.

"Of course not. Don't be silly, and don't you ever go around saying anything like that," said Jean, sounding quite annoyed.

"Come on, Mum, asking you isn't like going around saying things," said Lisbie indignantly. "Of course I wouldn't."

"Who *did* do it?" asked Fiona.

"Nobody knows," said Jean heavily. If she didn't answer they'd go on at her for ever. "Stella found him when she came home from doing her shopping."

"I bet it was Mr. Lumsden," said Lisbie through a mouthful of fish. "He probably did it when he was drunk."

Jean looked at Steven, silently appealing to him to stop the discussion, but he seemed as interested as any of them.

"Don't talk with your mouth full," he said sternly to Lisbie, but that was all the help she got from him. Lisbie pulled a long fishbone out of her mouth with more of a flourish than was really necessary, but was otherwise undaunted.

There was a silence, eventually broken by Steven.

"Is Stella's sister still living with them?" he asked, spearing a green bean on his fork.

"Amanda? Yes, why?"

"She doesn't have any kids of her own, does she?"

"No. Apparently she's divorced, but doesn't want everybody to know about it."

Steven seemed to lose interest, and went back to his fish, but Jean wondered; Steven didn't often get into gossip, and when he said something it was usually worth listening to. And Amanda had certainly seemed unduly overwrought when she came through the front door and saw the house full of people. It was as if she already knew something had happened.

"I'll tell you something else," said Steven much later, as they were getting into bed. "That Amanda is in love with Dempster Lumsden, even though he is a drunk. Remember we saw them at the Armstrongs cocktail party? They were talking together in the garden and I saw the way she looked at him. Jean, I'm telling you there's something going on between the two of them. I'd bet my bottom dollar on it."

It was all over the front page of the *Perth Courier* and *Advertiser,* and the story even made the national Sunday papers, which were less restrained in their reporting than the *Advertiser.* The *Sunday Mirror*'s headline, "Baby Killer Stalks the Glens," was matched only by the *Sunday Sport,* which reported a ghoul interrupted while starting to devour a child left unprotected in a Perth home. The ghoul, still slavering, then vanished into the night, mists swirling around its horrific form.

Jean glimpsed the *Courier*'s headline as she ran out of the house the next morning, and turned the paper face down, but even that glimpse was enough to start up the thoughts quietly simmering in her head. In the course of her work, Jean often saw the appalling things that people did to each other, but usually there was no mystery; a man would stab his girlfriend in a fit of jealousy, a bank robber might shoot his partner to get both shares of the loot, but there was always a motive, however transitory, however ludicrous it might seem later in the cold light of the courtroom. But who on earth would want to kill a baby, especially a sick, epileptic one? Jean's whole being revolted against the thought, and her hands gripped the steering wheel hard. It wasn't even like the princes in the Tower; there was no kingdom for the poor little mite to inherit.

Maybe there *was* an insane killer around. The thought made the hairs rise on the back of her neck. Nobody had escaped from the prison recently, none that she knew of, anyway, but with the new policy of emptying the mental hospitals, there were all kinds of strange people roaming around these days. She felt pretty sure that Douglas Niven would call in during the day for a chat; she could ask him then. Maybe by now they'd already found out who had done it and caught him. A feeling of sadness, almost of doom, descended on her. *Somebody* had done it, and had immediately separated himself from human society, irrevocably and for ever. Who on earth could possibly afford to take that risk? Especially as Jean was beginning to think that maybe it was someone

in that quiet, successful group who lived around the
Lumsdens.

A quick vision of all those people paraded past,
Stella Lumsden the distraught mother, her highly
strung sister Amanda Delincourt, Evelyn Ross, their
neighbor and friend, and Graham her banker husband . . . A thought flashed into Jean's head. Why
hadn't Graham come over yesterday? He must have
seen and heard the police cars going past his house.
And Keith and Danielle Armstrong, who lived in the
house opposite the Rosses; Keith the body-building
weaver with his big flat hands and curly red beard,
who watched and listened at parties but said little,
and his wife Danielle, a little quick-silvery woman
who fluttered nervously around him like a moth
around a flame. And lurking somewhere in the background of her mind, his fleshy, once-handsome face
bobbing above the surface of her thoughts, was the
Honorable Dempster Lumsden, ex-playboy, bon vi-
veur, husband of the beautiful Stella, and now a confirmed alcoholic. Jean thought about that for a
moment; in her experience, there were three kinds
of alcoholic: those whose genetic flaw was passed
down to them, then the leisured social drinkers who
became dependent without even realizing it, and finally those who turned to alcohol in suicidal despair.

Could the jovial, arrogant Dempster Lumsden
have come creeping back home yesterday to kill his
own child in cold blood? The thought made Jean feel
physically sick, and Eleanor looked at her with concern when she walked through the door into the
surgery.

"Are you all right, Dr. Montrose?"

"I'm fine, thank you, Eleanor." She looked questioningly at her. Eleanor usually called her Doctor

Jean, and when she used her surname, it was usually to warn her that somebody was waiting to see her in the inner office. It must be Doug Niven.

"Inspector Niven?" she mouthed.

"No, certainly not!" Eleanor had a profound distrust of the police; in her mind, Inspector Niven's occasional visits to the surgery did nothing to enhance the Wee Doctor's reputation.

"It's Mr. Armstrong. You know. . . !" Eleanor spoke in a theatrical whisper and rolled her eyes. She obviously knew about the Lumsden baby's death and thought Keith must have come in to confess his crime to Jean.

Jean didn't particularly like Keith; at parties she'd often look up and find his eyes on her. It made her uncomfortable, but once when she happened to mention it to Steven he just laughed. She braced herself and went in. Keith was sitting in the patients' chair, and his bulk seemed to fill the room. He got up when Jean appeared, and bowed clumsily. Jean's dislike took a quantum leap, but she couldn't have explained why.

"Keith, good morning, what brings you to this part of town?" She sat down behind her desk, which suddenly seemed a frail barrier between the two of them.

"Well, Jean, you never come out to see me, so I thought I'd pop in and see you!" His tone had a kind of jovial bantering quality that put Jean's teeth on edge. She waited. His eyes never left her face, and he must have seen something there, because he became a little flustered.

"This may sound strange, me telling you this, but somebody should know . . ." He took a deep breath and moved on his chair. It creaked. "When I left home to go to the shop yesterday, I saw Dempster Lumsden's car pass by on the main road. I'm almost sure it was him, although he was going quite fast. I know he's been . . . away; that's why I noticed.''

"Why shouldn't it be there?" Jean's voice was sharper than she wanted it to be. "After all, that's where he lives.''

"I know, but with what happened . . .''

"He could have come home to get some fresh clothes, or something," said Jean, remembering with a shock what Stella had said: "I don't know . . . He hasn't been home for three days." "Anyway, I'm not the person you should be telling this to. You know Doug Niven, don't you?''

Keith's eyes flickered uncertainly. "Yes, I know him. But he hasn't been around here too long, and you know about everything that happens here, you're like the mother confessor.''

Jean got up. "Tell Doug. He's a very good man. I agree with you, it may be important, and he should know about it.''

Keith got up. "Thanks, Jean, I just wanted to know what you thought." He stuck out his hand and Jean shook it. It was huge, and Jean had a sudden horrifying image of those hands picking up a baby by the legs and swinging it . . . For some reason, she wanted to spray some disinfectant around the room after he'd gone.

There was a pile of correspondence on her desk, and Jean started to work her way through it. Eleanor came in with a cup of tea and the usual two digestive biscuits on the saucer. She was obviously dying to hear what Keith Armstrong had said.

"He's really a big man, isn't he?" she said, hovering.

"Right. Can you get me Dr. Ramasandra on the phone? I want to know how Jimmy Castle's doing." Disappointed, Eleanor retreated into her own domain. While she dialed the hospital, she rehearsed a description of Keith Armstrong, his bristling red beard, his shifty, guilty expression. Her friends always expected her to have the inside story on everything, and she wasn't above doing a little embroidery for added effect.

Jean went back to her mail. There were a couple of letters from consultants about patients she'd had in the hospital, a letter inviting her to borrow up to £10,000 on her signature alone, an urgent warning about unsuspected side effects of a new drug . . .

Helen Inkster, her partner, put her head round the door.

"How is it you're always involved in everything exciting or criminal around town?" she asked. "One of these days, somebody's going to put two and two together!" She came in and closed the door behind her. She was a big, rather ungainly woman who liked tweedy clothes and wore no make-up on her large, plain face. She had played hockey for St. Andrews, where she had qualified near the top of her medical school class. Helen had started the practice, and worked in Perth for several years before taking on Jean as a partner. Her manner was too cold for her to be very well liked, but professionally she was highly thought of in the town.

"Eleanor's dying to hear why Mr. Armstrong came," she said, dropping a newspaper on the desk. "It all sounds rather lurid."

"It's just dreadful," Jean burst out. "I can't imagine who could have done such a thing."

"The police seem to know who did it," said
Helen. "Did you read the paper?"

Jean opened it up. After describing the findings
with fair accuracy on page one, on page three Detective Inspector Douglas Niven was quoted as saying that they were looking for a man who had been
seen that morning near the scene of the murder. The
description was so hazy as to be useless. In addition,
Niven said, they were appealing to Mr. Dempster
Lumsden, the child's father, to come forward, as he
might be able to help them in their inquiries.

"That bit about the man seen in the neighborhood, that's flannel," said Helen, with a wise look.
"They just don't want to scare Dempster Lumsden
away."

"I can't imagine him doing anything like that,"
protested Jean. "Can you?"

"Did you know he almost killed somebody in
some kind of drunken brawl a few years ago, up in
Aberdeen? It cost his father a packet to hush it up
and keep it out of court, and out of the papers."

Jean digested this piece of information. It seemed
that her ideas about people, even people she thought
she knew quite well, were often frighteningly wrong;
but on the other hand, she hoped she wouldn't suddenly start to see the skulls behind the faces of her
friends and everyone she knew.

Douglas Niven hadn't come to the surgery by midday; he was probably too busy tracking down
Dempster Lumsden.

After lunch, Jean drove out to Lossie House to see
how Stella was faring. There were several press cars
parked in Lossie Road. Someone, probably a re-
porter, was in the phone box at the end of the road
and another was waiting outside. A photographer had

his camera set up on a tripod at the entrance to the drive, ready to catch anyone coming in or out.

Stella was quiet and seemed calm. One of the policemen yesterday had taken pity on her and scrubbed down the wall in the bedroom after they'd finished taking photographs and done all the other tests.

"Any news of Dempster?" asked Jean.

Stella hesitated. "Nothing," she said, her eyes on the floor. Jean paused, then understood. Stella was embarrassed by her husband's continuing absence.

"Did his brother come down from Inverness?"

"Alexis? Yes, he went to see the . . . undertakers. It was very kind of him; I simply couldn't bear to."

"Well, it's certainly a blessing that he's here," said Jean. "How is Amanda holding up?"

"Not too well. I know she didn't sleep, and this morning she looked as if she'd been crying all night."

"And what about you?"

"I'm numb. My brain hasn't taken it all in yet, and I'm scared of what'll happen when it does."

Jean felt a vast compassion for Stella. The girl was putting on a brave face, but Jean knew how much she must be hurting, not just from losing the baby, but because she had been left alone when she most needed her husband's help and support. Jean couldn't help thinking how Steven would be in such a situation, and then she shuddered at the very idea of a death in her own family.

Jean looked round. "Did the policeman leave?"

"Yes. Inspector Niven said there wasn't any danger anymore."

"Good. That's a relief, anyway." Jean wondered how Doug Niven could be so sure. "Stella, I'll be in the surgery, or if not . . ." She pulled a piece of paper out of her pocket and wrote on it. "That's my home telephone number, so if you need anything at all, you let me know, all right?"

As she left Jean happened to look up at the windows on the front of the house, and thought she saw Amanda's face staring down at her. Without thinking, she waved, but there was no response. Of course the poor woman must be having a terrible time, just like the rest of them.

Then there was Stella's brother-in-law Alexis, having to go down and discuss the baby's funeral . . . Where was Dempster? The papers had been full of the murder, and Jean couldn't imagine that he was so drunk that he couldn't come home to take care of things himself. It was really shameful. Unless . . . Jean put the thought out of her mind. Dempster might be a drunk and a spendthrift, but she couldn't see him as a killer. But at this point Jean was feeling so insecure about her own judgment that she felt anything was possible, even that.

She had her photograph taken as she turned out of the drive, and hoped it wouldn't appear the following Sunday in the *News of the World*.

Chapter Five

It wasn't until almost nine in the evening that Doug Niven finally appeared on the doorstep of Jean's house. There, people came and went all the time, so nobody was surprised when the doorbell rang.

Fiona went to open the door, and Jean could hear her voice. She could tell that Fiona liked Doug.

"Come on in." Fiona opened the door wide. "She's in the living room."

Steven was sitting in his comfortable chair reading the paper. He looked a little put out when he heard Douglas's voice, folded his paper and escaped upstairs as soon as he could.

Fiona made coffee for Doug and her mother, to give her an excuse to sit and listen to what Doug had to say about the Baby Lumsden case, as it was now being called, but Jean sent her off; it was none of her business. Doug settled back in the easy chair which was still warm from Steven, and loosened the button on his jacket.

"Well, that's an attractive, well-turned out young lady you have there," he said, meaning Fiona. "I bet she has boys around her like flies."

"Not particularly, I don't think," said Jean, sounding a little vague. Maybe she does, now she thought about it—there certainly were lots of phone calls for Fiona, and she was out late often enough. But she was pretty sure there wasn't anything serious going on.

"Terrible business, that, about the Lumsden bairn," said Niven, taking a sip of coffee. He would have much preferred a good stiff Glenfiddich, but she knew he was driving, and would not offer it. The Wee Doc really is quite a character, he thought, smiling to himself, looking at her sitting there, a bit dumpy, a piece of crochet in her lap and a boxful of medical reports still to go through. He could not imagine her just relaxing, doing nothing and enjoying it.

"Yes it is," agreed Jean, her eyes on the crochet hook, noticing that he sounded genuinely upset. He's really compassionate, for a policeman, she thought. Douglas moved around on the comfortable armchair; to Jean, he looked tired, seemed to have a lot on his mind, and didn't appear to be quite sure where to start. Poor fellow, she thought. He's a nice, good-hearted man, but he surely can't have much of a home-life. Here he is, after nine in the evening, and still working.

"You've been in this town a lot longer than I have," he started, as he usually did when he needed some information. He was clever in his questions, and Jean always had to watch her step not to tell him anything that would be a breach of professional confidentiality.

Niven scratched his ear, trying to sound nonchalant. "Can you tell me a wee bit about the Lumsdens?"

"What do you want to know?"

"Oh, just generally, who they are, were they brought up here, that kind of thing. Being just a

Glesga lad myself, I don't know all the local people that well . . ." Jean didn't wait for him to finish his sentence; the only thing that sometimes irritated her about Doug was the way he talked, and she didn't have too much patience with the Clydeside accent he was now exaggerating.

"Dempster's thirty-four, maybe thirty-five. His father's Lord Aviemore, and they have big estates around Aviemore and up near Inverness, but Dempster isn't interested in forestry or land management or any of that. He used to be quite a playboy . . ." Jean glanced up at him and smiled. "That's what I heard, I don't know personally. Anyway he was quite Jack the lad until he met Stella about four years ago."

"Was he married at the time?" asked Doug, pulling out a packet of cigarettes. He put them hurriedly back when he remembered that Jean didn't encourage cigarette smoking in her house.

"No, he was never married before, as far as I know. But he really fell for Stella, who was really beautiful, as she still is."

"Somebody said they'd only been married for a couple of years. That makes it a long courtship, wouldn't you say, by today's standards?"

"By yours, anyway," retorted Jean. "I know how long you took to turn your Cathie's head—a week, wasn't it, or ten days, the poor bairn?"

"She wasn't a bairn, she was all of seventeen," grinned Doug. "Anyway it was her that ran off wi' me, even though I was almost twenty at the time!" He sat back, and loosened another button, wishing he could take off his shoes.

"I heard there was a bit of rivalry for Stella between him and his brother,'' reflected Jean. ''Maybe that slowed things down, too.''

''You know he was at his house today?'' Niven sounded elaborately casual.

''Dempster? Well, I don't know how far I'd believe that story, considering the source. Did anybody besides Keith actually see him?''

''Not that I'm aware of.'' Doug watched Jean carefully, but she was concentrating on her crochetwork. ''You don't think that Keith is telling the truth?''

''I didn't say that,'' said Jean carefully, her fingers now going faster. Doug looked at the round piece she was working on and tried to guess what it was going to be.

''Why do you think he'd make up a story like that, then?''

''I don't know,'' retorted Jean. ''I'm not the policeman.''

There was a brief silence.

''I wish Dempster would come forward, though. Maybe he saw the person who did it.''

''Where do you think he is?''

''Who?''

''Dempster.''

''Stella thinks he goes to Glasgow when he's on a binge,'' said Niven. ''I still have some friends on the force there, and they're checking some of the places he might hang around.''

Jean finished the piece of crochet, and cut the end of the thread with a little pair of scissors. ''Doilies for a wedding,'' she said, catching his glance. ''Don't mind me, I'm listening.''

''What about Stella?''

''I don't know too much about her,'' said Jean.

"She's not a local girl; she's originally from around Inverness somewhere. I think she did some modeling in London, was in the theater for a while—nothing very serious—then spent some time in New York. She's quite a cosmopolitan young lady."

"It must be rather dull here in Perth for her, don't you think?"

"I don't know, the Lumsdens are quite social . . . or at least they were until he started drinking so heavily."

"About when was that?"

"Oh, I understand he always liked a drop, but he really started to hit the bottle about a year ago, maybe a bit longer . . ."

Doug thought about that for a minute, while Jean lifted the cardboard box on the table beside her and started on her office notes and a small stack of letters about patients she'd referred to consultants. She watched him, under cover of her work. He was quite young to have such a senior job; Doug must be in his early forties, she estimated. He tried to make himself look more policemanly, with his short, military haircut, but the gentle gray eyes behind his round glasses, the pale face and pointed, rather elongated nose and chin gave him an ineffably professorial look. Doug had put on a little weight lately, and all in all he had the comfortable look of a placid, slightly confused academic with an established and not too demanding routine. That just shows that one shouldn't be taken in by appearances, she thought. He's a complex, clever, persistent chap, a good man to have on the force, and one to be reckoned with.

"What about his neighbors?" he was asking. "That whole group of houses, the Lossie Estate, do you know the other people who live there?"

"Come on, Douglas," said Jean sharply. "I don't have the time to give you the life histories of all those folk, even if I knew them. Who are you thinking of in particular?"

There was some noise from the front of the house; laughter, the sound of a door closing. Jean ignored it; maybe she didn't even hear it.

"I was thinking mostly of the Armstrongs and the Rosses . . ." A thought struck him. "Who lives on the other side, next to the Lumsdens?"

"That was the Kennealys' house," said Jean. "It's been empty since they went to Arbroath, six months ago. They're asking far too much money for it. They're just greedy—I know what they paid for it."

"Evelyn Ross," murmured Doug. His voice was casual again, but his eyes were not.

"I have to be careful here," said Jean. "She's a patient . . . Why don't you tell me what *you* know about her; maybe I can add something as you go along."

Douglas thought for a moment. His police training told him to start with a physical description—female, five foot ten, slim, a shade over nine stone, with long, very dark hair, regular features, elegant dark, arched eyebrows, no other major distinguishing features—but he was tired, and his mind slid off into a completely unprofessional spiral and he told Jean that he found Evelyn Ross very beautiful and sexy and moody and unsociable and possibly completely crazy and married to a bright up-and-coming banker whose career had inexplicably stalled.

"It's funny how she affects people," mused Jean. "There's a few who really love her, but generally she's not at all popular. They think she's a snob, standoffish, and, well, erratic."

"What about him?" Doug pricked up an ear; there had been a dull thump from the basement.

Jean shrugged. "It's just the girls," she said, then went on. "Graham? Well, nobody knows quite what's going on with him. When he came as the new manager, the bank people said he was on the way to the top, and he'd only be there for a couple of years before being moved to the head office in Edinburgh. But that was well over four years ago, before you came to town."

"What happened? Did they catch him with his hand in the till, or was he having it off with one of the tellers?"

"Douglas! What an idea! No, of course not! He's perfectly moral and does a very good job, or so I've heard. I don't know, but I think the problem may have had something to do with her. She's not at all social, doesn't like to entertain, and she's been known to snub the wrong people. She once had a public argument with Graham, and she chose the annual bank ball to have it. But she's basically a nice woman, kind and thoughtful. She's a depressive, though, and that's what causes most of her problems."

Doug sat there thinking. He looked really tired, Jean thought. "Douglas, don't you think it's time for you to go home? I bet you haven't even had supper."

"Yes I did, thanks. Cathie wasn't exactly delighted to see me going out again, but she said it was all right if it was you. She said to say hello, by the way, and are you coming to the garden show?"

"Of course. Steven has some nice phlox he's thinking of putting up. You know he got the Best Flower award last year." Jean was so proud of him she sounded almost complacent, then immediately

Doug saw she regretted sounding so boastful. "The competition's going to be a lot tougher this year, though."

"Good, I'll tell her. She'll be glad you're coming." He paused. "You're right, though," he said struggling out of his chair. "It is time I went home. Sorry for taking up your time like this . . ." He buttoned up his jacket. There was some noise outside the door, followed by the sound of suppressed giggling. The door opened and Fiona and Lisbie appeared.

"We're just going out for a while, Mum," said Lisbie. Doug thought he saw two shadowy male figures in the background.

"Have a nice time," said Jean placidly. "And don't be home too late, all right?"

"Bye," said the girls in unison. "Goodbye, Doug," said Fiona, smiling rather boldly at him.

By the time Doug was ready to leave, their car was already roaring down the hill. Passing the door to the basement, Doug sniffed and looked enquiringly at Jean.

"They must have been cooking something down there," she said. "There's a little stove they can heat pizzas and things." Doug looked at her in amazement. That sweet, smoky smell certainly wasn't pizza.

At the front door, Jean turned to face Doug.

"You think it was Dempster, don't you?" she asked.

Doug adjusted his tie, glancing in the hall mirror.

"I'd certainly like to talk to him about it," he replied. "It doesn't help his case to stay hidden like this. If there's one thing we cops are good at it's finding people. He won't stay lost for long, I can assure you. Anyway, thanks for your help, and for the coffee.''

Jean watched him leave, and waved as the car pulled away. He hadn't asked a single question about the Armstrongs.

"Now Mrs. Leuchars, I want you to listen to me," said Jean sternly, pulling her stethoscope back in the pocket of her white coat. "I've checked your blood pressure, your eyes, and your reflexes, and everything's just how it should be. There's absolutely no sign of a brain tumor."

Mrs. Leuchars sat, despondent, looking as disappointed as if she'd been hoping for bad news. "That's how Maggie Nairn's one started, though, with headaches, and pains in her een like that . . ."

"Do you remember when you started to get your eye pains and headaches?"

"February . . . About the middle o' the month."

"Do you remember what other things happened then?"

"Aye, they put Maggie in the ground on the thirteenth."

"What else?"

" 'At's when Willie was killed." Mrs. Leuchars's eyes filled with tears. "Not ten days later." Her son, a linesman for the Electricity Board, had been killed in a freak electrical accident, only a week after her neighbor died from a brain tumor.

"I'm sorry to be bringing all that up, Mrs. Leuchars," said Jean gently, sitting down beside her. "But it was just to show you that when bad things happen to people we love, we often take on the burdens they left off. Do you see what I mean?"

"Aye, I suppose so . . . I just wish I was dead and done with it all."

"I know, I can understand that, but you'll get over it eventually. Now, meanwhile I'm going to give you some pills for your depression. Make sure you take them regularly; they'll give you a dry mouth and make your eyes blurry for a week or two."

After Mrs. Leuchars had gone, Jean checked the waiting room. It was empty.

"Well, Eleanor," she said, sitting down with a thump on the chair beside the secretary's desk, "there were a lot of them this afternoon, weren't there?"

"You're getting busier by the week. Everybody wants to see you, for some reason."

"It's not just me," said Jean. "Helen's getting more too."

"There was a time here in this town when nobody would come to see a woman doctor for love nor money," said Eleanor. "And that wasn't so long ago." She pushed a pile of NHS forms across to Jean for her signature.

"You know, we're very lucky in this practice," said Jean, looking up with that sudden wide, attractive smile of hers. "We have such a lot of really nice patients."

Eleanor smiled tolerantly. They're all nice to you, Jean, she thought, because you're so good to them. And because of that, you don't always see what some of these people are capable of.

Helen came clumping out of her office.

"Are you done?" she asked Jean.

"Here, yes," answered Jean. "I'm on my way out. I've got about four calls to make . . ." She looked at her watch, and an expression of dismay came across her face. "Oh dear. They're starting the postmortem on Magnus Lumsden in about ten minutes. Dr. Anderson asked me to go, and I suppose I should." She got up and took her coat off the peg, while the other two women watched her.

"She's going to run herself to death, that one," said Eleanor when Jean had left.

"She may be little," said Helen, "and she may look and sound vulnerable, but she's really tougher than you and me put together, I can tell you that!"

Autopsies of victims of criminal activity in Perth were usually performed in the larger facilities in Dundee, but due to a backlog of cases at the Western Infirmary in their Pathology Department, Dr. Anderson had been told to go ahead and do it in Perth.

"It's a bit different with babies," he said, grinning when Jean arrived. He had on a big bloodstained rubber apron that reached almost to his feet, making him look like a Breughel butcher, and Jean wondered at his obvious enthusiasm. I couldn't do this kind of work, she thought, not in a million years.

Magnus was in a sealed bag, and it was opened in the presence of a young policeman who wrote down the time in a notebook.

"Seeing you're here, quine, you might as well identify the bairn." Anderson's broad accent made Jean smile in spite of herself. She hadn't been called a "quine" for some time. The identification made, the policeman wrote down her full name and address. Jean noticed that the young chap looked gray, and his hand was none too steady.

The technician put the baby on the table. It was stiff, the knees partly bent, arms away from the body.

It looked like an ill-used doll, with its dreadful head injury, and the blue jacket still covered the tiny chest.

"In murders we leave 'em wi' their claes on," explained Dr. Anderson. "In stab wounds, for instance, it'll help tae tell us the direction the knife went in."

Anderson came up to the table. Jean had rarely seen anybody who so relished such a gruesome job. He examined the body carefully, and dictated his findings to the policeman, who wrote it all down in shorthand.

"Extairnal appearances," he said. "The body is that of a sma' infant, who looks the stated age and shows postmortem mottling in the back and lower extremities." He looked around. "Did you get that?" he asked, staring at the young policeman. "Because if ye didn't, you'll just have to write faster, m'loon!"

The technician cut the jacket and the little shirt and placed the stiff, naked body back on the table. Jean looked at it with motherly pity; it looked so small, so cold, and so utterly defenseless.

Dr. Anderson picked up a long scalpel, and Jean involuntarily winced when he made a small incision in the center, just under the breast bone, then took a pair of heavy scissors and cut upward through the sternum, opening up the chest. Some dark blood welled up and ran down the baby's side. Anderson, working rapidly and with a kind of assurance that bordered on bravado, made a cut with the scissors on the inside, at the level of the baby's throat, and pulled out the heart and lungs all together with a loud slurping sound. Jean instinctively stepped back, feeling slightly sick. Dr. Anderson took the organs over to the sink, took a knife and cut pieces out of the lung for later microscopic examination. With a smaller pair of scissors, he opened the heart.

"Well, look at this!" he said, holding the plum-sized organ under the tap to wash all the blood out of it. With a slender probe, he poked excitedly at a small hole between the right and the left ventricles. "He's got a VSD, a ventricular septal defect!"

He makes it sound as if he'd just won the pools, Jean thought, then shrugged to herself. A man has to take his pleasures where he finds them. Anderson turned to the abdomen, putting two fingers inside the opening, then with a knife in his other hand cutting down between his fingers through the skin and muscles down to the pubis. Again, Anderson found something to fascinate him. He held up a little outcropping of the small intestine.

"D'ye ken fit that's called?" he asked Jean, holding it up. Jean shook her head. All that gray, slithery intestine looked pretty much the same to her. "Well, it's called a Meckel's diverticulum," he said, a note of satisfaction in his voice. "You get that in about two percent of all pairsons." There was a sound behind him.

"Would you spell that for me, Doctor?" asked the policeman. He was not looking well, and Jean feared she might have him as a patient before the autopsy was over. She went over to the end of the room and brought back a plastic chair.

"Sit you down there," she ordered the bobby, and he didn't argue.

"I'm keeping the heid for last," said Anderson, as if it were dessert. He worked fast and efficiently, though, and Jean began to think his callous attitude was merely a defense mechanism. The head was more complicated, but easier to deal with than an adult's, as the skull bones were still mostly made of cartilage and Anderson was able to cut them easily with the heavy scissors. There was a massive fracture on the left side, involving the orbit and the whole side of the head, and underneath, the brain was haemorrhagic and disrupted.

"That was quite a blow," said Dr. Anderson finally as he washed his hands at the big rounded white sink. "Likely a man did it, and a big man at that."

The policeman stood up, then sat down again suddenly, leaned forward and put his head between his knees. Jean kept an eye on him, not wanting to embarrass the lad, then when he had got up again and left—rather unsteadily—she went off herself. She had four visits to make, and wouldn't have time for lunch. Anyway she didn't feel hungry. She patted her tummy as she walked to her car; it was probably just as well.

Chapter Six

Douglas Niven might have been uncomfortable in the rarefied social level of the Lumsdens, but when it came to routine police work there was nobody to beat him. Douglas Niven never leaves a stone unturned, his last boss had said, and added, whether it needed turning or not.

The problem he kept bumping into was economic; doing a job thoroughly cost time, and time cost money. He would have liked to instruct the Glasgow and Edinburgh police forces to scour their respective cities until they found Dempster Lumsden, who initially seemed most likely to hold the answers to the murder, but, of course, they had neither the time nor even the inclination to do very much. To satisfy old friendships, and with the well-known solidarity between the upper echelons of the Scottish police forces, the Glasgow and Edinburgh brass did issue a station bulletin, which was passed on to their patrol cars, to look out for him. Dempster's photo, after multiple reproductions on overused and out-of-date police copiers, could have represented anybody from Idi Amin to the Prince of Wales.

By the time Doug had organized his colleagues, he was already beginning to have doubts about the case. It wasn't anything concrete, but he had enough experience to pay attention to instinct and intuition. In this case it was his instinct and Jean Montrose's intuition. From the beginning, his dealings with what he called the Lossie set had been uncomfortable; he didn't know these people, with their English public-school accents, who shot grouse in August and went skiing in Davos in January. The only thing Douglas had ever fired at was the target at the Police Academy training ground near Kirkaldy, and the closest he'd been to skiing was the Bijou skating rink off Sauchiehall Street, where he and Cathie used to go on Friday nights after they were first married.

But now, with the perspective provided by Jean, he was able to see that there was more going on in the Lossie Estate than just their self-protective upper-class posturing. There was an undercurrent of dissension, of bitterness, even hatred among these so-civilized people, and Douglas was beginning to think that the murder of the Lumsden baby might be a part of something else, rather than an isolated incident of mindless brutality.

And in that, the Lossie set were again different; in the Gorbals, where he had spent several years as a constable and later as a sergeant, there was much more crime, at least of the visible sort, but there a man knew where he was, most of the time. When somebody got seriously upset with somebody else, they'd go after them directly with boot, bottle or knife. Everybody knew who did what, and to whom, although of course they were rarely willing to share that information with the police. In the Lossie Estates, they stabbed each other invisibly, with a smile, and nobody but the victim was any the wiser.

Douglas knew very well that unless he was careful, his working-class background and prejudices could get in the way of his work; his father had been a trade union official and used to come home with hair-raising tales about the treachery and duplicity of the pit owners, and Douglas had been an ardent Labor supporter all his working life. Jean Montrose had seen that, and although her own roots were middle class, she had gently warned him that people like the Lumsdens were not basically any different. They were motivated by the same passions—love, fear, greed—and they were vulnerable to the same deadly sins as anybody else. They just had a tendency to respond differently; with them a prime consideration was to avoid discovery and the appearance of doing wrong.

Thus, according to Jean's theory, there was something fatally flawed about Dempster Lumsden as the chief suspect in the murder. Even drunk, even furious, and however much he might be tempted, he would have recoiled from such a cowardly deed because he would certainly be caught, and he and his family disgraced and humiliated. Dempster could never have accepted that. In any case, had he done the deed, he would be much more likely to stay and brazen it out with the police, claiming it was an accident.

But who else would or could have done it?

In his meticulous way, Douglas had made detailed file cards on the people principally involved in the case, whether he felt they were suspects or not. "Everybody's a suspect" was one of the dicta drummed into him when he was learning his trade as a detective, but in fact it didn't make too much sense; if one took it seriously it diluted the effort among too many potential suspects. It made more sense to narrow the list down as early as possible and accept the possibility of error.

Doug reached up to the shelf above his head for the cardboard box with the filecards and put it on the corner of his desk. Some of them were already beginning to look dog-eared.

They were alphabetically arranged, and at the top of each one was a brief biographical summary. Where the information was unconfirmed, the source was marked with the initials of the person giving it. Doug flipped through the cards; there were still far too many blank spaces, too many unanswered questions. Look at Stella's sister, Amanda, for instance. She had been right there, or close by, when the murder was committed. She was a divorcee of two years standing, a long time for a woman as attractive as she was to remain alone. And she'd been coming to Lossie House every few weeks . . . Was it really to spend time with Stella, as she said, or did she come up to see someone else? Dempster? Or maybe some other person who lived nearby? Jean had not been able to help him on that; all she knew was that Amanda had finally got tired of her husband's infidelities, and that as far as she knew there was no other man. Or woman, Jean had said, then became acutely embarrassed and blushed bright red.

Doug shook his head and flipped up the next card for a moment. It was Dempster's, and he pushed it back down. Then came Stella's card, and he looked at it thoughtfully. Stella, because she had been there, was just as much a suspect as Amanda, even though his knowledge of human nature made him automatically reject her as a killer of her own child. Maybe she was having an affair with somebody who had become jealous or angry and had smashed the baby against the wall . . . If that had been so, Amanda would have had to be aware of him, and she wouldn't have been able to hide it when Douglas interviewed her, of that he was quite certain. But then Amanda had seemed so strange, almost wild, when she came back into the house after the murder, with the ambulance men and all the other people who had suddenly invaded the house.

Douglas shrugged; his head was beginning to throb. Maybe it was a mistake to be looking into everything in such detail; as long as he didn't examine things too closely, the case was clear cut enough.

After thinking about it for a while, he had opened a card on Alexis, Dempster's brother, although there didn't seem the faintest possibility of his being the killer. In fact, Jean Montrose had spoken to him in Inverness the same day to tell him about the murder, which gave him a cast-iron alibi. Probably another case of a stone which didn't need turning, but nevertheless . . . Alexis was the second son of Lord Aviemore, a couple of years younger than Dempster. He lived with his widower father on the principal estate near Inverness. He had gone to Aberdeen University where he studied agriculture, getting a good degree. According to Doug's sources, Alexis was capable, hard-working and ambitious to improve the existing level of farming on the estate. Doug turned the card over. That was all. Not much, but he didn't really need more anyway. He'd met Alexis the day after the killing and got a good impression; he was a nice-looking young chap, not at all arrogant, and cooperative, quietly doing things like arranging for an undertaker and making telephone calls to their numerous relatives around the world. Stella would have been lost without his help.

At the front of the stack was a card for each of the Armstrongs, Keith and Danielle. Now they were different, not upper class by any means, and people he could relate to more easily. Keith was a weaver, a big man who had no hesitation in calling a spade a spade. They had come to the Lossie Estate about a year before, and Doug thought Keith had some kind of business connection with Dempster Lumsden. He made a note on his pad to check up on that. Danielle was a small, rather colorless woman whom Doug saw from time to time in Perth, usually on South Street, carrying a shopping bag. She looked like a mouse, with bright eyes, a gray coat and no make-up, and a general air of wary alertness as she scurried around the shops on Saturday mornings.

Keith had been home, asleep, at the time of the murder; it had been Danielle's day to mind the shop, a converted loft down near the harbor. Doug had talked to both of them at length, but neither one had had anything to add. Keith had seen nobody suspicious, apart from his doubtful sighting of Dempster's car that afternoon. When Douglas questioned him closely about it, it turned out that all he had seen was a Land-Rover of the same color as Dempster's going fast on the main Dunkeld road later that day, and that hardly qualified as a positive identification. Danielle had been at the shop all morning, sounded very upset, but seemed even more concerned for the safety of her own two small children who were at school at the time.

With an increasing sense of frustration Doug put the cards back into the pile. Maybe he shouldn't bother with all this data; it was just confusing him.

The Rosses; Graham and Evelyn. Graham had come home at midday on that occasion—rather unusual, but he had a perfectly satisfactory explanation; for once he had no lunchtime business appointment and decided to take Evelyn out as it was her birthday. Doug didn't even look at Evelyn's card; he had memorized all the relevant information he had about her. Could she legitimately be considered a suspect? The timing of her arrival just after the discovery of Magnus Lumsden's little body was maybe just a coincidence, but Douglas thrived on coincidences. And there had been such a calm about her, such poise . . . In retrospect, Douglas felt that she had actually enjoyed the whole thing. But why would she have killed the baby? What conceivable reason could she have for doing such a thing, especially now that she and Stella were such good friends?

One other possibility existed and that would have to be checked again; several days before the murder, one of the tradespeople down at the shops near the Estate had reported a strange man hanging around the neighborhood. He'd bought a packet of cigarettes, smoked one outside the shop, then gone off along Lossie Road. He hadn't done anything suspicious, it was simply that he was shabbily dressed and they didn't know who he was. The duty sergeant had sent a car, but they had found nobody; the man had disappeared.

Douglas opened the top left-hand drawer of his desk and pulled out a small bottle of aspirins. He put two in the palm of his hand and swallowed them, but they stuck halfway and he had to go down the hall to the staff lavatory to get a drink of water.

He found Constable Jamieson standing by the open window, smoking a cigarette.

"Solved the case?" asked Douglas tartly. The water tap would only run as long as he pressed on it, and he couldn't get much water into one cupped hand.

"Yes, sir," said Jamieson, looking quite serene. "It was Mr. Lumsden who done it."

As he walked back to his office, Douglas acknowledged that Jamieson was probably right. In real life, the most obvious answers were nearly always correct.

The telephone was ringing when he opened the door. It was Cathie; she usually called about this time. She'd got a nice piece of cod at the fish shop, and would he like it in a cream sauce or just boiled? They chatted for a little while, inconsequentially. These phone calls, although he'd frowned on them at first, had become one of the highlights of his day. As he put the phone down, he wondered what they would be having for dinner up at Lossie House. Pheasant under glass, maybe, or a haunch of venison, followed by Evelyn Ross's trifle . . . Now then, he told himself, you're sounding childish and jealous. Would you really trade places with those people, with all their money, all those estates, if you knew that your baby was lying stiff, cold and gutted in the mortuary? Douglas gave an involuntary shiver, and felt glad that Cathie and he didn't have any children to worry about.

Douglas turned to the stack of unopened post on the desk. There was a copy of a report to the Scottish Home Secretary about a recent disturbance at the prison, a computer-generated list of car thefts in the area last month, and a note from the superintendent concerning an item on Douglas's expense account. He crumpled the scrap of paper in one hand

and threw it angrily at the round metal wastepaper basket, missing his target. As he bent to pick it up, his sense of frustration increased and the pressure made his head throb again. The whole thing didn't make any sense; it was getting more and more obvious that the only hope of really clearing the case up was to find Dempster Lumsden.

Chapter Seven

Driving back into town after the autopsy on Magnus Lumsden, Jean joined the traffic leading into South Street, as usual crowded with shoppers. Several people waved to her; the little white Renault was a well-known sight around Perth. She turned the corner, stopped briefly at Mackays for some spaghetti, a bag of frozen prawns, and some grapes and biscuits for her mother. She had a tin of bolognese sauce at home, she knew, and dinner wouldn't take long to prepare. If Fiona or Lisbie came home before she did, they could make it. What a blessing those two girls were! They were always ready to help, even when they were tired after a day's work. She dropped her purchases off at home, left a note for the girls, checked her list of patients to visit; the first one was in a housing estate just beyond the nursing home where her mother stayed, so she decided to stop and spend a few minutes there before going on.

Jean was feeling queasy, and it took her a second to remember why. That poor baby! She saw it again on the stainless steel table, white, eviscerated, emptied. Poor Stella, more like. It was the survivors who suffered, not the dead. If she had time, she'd call in later to see how Stella was doing. At least she had friends who would take care of her, and her brother-in-law was there. And maybe by now Dempster had heard about the tragedy and come home.

By the time Jean had spent half an hour with her mother and finished her rounds it was late, and beginning to get dark. She sat in the car outside the home of her last patient, allowing herself the luxury of feeling tired. All she wanted to do was go home and put her feet up for five minutes before starting on the dinner. She hesitated for a moment. Stella would be all right, surely, it wasn't really necessary to go all the way out there to see her. Then, as she knew she would, and suppressing a sigh at her own inability to leave any work undone or a patient unseen, she fastened her seat belt, started the engine, pushed in a tape and headed toward the Dunkeld road.

She reviewed the events of the past couple of days, absently humming the music along with Richard Strauss. It was amazing that she'd been right there, so soon after Magnus's murder. She could have easily passed the murderer on the road while she was driving there. Surely there had been something, some clue, some indication of who could have done it. What had she missed? What had she seen but not noticed? She forced herself to go through the entire dreadful sequence in her head; the drive there . . . There hadn't been much traffic, but the only vehicle she could actually remember seeing was a truck from Bell's distillery which had pulled out too close in front of her . . . then pulling up outside Stella's house . . . it had stopped raining about ten minutes before, but only just. Had there been a dry patch outside the Lumsdens', where a car—Dempster's car—might have stood? She racked her brain, but simply couldn't remember. If only she'd known at the time that it was important to look . . . Then Stella's horrified expression when she came out of the bedroom, the strange ambulance men, Amanda . . . Jean stopped short, right on that thought. Amanda had known something, there was no mistaking her look. And it wasn't just the fact that a police car and an ambulance were outside, there had been something in her expression, as if she were saying, Oh God, it's finally happened . . .

Evelyn Ross. Jean hadn't told Doug Niven everything she knew about her, not by any means, although she'd given him as big a hint as she could. Evelyn had been in mental hospitals on at least two occasions that she knew of, and maybe more. In addition to having recurring problems with severe depression, Evelyn had two more severe episodes of paranoid schizophrenia, when she thought people were out to kill her. The first time it happened, she had arrived at the surgery, dressed up rather formally. She seemed entirely normal; they chatted briefly about the hot weather they had been experiencing, then, quite calmly, as if she were reporting something she'd read about in the paper, Evelyn told Jean that her neighbors had been sending poisonous gases under her door and whispering about her in the streets. That time, she had responded quite well to treatment. Poor Graham, he coped as best he could, but it wasn't easy for him. And there was not much doubt that she was the reason for his lack of promotion. It was really a shame, because he was a clever and capable banker. He was caught in a trap, the poor chap, because if he divorced Evelyn, his stuffy bosses at the National Bank would be just as disapproving of him as they now were about Evelyn.

Jean turned off the main road. It was quite dark

now, and the row of shops was closed. She slowed again coming up to the sharp turn into Lossie Road. She could see an unusual number of lights in the houses through the trees as she went past; they must be nervous, Jean thought. The empty house before the Rosses' was shrouded in darkness, like a missing tooth. There was something eerie, frightening about the place, but that was probably just because it had been unoccupied so long. The grass around it was a foot high, the gate was ajar, and the front garden all overgrown.

As she slowly passed by the Armstrongs' house, she saw a flash of light from the front door and the huge silhouette of Keith Armstrong appeared for a moment, then vanished. Jean gave a shiver of discomfort; there was something unusually unpleasant about that man. Poor little Danielle; Jean wouldn't have liked to be in her shoes.

She negotiated the turn into the rhododendron-lined drive, her headlights making a tunnel through the darkness until it widened in front of the house. She parked just beyond the well-lit porch of the Lumsdens' house, and with a strange retrospective attention, Jean noted every detail of her short walk to the Lumsdens' front door, which was lit by floodlights fixed to the outside wall of the porch. On the opposite side of the drive, Stella had planted rosebushes, lots of them, long, elegant yellow and pink tea roses on the right, and robust dark red floribunda on the left. They had still been in bloom two weeks ago, but now were reduced to bare, skeletal stems. Jean hesitated for a second. Everything was silent, except for the regular drip of water from a gutter out of sight above her head. And everything had changed from the time she and Steven had come here for dinner only a few weeks ago, when it was a cheerful, open, welcoming country house with nothing but smiles in its past. Now it was a silent, brooding place, marked among human habitations for the violent death within its walls, a place where the ghost of little Magnus Lumsden would abide until its stones were pulled down one by one. Jean suppressed a shiver at these morbid thoughts and rang the bell.

Stella opened the door after a few moments, and stared at Jean for a fraction of a second before smiling and inviting her in.

"I wasn't expecting to see you," she said. "I've never known a doctor as nice and considerate as you." Impulsively she put her arms around Jean and hugged her.

Amanda was there too, looking hollow-eyed and sleepless, standing by the fire beside a tall, good-looking young man with a shock of long blond hair which hung rather rakishly over one eye.

Jean walked toward him and put out her hand. "You must be Alexis—I'm sorry to be meeting you at such a sad time." So this was Dempster's brother; he didn't look much like him, but over the last year, the booze had really affected Dempster's appearance; his nose and cheeks had become red with little veins, and his face, handsome in a rather heavy, military kind of way, had suffused and bloated. But this Alexis was quite gorgeous, she thought. She glanced over his immaculate Savile Row suit, handmade shirt and Italian shoes; he would be a nice person for Fiona to meet.

"Stella and Amanda have told me about you," he said. His accent was hard to place—Scottish blended with a good English public school. "I'd like to thank you for all the help you gave them."

"Do sit down," said Stella. She was quite self-possessed now, and her grief seemed to have made her even more beautiful. "Can I get you anything? A glass of wine?"

"A wee sherry would be nice, if you have it," said Jean. She felt a bit uncomfortable in the company of these elegant people. "I just wanted to be sure you were all right . . . Are you getting some sleep?"

"Well, not much." Stella poured sherry into a small crystal glass. "This is Bristol Cream. Will that be all right, or would you like a drier one?"

"Oh, no, that will be just fine, it's my favorite, thank you." She turned to Alexis. "Has there been any word from Dempster?"

"Nothing at all, I'm afraid." He flicked the hair out of his eyes with a graceful gesture, and Jean noticed a scar, so well-healed it was almost invisible, on the side of his nose and up on to his forehead. "Tomorrow I'm going to Glasgow to look for him. We're all sure he had nothing to do with what happened yesterday . . ." He looked at Stella for confirmation and she nodded vigorously.

"Dempster is such a gentle person, he wouldn't dream of hurting anybody, let alone his own baby."

Somehow her words sounded strange to Jean; she would not have immediately characterized Dempster Lumsden as gentle, but Stella was his wife and she should know.

"Amanda," said Jean, turning to her quickly to give Stella a chance to recover the poise she looked about to lose, "how are *you* doing? I know this has been as much of a shock for you as for anybody."

In face, Amanda looked as if she were the bereaved mother; she was so haggard.

"I'm fine," she answered shortly. "If you'll excuse me, I was in the middle of cooking dinner." She left the room almost at a run. That woman looks at the end of her rope, thought Jean, anxiously following her with her eyes. She's taking this worse than I could ever have expected.

"She's terribly upset about Magnus, and about Dempster, of course," said Alexis as he accompanied Jean to the door a few moments later. But to Jean it seemed as if there were more to it than that. Amanda seemed to be bearing an even greater burden than Stella, and at that thought her heart sank once again. Before this awful business was over, she knew, the pain would have spread to many others, like a plague.

Outside, the night was crisp and moonless, and the stars sparkled in the cold air. There was no wind, and the silence was absolute. She stood beside her car, absorbing the peace, but only for a moment. The restlessness of her spirit didn't allow her to do anymore than pause in her headlong rush through her life. She drove slowly down the drive and into Lossie Road. For no real reason, she slowed, then stopped outside the empty house next to the Rosses', and sat in the car with the window down. A tiny sound close by attracted her attention. It seemed to come from near the gate. Curious, Jean got out of the car, and heard a quick scampering. It must be a mouse, or some other small rodent . . . She looked beyond the gate toward the house. The dark bulk of it stood stark against the sky, and somehow it seemed to beckon to her. It didn't even occur to Jean to be scared, and before she knew it she was walking along the path, the long grass rustling as she passed, then along the side of the house, finding her way by the light of her pocket torch, the one she used to look into the back of people's throats. Out of sheer curiosity, she tried the back door, and to her astonishment it opened with a creak. Some estate agent must have forgotten to lock it, she thought, and went in.

The kitchen was bare, the cupboard doors gaped open like unfed mouths, and her steps echoed when she stepped cautiously into the hall. She thought of switching on the lights, then remembered the electricity was sure to have been turned off, and anyway, if somebody saw a light there, they might call the police. She sniffed. There was the faintest odor of smoke. Somebody must have smoked a cigarette here within the last few days. On her left, the door of the dining room was half open, and the shadows leaped wildly around her as her torch moved. She went through the door, and stopped suddenly. In the far corner, beside a rolled-up carpet, was a kind of pallet, with an old blanket and a tattered army haversack beside it.

Jean didn't hear anything come up behind her. Suddenly a hand reached around her neck and covered her mouth. She tried to scream, and twisted to get out of the grip which threatened to choke her. She brought her heel up sharply behind her, jabbing her elbow backward as hard as she could. She heard a gasp, and the grip was released. A bright light shone in her eyes and she put her hands up to shield herself, blinking painfully.

"My God!" said a familiar voice. "It's the Wee Doc!" The beam was immediately directed to the ceiling, and she saw Douglas Niven standing there, looking at her in shocked surprise. The other man was still on the floor, gasping.

"Get up, Jamieson," barked Doug. "You're embarrassing me!" Then to Jean, "What on earth are you doing here? We were waiting for the person who's been squatting here . . ." he indicated the bedding.

"Oh my," said Jean, "what a scare you gave me! I was just curious. It occurred to me that whoever it was who killed that baby could have hidden here."

"And you came in looking for him, in the dark? You're completely daft, woman!"

"Not so daft, Douglas, and I can take good care of myself." She glanced at Jamieson who was getting to his feet, breathing hard.

"Jamieson, see Dr. Montrose back to her car, please, and make sure she gets off safely." Douglas's voice brooked no disagreement.

"Are you all right?" Jean asked Constable Jamieson, genuinely concerned. "I hope I didn't hurt you."

Jamieson pulled his cap on savagely and muttered something which fortunately neither of the others heard clearly. Silently he led the way back, his torch making a splash of light which Jean obediently followed.

"You probably lost us our man," said Jamieson in a furious whisper, holding the car door as if he'd like to slam it on her.

"Your stomach'll feel a wee bit bruised in the morning," she whispered back. She spoke in a consoling tone, but he could feel the sharp ironic edge on her sympathy. "Take a couple of aspirins when you get home, then it won't be so bad."

* * *

Nobody was very pleased with Jean when she got home; her iron rule that everybody should eat together had rebounded on her. The girls said nothing, but looked at her reproachfully. Steven didn't bother to conceal his irritation.

"If you can't be home at meal times, you can't insist that we wait for you, you know," he said.

"Well, I'm sorry," said Jean, smiling. "It doesn't happen often, now, does it?" She looked into the kitchen. Fiona had cooked the spaghetti, but it had sat in the pan for too long without water and was pretty well solidified. Jean quickly ran the hot water until it was almost boiling, filled the pan, put in some olive oil, put it on the high gas and stirred vigorously for a couple of minutes. The sauce was a little crusty around the edges of the pan but that was also cured with a brisk stir.

"Right! We're all set!" she said, and everybody sat down round the big dining room table. Steven, still looking a little tense, served the spaghetti, and his lips tightened when the telephone rang.

Lisbie ran to answer it. She came back into the dining room a moment later, dragging her feet. "It's for you, Mum. It's the hospital."

Feeling guilty, Jean got up. When she came back, she was white, and the others all stopped eating when they saw her expression. She sat down and tried to go on with her meal.

"What is it, Mum? What happened?" Lisbie, so sensitive that when something upset one of the family it made her almost ill, went as pale as her mother.

"That was the police. They're just sending Amanda Delincourt to hospital by ambulance." And try as they might to get more information out of her, that was all Jean told them, except that it wasn't something she could deal with, but she would go to the hospital to see Amanda in a couple of hours.

Chapter Eight

When Jean got to the hospital, the car park was almost empty, except for a little clump of cars belonging to the night staff, huddled, as if for mutual protection, near the back entrance. Jean left her car in the doctors' parking area and walked across the darkened expanse, stepping round the puddles, her footsteps resounding metallically in the silence.

She'd waited for two hours before coming to the hospital; Niven had told her Amanda had cut her wrists, and there was no point in getting in the way of the emergency doctors who would be taking care of her.

The woman in the reception area checked the daysheet.

"She's on McDonald ward, on the first floor, Dr. Montrose," she said. "They just got back from theater about ten minutes ago, but they said she's awake."

Stella and Alexis were sitting on a bench outside the ward, and they both got up when they saw Jean.

"They just took her back," said Alexis softly. "She seems okay, she recognized us."

Jean hesitated for a second. No, she decided, she'd wait until later to ask them what happened.

Amanda was in the bed next to the door, so that

the comings and goings would disturb as few people as possible. The curtains were drawn around the bed and the light was the only one in the darkened ward. Jean pulled the curtains open, and saw Amanda lying with her head back, eyes closed, an intravenous drip in one arm, and bandages on both wrists. Detective Inspector Niven was sitting by the bed; he looked up when Jean arrived.

"Dr. Montrose," he murmured, partly as a greeting but also to let Amanda know she had another visitor. Amanda didn't move. Jean pulled a chair from beside the next bed and pulled the curtain closed behind her. She put her hand on Amanda's long, pale fingers, only the tips of which were showing beyond the bandages, and looked at Niven. With both hands, he mimed cutting wrists with a knife.

Why? she mouthed. He shrugged. That's why I'm here, he indicated.

"Amanda?" She opened her eyes. Without any make-up Amanda looked awful, her skin gray and lined, bags under her puffy eyes as if she hadn't slept for days. Jean had difficulty remembering that she was only in her late twenties.

"I'm sorry . . ." Her lips were dry, cracked, and her eyes fixed on Jean like a limpet. Jean got up, dipped a face-cloth in the glass of water on the bedside table and gently moistened Amanda's lips.

"Why, Amanda, why?"

Amanda didn't reply, just shook her head as if to dislodge thoughts stuck inside it.

"Amanda, is there anything you want? Anything I can do for you?"

"Yes, there is." Amanda was suddenly alert. She tried to sit up, her eyes fixed on Jean's face, but her wrists hurt, and she fell back on the pillow again. "Can I get ECT?"

"ECT!" Jean stiffened. "Is that what you mean, Electroconvulsive Therapy?"

Amanda nodded, but Doug looked blank. Jean spoke to him in a quick aside. "It's often called electric shock treatment," she said putting her hands up to her temples to indicate the placement of the electrodes. She turned back to Amanda.

"Whatever do you want that for, Amanda? That's for people with terrible depression that can't be treated any other way . . . Or were you thinking of something else?"

"No, that's it. I read about it in *Vogue* . . . how it makes you lose your memory. Is that right?"

"Yes, some people think that's how it works against depression."

"Well that's what I want," she said, her voice beginning to rise, "that's what I want!" A young nurse appeared silently at the curtain. Her dark hair was drawn back tightly on each side of her head, giving her a look of dedicated severity.

"It's time for your injection," she said to Amanda, and Jean made room for her to pull up Amanda's loose hospital gown. Doug discreetly looked the other way. With one hand the nurse gently pushed her over to expose her buttock, then stuck the needle in expertly with the other and pushed the plunger of the syringe with her thumb. "Pethidine," said the nurse, glancing at Jean. And then very quietly, "She seemed very disturbed when she came in."

"Why do you want to lose your memory, Amanda?" Doug asked gently after the nurse had gone, but Amanda's eyes were closed, and she seemed to have gone to sleep.

Jean got up. "Are you staying?" she asked Doug, and he nodded. Big deal, his shrug said, what's one more night away from home?

"I'll let Stella and Alexis in?" Jean's words were more of a question.

"Not yet, if you don't mind," replied Doug. "I'd like a chance to talk to Amanda by herself. I'll let them in later."

Stella and Alexis were still sitting silently on the bench when Jean tiptoed out of the ward.

"She seems all right now," she told them. They both looked drawn and haggard in the semidarkness.

Jean sat down next to Stella.

"Can you tell me what happened?"

"Well, it was soon after you left . . ." Was there a tone of accusation in Stella's voice? Jean looked sharply at her, but she must have been mistaken. Her expression hadn't changed, it remained just tired and sad.

". . . She was saying she couldn't stay in the house any longer, and she ran upstairs. Alexis went to see if everything was all right in the kitchen— Amanda had burned some rice earlier, she couldn't seem to concentrate on what she was doing—and from the hall he could hear that she had gone into the small bathroom on the first floor landing. She was making noises, like little screams." Stella looked over at Alexis for confirmation. He nodded, and took up the story.

"I went into the kitchen, did a couple of things there, then went back into the living room. Everything seemed quiet, then . . ." Alexis took a deep breath. "There was this horrible scream and she came running downstairs.'' Jean could feel Stella shudder beside her at the recollection. ''There was blood dripping from both her hands . . .'' Jean sensed, more than actually saw a quick warning look pass from Stella to Alexis. He stopped talking suddenly, as if he weren't quite sure what he'd said wrong.

''Then what happened?'' asked Jean.

Stella took up the account. ''I ran to get a towel while Alexis called for an ambulance. I wrapped up her wrists as best I could. There was quite a lot of blood, but I didn't think she'd hit the artery.'' Maybe it was the lateness of the hour, or the fact that they were conversing in whispers, but Jean's possibly oversensitive ears felt some very strange vibrations in Stella's voice. As if she wished that Amanda *had* hit the artery, and on both arms.

Just then Douglas Niven came out of the ward and signaled to Stella and Alexis to come in. Jean said a whispered goodnight to all of them, and headed toward the stairs, feeling sad and quite alone with the terrifying speculations that twisted and writhed like a thousand maggots inside her head.

The whole hospital seemed shut down for the night, and the few people she saw on her way out moved quietly around like ghosts on soft rubber soles.

The clock on St. John's kirk struck twelve as she got into her car. Midnight, the witching hour, the hour of bogles and long-leggity beasties . . . Amanda . . . What was it she wanted so badly to forget? Maybe her husband, who had divorced her? That she hadn't been around to defend her nephew Magnus from the killer? And what was it that had compelled her to cut her wrists? Was it a cry for help, or was it a real attempt to kill herself? If so, why did she scream and come running down the stairs like that? She must have known what a horrific impression that would make on Stella, whose son had been so recently murdered in the same house. Maybe Amanda had done that purposely to horrify them? Or had she cut her wrists in a paroxysm of guilt? Was that why she wanted to be given ECT? Was it so she could forget what she had seen, or . . . done?

Jean drove slowly home, automatically, her mind filled with dread. The only thing she felt she knew for certain that night was that the pit of horrors was far from empty; if she stopped for a moment to listen, she could hear the hissing of the snakes.

Danielle Armstrong had made few friends since coming to Perth; her two children were too small to have their own friends, and Keith . . . They'd been asked out a few times when they first came, but she could sense that Keith wasn't liked; it wasn't just his size, obviously, that turned people off, but it seemed to compound the repressed violence in his nature. It was that, blended with a kind of unconvincing desire to please which made people nervous of him.

Of course, things had improved for a while since coming from Aberdeen, but that wasn't much consolation; they couldn't have got a great deal worse.

Danielle had always been a popular person, ever since she was a child, so feeling like a social outcast now made it all the more difficult. At Aberdeen University she had been dynamite, establishing a new women's 100 meter sprint record in her second year, elected president of the women's union in her third, and gaining a 2.1 in modern languages in her fourth. As one of her professors said, inch for inch—Danielle was almost five feet tall—and pound for pound—she was tiny—she was the best thing that had happened to the University for years. Then she met Keith, clever, unpredictable, who'd given up a promising career as a stockbroker to become a weaver, of all things. It was maybe the size of him, the contrast, the hugeness that gave her an orgasmic thrill just from watching him. Nobody believed her when she said she was going to marry Keith Armstrong. Her mother, also a tiny woman, tactfully suggested that the disparity in size would present some major and possibly painful problems, but even that thought had only given her a wild quiver of anticipation.

Keith had begun to make some really good things on his loom. He had developed a style which blended some of the characteristics of ancient Mayan patterns with the more traditional Scottish ones, and it had attracted enough attention for him to set up a tiny workshop. Keith had no idea about accounts or any other aspect of business matters, even though he had dealt in stocks and shares, and soon after they were married, Danielle had made the error of offering to keep the books, take care of the bills and so on. But even in those early days she'd already begun to feel the fear of him which never left her now.

Far from being a gentle giant, he turned out to be a petulant bully, who excused all his scenes and rages by saying it was for "his art." He also believed strongly that punishment should follow crime, and anything that happened to displease him was by definition a crime.

He was only slightly drunk when he came home in the early afternoon one day when they were still living in the tiny ramshackle house off MacIver

Street. They had been married a mere few months, but Danielle had already learned that this stage of drunkenness was when he could be at his worst. When he became more intoxicated, she easily avoided his flying fists; after all she presented a small and still very athletic target.

She could hear him singing, if you could call it that, just before the front door crashed open downstairs. Actually it was half shout, half hum, and it was always the same tune, "Scotland the Brave," and he marched briskly to his own music like an Assyrian wolf on his way to the fold.

He started to come up the stairs, the boards creaking under his weight, and Danielle braced herself, determined not to do anything that could annoy or upset him.

He stood in the doorway, redhaired, shaggy and dishevelled as a Highland bull, his feet apart, the third finger of his left hand squirrelling up his nose. He looked at her with a kind of boozy jollity. Maybe it was going to be all right . . .

"Here, gie' us a hug!" He stood there, opening his arms for her. She ran over to him, full of relief, and he put his arms around her and squeezed, and squeezed . . . She thought she was going to die; she couldn't speak, just looked at him. When he let go, she dropped on her hands and knees in front of him, wheezing, faint, unable to speak.

"And where the fuck is the alizarin red wool you were supposed to order from Shetland?"

And of course, he refused to listen to her explanation.

"Take your clothes off," he said, aloof and dominant like a Roman emperor, and when he impaled her and she screamed with the vicious, deliberate pain of it, he put his huge hand over her whole face, so she screamed silently, biting her tongue without even knowing it.

Yet in company, there was no one like him. At parties, he brought chairs for her to sit on, he opened the car door and handed her out like a Duchess, he deferred gently in mixed conversation, but when she glanced at him she could see from his bright, pitiless expression that this was just another cruelty he was practicing on her.

"I don't know what you've done to change him," said a mutual friend, marvelling. "He used to be such a pig; we were really worried about you marrying him."

About four years and two children later he met Dempster Lumsden at a party, and for weeks thereafter, it was nothing but Dempster this and Dempster that. The two men went for long walks together, talked about art, the resurgence of Scottish crafts, the vicissitudes of life. Keith smoked Dempster's cigars, ate his dinners. After all he was poor and Dempster was rich.

"Why don't you get a studio with a shop in Perth?" Dempster said one day, looking at a new piece still on the loom. "There are lots of visitors during the summer, and you'll become rich and famous a lot faster there."

Keith laughed his famous sardonic laugh and explained that there was a little thing that stood in the way of that otherwise excellent idea, and that little thing was called money.

To Dempster, good-hearted and full of admiration and enthusiasm for Keith's genius, this was only a minor problem. He would loan him enough money to buy a place in Perth where he could set up his looms and sell his fine woven blankets and dress material. And there was a vacant house in the Lossie Estate, almost next door to where they lived. Dempster would arrange a lease with an option to buy; the rent would be deducted from the price if he decided to purchase the house. Dempster had a vision of the beginning of an artistic enclave, a colony of artists, writers and craftsmen who would renew the cultural life of Scotland.

Everything went perfectly; Keith was soon established in a workshop near the harbor, although few people seemed to feel quite the same enthusiasm for his work that Dempster Lumsden did, and the house was perfect, larger and finer than anything either Danielle or Keith could have imagined.

The two men often went drinking together, always out of town, sometimes staying out overnight if they didn't want to take the risk of driving home. Neither Danielle nor Stella knew where they went, and they never asked, although Stella thought it was probably some low pub in the Gorbals area of Glasgow.

For Danielle, this was a charmed period; Keith treated her with a kind of rough contempt, it was true, but he wasn't nearly so violent and the children, who used to start crying when they heard him come home, developed a wary love for him.

Then disaster struck. Danielle never knew what had happened, but one day, a few months before Magnus Lumsden's murder, Keith came home in a white, blinding rage and Dempster never spoke to him again, communicating only through his solicitor, and only about the money Keith owed him for the house and the shop.

And now, Danielle was in the grip of a new terror. She tried to keep herself and her children out of his way, but things were not going well at the workshop. Keith seemed consumed by rage; he stalked about the house, talking to himself and looking at her occasionally with a red, homicidal fury. But he didn't touch her, and she was thankful for that. She thought of leaving him, taking the children with her, but the thought of his anger, and what he would do to them when he finally caught up with them, kept her at home, hoping that one day he might have a fatal accident.

After the Lumsden baby murder Keith seemed to improve, maybe because he enjoyed the fact that the Lumsdens were suddenly in such trouble. He even said to Danielle once that if Dempster didn't ever come home, Stella would be a lot easier for him to deal with, meaning the loan, the house, and the other financial dealings presently all snarled up in their antagonisms.

Danielle, awake and shivering at her own imaginings, lay next to Keith's huge slumbering bulk, wondering poisoned thoughts . . . Could he have done it? Danielle ticked off all the factors in her mind. Keith had been alone in the house on the morning of the murder. He could see the comings and goings at Lossie House from the bedroom window, so he could tell when the house was empty. He had all the strength it would take to kill an adult person, let alone a baby. He had all the hatred for Dempster, all the rage it would take to commit such a crime. All in all, whichever way she looked at it, the answer was an unequivocal yes.

Chapter Nine

Jean was surprised that Stella Lumsden decided to have Magnus buried before Dempster had come home; she would have expected it to be a private funeral. It turned out later that Doug Niven had applied some pressure on Stella and Alexis to go ahead with it; a well-publicized funeral would surely draw Dempster Lumsden out of wherever he was hiding. Niven was getting increasingly frustrated by his inability to track down Dempster. He had put in quite an effort to find him, and he'd asked for help from his old colleagues in Glasgow, but as it was a case from out of town and without much potential for good publicity, the Glasgow police had neither the incentive nor the manpower to spend time and energy searching through every sleazy bar and pub in and around the city.

Jean, of course, felt she had to go to the service. She always tried to put in an appearance at the funerals of patients who had the misfortune to die. Steven wouldn't let her go to the service for Magnus by herself, and the girls insisted that the whole family should be represented, so on the appointed day they all set off in Steven's car which he had washed and waxed for the occasion.

Jean's dark suit and white blouse looked nice, but

the height of her heels made her look uncomfortable and off balance. She wondered about wearing a hat, but Steven laughed and told her nobody wore hats these days.

"Just as well," replied Jean, "because I don't have one."

Lisbie wore a royal blue dress with matching shiny leather belt, and Fiona started off with a fluffy-looking pink and white dress with a short skirt which showed more leg than was strictly necessary, but both her parents thought it was unsuitable and made her change into something less "summery," as Jean tactfully put it.

The murder was recent enough to attract a crowd around St. John's Kirk. Steven parked the car round the corner, and Jean's eyes ran quickly over the crowd; according to Niven, there would be plain-clothes members of the CID scanning the faces for Dempster Lumsden. Niven's theory was that even if he wanted to stay in hiding for whatever reason, he would somehow manage to join the crowd outside in a separate mourning.

A television crew stood by their van, parked near the main entrance of the church, the cameraman waiting patiently with a video camera on his shoulder, his assistant holding the long cable, ready to follow at a moment's notice.

"Aren't you glad now you didn't wear that dress?" Jean whispered to Fiona, who sniffed and glanced at the camera crew. That dress would have got her on the telly, she felt pretty sure of that.

Inside, all was cool and quiet; not many of the public wanted to sit through the entire ceremony, and only close friends, neighbors and a few reporters who wanted to get out of the cold were inside.

Jean led her little group, and they sat down about five rows from the front, behind almost everybody.

It was a good vantage point, although Jean was the only one to whom that idea occurred; she was getting sly and treacherous in her old age, she thought, and it made her sad that she should even think in these terms.

"Who's that with Stella?" asked Fiona, who was taking it all in with round eyes. Jean looked at the front row, expecting to see Alexis, Stella's brother-in-law, but instead she saw a very old white-haired gentleman, sitting erect, staring straight in front of him.

"That must be Mr. Lumsden's father," she whispered back. "Lord Aviemore." Fiona's eyes grew bigger; it was the first time she'd ever seen a real Lord except at the Braemar Gathering, and there they'd been too far away to get a really good look.

Jean looked around for Alexis, and at that moment he came into the church, looking spare and distinguished in an immaculate dark suit and black tie. He saw Jean sitting next to the aisle and briefly put a hand on her shoulder and smiled as if to say thank you for coming, before he went on to join Stella and the rest of his family. Amanda was there, of course, next to Stella, wearing a long-sleeved black dress. She had apparently recovered well from her suicide attempt; the doctor at the hospital had said her injuries were superficial, and she'd only had to stay in the hospital that one night. Amanda turned, caught Jean's eye and smiled, a thin, wan smile. Jean was very worried about her; she had refused a psychiatric consultation, and had also refused to tell anybody what had precipitated her self-destructive attack.

The organ was playing, "Jesu, joy of Man's de-

siring," and Jean recognized the quiet, mournful
music; she had it on one of the cassettes she kept in
her car. The Rosses were sitting behind the Lumsden
party and Graham was leaning forward, saying
something to Stella. Evelyn was looking on, and
Jean, to her horror, caught sight of her giving one
of the most malignant glares she had ever seen. It
was enough to make Jean catch her breath, and before she could see who it had been aimed at, it was
instantly replaced by Evelyn's usual benign, if
slightly distant smile. Jean looked at Steven for a
second to see if he'd noticed, but he was busy trying
to read the dates and inscriptions on the battle-
standards of the Highland Light Infantry in the Lady
Chapel opposite. Jean looked back at Evelyn, who,
her expression entirely normal, was now saying
something to her husband. Graham was splendidly
attired in full Highland dress, complete with plaid
and cairngorm brooch. Surely she'd imagined it; the
light wasn't very good, and Jean knew that shadows
could be misleading.

The church door opened again and Keith Armstrong came in, followed a few paces behind by
Danielle, who looked tinier than ever. He marched
past Jean; he had made no attempt to dress for the
occasion and wore a gray-green Harris tweed jacket
with bone buttons and light green polyester trousers.
The man was so big that Jean felt the draught of his
passing. Danielle slowed, hesitated, and gave Jean a
look that startled her completely. It was a beseech-
ing gaze, but Keith stopped two pews ahead and
looked round for her, so she went on without stopping; Jean was certain she'd been about to say something, but didn't want to be seen by her husband
talking to the Wee Doc.

The pew creaked when Keith sat down, and Stella looked across the aisle. She must have caught his eye for a fraction of a second, because she seemed to flinch momentarily before turning away. Steven saw it too, and they exchanged glances. Jean couldn't believe all the undercurrents of emotion that she was witnessing at a time when everyone's mind should have been fixed on the sad little body in the varnished coffin in front of them.

She made an effort to compose her mind to do just that, and kept her eyes firmly on the bier. The Very Reverend Vernon Paisley walked in with his attendants, his face masked with professional sorrow, and the organ swelled in a muted diapason, soon dropping to an almost inaudible tone as he started the service with a sonorous "Dearly beloved, we are gathered here to bid farewell to Magnus . . ."

It was soon over and the pallbearers carried the pathetic little coffin down the aisle and slid it on the rollers into the hearse. Lisbie, more sentimental and soft-hearted than her sister, wept into her hankie as the sad procession passed, but Fiona seemed more interested in how the women were dressed. Not that she was heartless, by any means. Fiona had no well-defined concept of death; she had never lost a close relative, and to her, Magnus Lumsden's death was just a cessation, a disappearance. His parents would miss him, she had no doubt, but they could always make another baby if they wanted to.

When they came out of the church, the TV crew had gone, and only a few stragglers were left to gape at the mourners. Jean felt unaccountably sad and apprehensive that Dempster had not made it; could he really be so perpetually drunk that all the events of the last few days had passed him by? Jean still could not believe that he could have killed his own child, but she knew that as the days went by without any word from him, Doug Niven's attitude was hardening against Dempster, and his suspicions were getting more difficult to dispute.

Graham Ross left the funeral and walked to the car park behind the theater where they had left their Vauxhall. Evelyn was on his arm, and they looked a fine couple with him swinging along in his kilt and her walking alongside him in a green sweater and Ross tartan skirt. Graham was thirty-seven, sturdily built, going to fat, with thinning blond hair showing a pink, rounded, bullet-shaped scalp. His collar looked tight round his short neck, and a fold of flesh rolled over the back, like a sealion. His eyes were small and intelligent, but in spite of his purposeful stride and erect posture there was something beaten, something defeated about his expression. People said that it was because he hadn't made the expected big move to the main office in Edinburgh. When he first came to Perth almost five years before, he was billed as a brilliant, up-and-coming young banker who would spend a couple of years at most running the Perth branch before moving up the executive ladder, probably finishing up as chairman of the board. But then he'd married Evelyn . . .

It had been a classic story—he was a hard-working, studious man who didn't socialize too much and had had only a few transient and unsatisfactory relationships with women. He was in his early thirties, and his bosses tactfully suggested it was time he married, developed a social life and better social skills. In the upper echelons of banking, they hinted, a considerable amount of entertaining was expected, and he should consider getting a wife whose talents included those of being an agreeable and sophisticated hostess. There was never any question about his competence; Graham had developed a system for marketing foreign securities using computer-generated data which had caused a major stir in that rather arcane field, and he was clearly marked for stardom. His whirlwind romance with the beautiful but deeply troubled Evelyn McArdle, eight years his junior, resulted in a fine wedding in St. Giles Cathedral in Edinburgh. Her father, a psychiatrist, was so relieved to have her off his hands that he spared no expense, and the wedding hit the society pages of the newspapers even in London.

"I'm surprised Dempster didn't show up," said Graham, looking straight ahead.

"No you're not," replied Evelyn, smiling and waving at Steven Montrose and his family getting into their car on the opposite side of the road. "I happen to *know* you're not."

"My, my," said Graham after a moment. His face showed no sign of his sudden apprehension, except for a slight tightening of his lips.

"You wouldn't happen to have been reading my business letters, by any chance?" Even as he said it, he knew it was impossible. All his correspondence with Dempster Lumsden was kept in the small safe in his office, and he'd never brought any of it home. They turned the corner in silence and went past the raised barrier of the car park. As he always did, Graham opened the passenger door for his wife and closed it once she was in. Everybody envied Evelyn; her husband was always such a perfect gentleman.

As he put the key in the ignition, he suddenly realized how Evelyn could have known about his dealings with Dempster Lumsden; they had always discussed their business affairs in Graham's office, except for just one time.

"Well, dearest, you must have been eavesdropping that time when Dempster came over." His voice had years of bitterness behind it. "You were so drunk that night, I'm surprised you remembered anything you heard."

It had been the culmination of a long, bad deal, the only one that had ever gone really sour on the normally cautious Graham. About two weeks ago, Dempster had come through their garden from his house and knocked loudly on the back door. Evelyn had jumped as if she'd been shot, even though she was already aggressively drunk. Graham had opened the door.

"Dempster!" he said, without much enthusiasm. "Come on in. My, it's cold out there."

Dempster nodded at Evelyn, who suddenly became distant and haughty, barely acknowledged his greeting and ostentatiously picked up a newspaper. Dempster followed Graham into his study.

"Well, Dempster," he said, trying to hide his anxiety, "I hope you have some good news for me."

In answer, Dempster held out a letter. The first thing Graham saw was the embossed blue coat of arms at the top, the Aviemore family crest.

"Just a second." Graham's hand shook slightly as he put on his reading glasses. "There is no reason why I should underwrite either your business incompetence or your investment follies . . ." Graham read, muttering the words almost to himself. He glanced at his visitor over his glasses. No emotion showed on Dempster's impassive face, only a slight pallor in his normally ruddy complexion. Graham read on, his voice just audible. ". . . I suggest that failing further financial assistance from your bankers, you should consider the possibility of starting formal bankruptcy proceedings. I trust you will make every effort to do this without further embarrassing our ancient family . . ."

Graham folded the letter and handed it back to Dempster, his mind racing. This was going to put the final nail in the coffin of his career; already head office had been sending worried memos, and next week someone was coming over from Edinburgh to discuss the Lumsden account. Both he and Dempster had depended on Lord Aviemore's fabulous wealth if for some reason the project failed. In fact, Graham had as security the deeds of a large estate in Midlothian in his office safe, but it had turned out that Aviemore himself would have to approve the sale of the land, and that approval was not forthcoming. So, as a security, the deed was worthless.

"So what happened?" Graham had trouble making his voice sound calm.

"We built the factory, all right." Dempster pulled out an envelope of glossy photos from his pocket and passed them to Graham. "Complete specifications, down to the projection system in the chairman's office, and the proper number of lavatories for the workers."

"So what happened?" repeated Graham, his voice rising in spite of himself.

"The Hokkaido Corporation bought another factory, in Dundee," replied Dempster. " 'Solly, so velly solly,' they said, when I asked them about it."

Graham put his head between his hands, trying to control his anger. Dempster didn't seem to understand what was happening to them both. He had the old, upper-class attitude to money; it was really beneath his dignity to have to talk about it, let alone deal with the stuff.

"But the contract, man! How could they renege on that?"

"The small print said that the contract was subject to ratification by their labor committee."

"Dempster, how did you miss that? How could you . . ."

"It was the local unions, apparently," Dempster went on, sounding quite insouciant. "They got paid a lump sum by the people who built the other factory. And you know how the Nips hate to have to deal with labor problems, especially at the start of a project . . . Now I'm quite sure we could fight it in the courts, but we'd be down the drain long before it came to a trial."

"Can't you sell the factory to some other country? After all, it's the most up to date . . ."

" 'Fraid not, old chap. Purpose-built, they call it. Not much good for anything else. We could rent it out as a warehouse, I suppose, but that wouldn't cover a fraction of the costs."

"Do you have any other source of financing?"

"Besides you? No, my tiny share of the family jewels are in hock somewhere already, not that they would do us much good anyway. I don't get anything more until the old man dies, and he's in better physical shape than I am."

Graham stood up, appalled. He could feel his legs shaking under him. The worst thing was Dempster's apparent lack of concern; if only the man could recognize that they were both facing disaster, maybe he'd be more inclined to do something about it.

"Couldn't you work on your father, threaten suicide, or something?'' Graham started to pace up and down the room in agitation. "There must be some way to get the old . . . gentleman to keep you from bankruptcy." And me from getting ignominiously fired and probably prosecuted, he added to himself.

"I think he stated his position rather clearly here, don't you?" Dempster smiled, waving the letter. Maybe the alcohol has scrambled his brains, thought Graham, and from then on his anxieties had to do with how he could get himself out of this disastrous situation. Dempster was on his own; he'd just have to take his chances.

Graham turned to Dempster. "Why don't you just disappear, go to South America or somewhere, stay out there for a while until the heat's off?" he asked. "If the burden suddenly fell on Stella, I'm sure your father would take over and get her out of the trouble you'd left her in."

"That's a thought," said Dempster, suddenly sounding brighter. "He certainly dotes on Stella. Yes, he'd probably do it for her if he thought I'd . . . gone. Let me think about it."

A week later, Dempster had obtained his passport and a ticket to Lisbon, and one from there to Rio de Janeiro, and was all set to go. Then, a few days before Magnus Lumsden was murdered, he backed out, quite suddenly and without any apparent good reason, merely saying he couldn't go through with it. The next day he disappeared, presumably on one of his binges.

Graham drove out of the car park, his face grim.

"There was one way of making sure Dempster wouldn't come back," said Evelyn brightly. "Wasn't there?"

"And what was that?"

"Kill his baby, and make it look as if he'd done it," said Evelyn. "Then Dempster would have to use his ticket, and go to Rio after all. Old Aviemore couldn't humanly refuse to help Stella, and that of course would get you off the hook with your bank. Good thinking, Graham. I wouldn't have guessed you had it in you."

Graham swerved, narrowly missing a cyclist on the new bridge. His hands were cold and clammy, and the sweat on his brow was incongruous in the cold gray morning.

"Not only that, you fat swine," Evelyn suddenly screamed at the top of her voice, "but I know you fathered that little bastard Magnus!"

Chapter Ten

When the Montroses went out *en famille* Steven always drove. It wasn't that Jean didn't drive well, it just seemed natural that way. He was the man, so he drove. They were all feeling a bit quiet after the funeral, and Jean suggested going for lunch to Crieff Hydro. Steven grumbled a bit, because it was a good twenty miles away, but the girls gave him no choice. He stopped for petrol at the Esso station on the far side of the bridge over the Tay.

"Did you see Doug, Mum?" asked Fiona, while Steven was out of the car paying for the petrol. "He was standing in the entrance of the Mall, looking at all the people waiting outside the church."

"Inspector Niven to you, Fiona," replied Jean automatically. "Yes, I did see him."

"Why didn't he come into the church?" Lisbie's voice sounded funny, and she made a snapping noise with her mouth. Jean looked sharply at her. "Are you chewing gum? You'd better get that out of your mouth before your father comes back."

"Somebody at the office said it was Stella and Dempster's brother that killed him, you know, the yummy tall one in the dark suit who was at the funeral," said Lisbie.

"That's just silly," said Jean sharply. "Alexis

Lumsden wasn't even there. You mustn't listen to nonsense like that. Nobody knows who did it.''

"I bet Doug was waiting for Dempster to show up," said Fiona. "I think Dempster did it." Fiona gave a delicious shudder. It was really exciting to be close to something so awful that had appeared on television and even in the *Scotsman*.

Steven got back into the car. "I smell chewing gum," he said. "It had better be outside before I count to three." A window wound down instantly, a piece of gum flew through the air, then the window went up again.

"Thank you," said Steven without looking round. He waited for a gap in the traffic, then swung out, enjoying the acceleration of the big Rover.

"Dad, where do you think Dempster's hiding?" asked Lisbie.

"How should I know?" asked Steven. "I can't imagine why he killed his baby, let alone where he went."

"Steven!" said Jean, shocked. "How can you say that? Just because Doug Niven was . . .''

"It's obvious," said Steven. "You know how drunk Dempster gets, and I've heard he can get really tough sometimes. He probably got fed up with the kid's crying, bashed him against the wall and ran. You remember what he said about throwing Magnus away and starting again, that time when we went out there to dinner."

Jean thought for a moment. "Maybe you're right, Steven," she said, not wanting to disagree too strongly, especially as her own thoughts were far from conclusive.

"I think so," said Steven confidently. "In real life, it's usually the obvious solution that's the right one, thank God. I don't think Miss Marple would have spent too much time worrying about this one, and Sherlock Holmes wouldn't have wasted his brain cells on it.'' He grinned at his wife; he knew how her mind functioned when she set herself to it; it was like a little factory that worked twenty-four hours a day, chewing on facts, and eventually coming up with what was, in retrospect, a perfectly simple and logical conclusion. The only surprising thing was that other people didn't get there first. But this time, there really didn't seem to be any problem. He slowed behind the stream of traffic. There were only two lanes functioning because of road works, and he would just have to be patient. Jean, he saw, was wearing a look he had come to know; her lips were compressed, and her eyes were slightly narrowed, as if she were looking into the sun, focused on a spot in the far distance. He sighed. Why did she always have to get so involved with other people's problems? It wasn't as if she didn't have enough with her own . . . Why couldn't she just be satisfied taking care of her family and her patients? Jean was the busiest person he'd ever met, and yet there she was, finding even more things to occupy her mind. A sudden flash of annoyance went through him. Why didn't she pay more attention to what was going on in her own family? It wasn't much fun for a man, when his turn didn't come until everybody else was taken care of, after she'd seen every last patient, gone resolutely to each late-night call.

The long string of orange cones ended, and the traffic speeded up. Steven put his foot harder on the accelerator than he'd meant to, and the car jumped forward. He glanced at Jean, was about to apologize, then saw that she was still miles away, her brain still sifting, evaluating. She hadn't even noticed the jolt. Steven set his lips tight; there was no reason in the world why a man had to put up with that kind of shit, day after day.

Steven drove slowly through the open gates of the Crieff Hydro Hotel, the sun shining on the wide, well-kept lawns in front of the main building. Through his open window, Steven could hear faint shouts coming from the direction of the tennis courts, muffled by the thick high hedges that hid them from view.

"Please, Dad, hurry!" As usual, Lisbie needed to go to the loo, and the closer she got the worse it was. Steven pointed out that there was a five-mile-an-hour limit posted at the gate, and five miles an hour was the speed he went. When they finally pulled up outside the main entrance, Lisbie was in tears, and she ran from the car into the hotel. Jean knew how embarrassed Lisbie felt; Fiona was different, it made no difference to her what other people thought.

Five minutes later when they all gathered in the bar next to the dining-room, Lisbie had regained her poise, but she had a smug little look about her. She knew what would happen. Fiona, two years older than Lisbie, always came roaring to her defense like a lioness protecting her cubs. She was simply more aggressive, less able to let things pass than Lisbie. And Lisbie knew Fiona wasn't going to let this one pass without a major counterattack. They both knew what the subject of the attack would be, but it was up to Fiona; one never knew about her, whether she would just indulge in a border skirmish, or point the big guns down the line. Lisbie waited, wishing she had the talent and the guts to do it herself.

It didn't take long. Jean had gone off to the ladies

when the manageress came to lead them to their table. After they sat down, Fiona zeroed right in.
There was no point waiting for her mother, it would
just upset her if she happened to be paying attention.

"Dad, I hear you took that lady from your office,
Pearl, out to lunch again."

Steven, who was scanning the menu, froze. Fiona
and Lisbie were watching him like a pair of young
hawks, and nudged each other; they'd got him, no
question.

He tried to ignore them.

"Do you want a starter?" he asked. "They have . . ."

"Come on, Dad," interrupted Fiona. "You didn't
answer the question." He looked over the menu at
them; they were both staring intently at him. He
would have to say something.

"It didn't sound like a question to me," he said.
"More like an impertinent comment."

"We also heard you were with her last Saturday,
over at Cowdray Park, and you were holding hands."
Cowdray Park was a wooden fifty-acre estate about
ten miles out of Perth, often frequented by courting
couples.

Steven blushed. They saw it and smiled grimly at
him.

"I'd like you to know that this is a free country,
and I can go anywhere I please, and whenever I like.
Miss Blaikie just happens to be a friend . . ." Both
girls started to giggle, and Steven became suddenly
angry. "The thing I like best about her," he said,
"is that she at least has time to talk to me." The
girls didn't even hear what he said, and he put the
menu up again to hide his annoyance.

When Jean rejoined them at the table, Fiona and
Lisbie were still convulsed with laughter.

"Well, what's so funny, you two?" she asked, smiling at them. She sat down, unfolded her napkin and put it on her lap.

"Nothing," said Fiona, finally controlling herself. "It was just something Daddy said."

Jean looked at Steven, who shrugged.

"Here," he said, giving Jean a menu. "Choose. The waitress'll be back in a minute."

Aladdin's Cave . . . Dempster Lumsden had decided long ago that there was nothing very magical about it except for what they sold. Its very dinginess, the crowds of raucous dockers and seamen who filled it nightly, the thick pall of cigarette smoke, the occasional fights, and of course the whisky, all combined to make a covering bandage, a kind of active noisy shroud in which he could wrap himself.

His misery was not of the passing kind. When he was at home he could cope with it for a while, but then everything would get too much and he would take off, away from home and the people he knew, to drink himself into a stupor, talking to no one, sleeping wherever he collapsed after the Aladdin closed its doors for the night.

This time it had been worse, of course, because of the fact that he was about to go bankrupt. Money had never meant anything very much to Dempster Lumsden; as a child, it never occurred to him that it had to be worked for, one way or another, by the sweat of the brow or by cleverness and skill. To him money was just there; it existed to be spent.

It gave him headaches to think about it. Money turns ordinary people into liars and thieves, and it seemed that the bill always finished up in his hands. All the drinking he'd been doing, that didn't help either. Dempster knew that he wasn't able to concentrate as well as he used to, and now, even the thought of that damned factory he'd built, and all the bills that were coming in, just made him want to run, get away, hide. And that's what he'd almost done. That's what that greasy little coward Graham Ross wanted him to do—leave the country, abandon everything, just to save Ross's own precious skin.

The Aladdin was always busy, and employed three full-time barmen. Dempster's favorite corner was at the far end of the bar where he could lean up against the end wall during his spells of dizziness. Arthur, the big Irish barman, kept an eye on Dempster. He had no idea who he was, and wasn't really interested, but recognized that he was different from the other customers; a good-looking man, he obviously didn't work down at the docks. His clothes were expensive, and at least in the first days of his binges, he looked and carried himself like class. After being mugged outside the bar a few months back, Dempster had taken to carrying his money in different parts of his clothing, and cut a slit in his jacket lining to hide a few ten-pound notes.

Dempster banged on the bar with his pint glass, once. Arthur brought him a small glass with whisky in it and set it down in front of him. Dempster raked through his pockets and brought out a crumpled five-pound note. A few moments later a heap of change suddenly appeared on the bar and it took Dempster a huge effort of concentration to realize it was his. He swept the coins up and put them in his pocket. A coin fell on the floor, but Dempster didn't bother to look for it. If Keith had been there, he'd have been instantly on his knees, groveling around on the floor, pawing under the chairs, then he'd put what-

ever he found into his own pocket . . . That dirty
bastard!

But they were all like that, more or less, all interested in feathering their nests at his expense. And
when he ran into problems, who was there to help
him? His father? Dempster gave a disgusted snort,
and the man next to him at the bar looked round.
Stella? Alexis? Not bloody likely, not any of them.
He looked at his glass. It was empty, although he
didn't remember drinking anything. He looked suspiciously at the man next to him. You couldn't trust
anybody. He banged on the bar, and Arthur brought
a pint of bitter. Dempster pulled out a handful of
change and slammed it down.

Arthur picked out some coins and left the rest. This
customer would last about another two rounds, he
thought, before he keeled over. He was getting worse,
there was no doubt about that. He hadn't always been
like this, when he used to come in with that other big
fellow; then they'd just drink like anybody else, one
evening at a time, and they rarely had any trouble
walking out.

Dempster was drinking alternate pints of bitter and
nips of Glenmorangie, and he had reached the stage
when he relied on Arthur to remember what was
next. He was on his fifth day, and Arthur figured
another two days then he'd vanish again. The inter-
vals between bouts were getting shorter, only about
three weeks the last time, and Arthur knew from
experience what to expect. This time, though, he
thought the chap would finish up in hospital; they'd
dry him out for a while, send him home, then after
a few weeks he'd be back. Arthur wondered vaguely
what kind of job the man could have which let him
take so much time off.

For Dempster, everything now was wooly, soft-edged; the lights reflecting from the mirror behind the bar and the white pumps on the bar had a blurry, disconnected look; only the sharp bite of the whisky had any reality now. The beer was just warm swill, and he drank it because Arthur put it down in front of him. His bladder was full, and he eased himself off his stool, stumbling sideways toward a couple of men drinking close by. A big arm came out, he heard laughter, and headed unsteadily round the corner. There was one step up, he remembered that, but had trouble with his zip and didn't quite make it in time.

He didn't realize somebody had joined him until he was back on his stool. Too drunk for surprise, he muttered an obscenity and turned away. There was nothing else he could do; he knew that if he tried to hit the person who was now talking to him, he'd just fall off his stool. He heard the voice talking, that soft repetitive, insistent voice, but the only word he understood was "home."

The next whisky tasted different, and there seemed to be some crumbly stuff at the bottom of the glass. Then something seemed to be happening to him, he didn't remember getting up, but the lights bobbed crazily past him as he went toward the door, the gentle pressure on his elbow propelling him forward. In the distorted light from the dancing wall sconces the shape behind him seemed gigantic, monstrous, but that could have been more a reflection of what he knew . . .

The air was cold outside, and the pavement felt uneven under his feet, further one moment, nearer the next, then the shiny car door, the ceiling light spiralling above, then the noise of the engine starting . . . The lights of the port shone yellow and

moved in the car as they flicked past, then they were
coming out of Leith and he felt as if he was going
to throw up, he'd have to get out, he was trapped,
he couldn't vomit in here . . .

Chapter Eleven

On the way back from the Crieff Hydro the subject of the Lumsden baby came up again, in spite of Jean's attempts to direct the conversation into more cheerful channels.

"Why did you have always have to see Magnus so often?" asked Fiona. "I mean before he got killed. Was it because his mother didn't know how to take care of him, or what?"

Jean was enjoying the scenery; it wasn't too often she had the luxury of sitting in the passenger seat, not having to worry about finding her way through the traffic.

"He was premature," she replied. She half-turned in her seat to face Fiona and sighed. She knew that that was not going to be considered an adequate reply. "That often means that the baby has weak breathing muscles and can easily get pneumonia, things like that." Fiona nodded, very interested. "Magnus was very sick for quite a while. They weren't even sure if he was going to live."

The whole thing had been one long nightmare. Right from the beginning, it had been a bad pregnancy. The day after Stella missed her first period, she started to be sick in the mornings and from that time on felt awful most of the time. For the first few months Jean was continually worried that she might lose the baby. Then poor Stella started to retain fluid in her body; her belly swelled up, her normally slim ankles thickened, and the tissues of her face puffed up, making her quite lovely features thick and bloated.

"God, just look at me!" she said tearfully, about five months into her pregnancy. "Nobody told me having a baby would make me look like this!"

Jean cut down on Stella's salt intake, put her on a strict daily water ration, but nothing seemed to help. Then one day Dr. Desmond Bruce, her obstetrician, phoned Jean, very concerned about Stella.

"Her blood pressure's gone way up," he told her. "She's twenty pounds over her expected weight, she's got albumen in her urine and I'm really quite worried about her. If it's all right with you, Dr. Montrose, I'm putting her in hospital. Yes, today, right now."

Even in the hospital things didn't improve much. They gave her medicine to bring her blood pressure down, but she had a bad reaction to it and couldn't get out of bed without fainting. Finally it was judged that both she and the baby were beginning to be in some danger, and although it was still six weeks from her due date, the doctors decided to induce her labor. Even then, nothing happened easily, and Dr. Bruce had already told the operating theater that he might have to do a Caesarean section when finally Stella cooperated and delivered the baby—a tiny, quiet, red little thing, with barely the strength to make a faint, mewling kind of cry. He had to be put immediately on a respirator and kept in a special incubator. For several days everyone was concerned about his survival.

Stella was exhausted by the delivery, scarcely able to get out of bed, and didn't even see her baby for the first week. The nurses would come in from time to time to tell her how things were going, and Dr. Bruce was as supportive as he could be. But Dempster, after dutifully bringing her to the hospital, had vanished immediately afterward, presumably off on one of his binges, and didn't reappear until Stella was almost ready to go home. He was full of remorse, and brought flowers and fussed over her continually, but it took quite a while for Stella to get over it.

And on the very day she was finally able to bring the baby home, in the midst of their quiet celebration, Magnus had his first epileptic attack.

"Do you think Stella'll have any more babies, now?" asked Lisbie.

Jean and Steven exchanged a glance.

"I don't really know, dear," replied Jean cautiously. "But I will tell you this. If I'd had that kind of trouble having Fiona, *you* wouldn't be sitting there asking me questions, you can be quite sure of that!"

It suddenly occurred to Jean that the girls were rather pointedly not addressing any of their comments to Steven, but that wasn't very unusual. Arguments and disagreements occasionally arose within the family, but as they usually didn't involve her, she wasn't always aware of all the details.

"You didn't tell me about the dance last night," she said to the girls, wanting to change the subject. "How was it?"

"Fiona's got a boyfriend," replied Lisbie immediately. "He looks like Tam-o'-Shanter's horse."

"That's not very kind," protested Jean. "I'm sure he looks perfectly normal."

"You mean like a normal horse?" Lisbie started to giggle.

"What does *your* boyfriend look like?" Steven asked her rather acidly, breaking his long silence, but the girls ignored him.

"He breathes like a horse, too," said Fiona, beginning to laugh. "You should have heard him, later, when he started to get all excited . . ."

"That's enough of that, I think," interrupted Jean. She should have known better than to raise that kind of topic. The two girls went on giggling quietly in the back between themselves.

"What's for dinner?" asked Steven as they approached the roundabout that signaled the Perth city limit.

"I don't know," replied Jean, startled. She had been thinking about Amanda's wrists; they weren't healing up the way they should. "How can you be thinking about food so soon after your lunch?"

"Dad has to keep his strength up, these days," said Fiona tartly, with a quick glance at her sister.

"You're right, dear," said Jean, abashed. "Of course. I'll make something specially nice."

Douglas Niven was feeling discouraged; there had been no trace of Dempster Lumsden at the funeral, and according to Stella and Alexis he had not phoned, written or made his presence known in any way.

"That's what he always does, though," Stella had explained to him. She told him about Dempster's disappearance when she had the baby. Nevertheless, Doug was beginning to wonder if Dempster had left the country. His routine inquiries had picked up the airline booking to Lisbon, but Dempster hadn't turned up for the flight. Maybe buying that ticket was just a red herring; by now he could be anywhere in the world. It would be embarrassing if he turned up in Turkey, or Venezuela or somewhere else abroad; Doug had had his chance to block the airports, but at the time he didn't really think that Dempster was the killer. There certainly wasn't any point in doing it now.

There was a crackling noise from Doug's portable radio. He'd left it in his jacket on the back of a kitchen chair, so he got up wearily, turned down the television, and went into the kitchen.

The message Doug heard on the radio was that the Leith police had traced Dempster Lumsden to a bar named Aladdin's Cave, down near the harbor, although he was not actually there when they arrived. They were presently talking to one of the barmen and would contact Doug as soon as they had anything definite to report.

"Leith, huh," muttered Doug, surprised. "They all said Glasgow."

"Well, the Mountie gets his man again," said Cathie, smiling. She had stopped to listen to the radio message, floury hands in the air, and was as relieved as he was to hear the news. Doug had not been the easiest person in the world to live with over the last few days.

"Tracing isn't the same as having him in custody," Doug reminded her, a little heavily, but he still felt a weight coming off his shoulders. He'd know immediately if Dempster was guilty; it wouldn't take him five minutes of face to face confrontation, he was sure of that. Dempster was not used to lying; why should he be? He'd never needed to learn to lie, being a member of the rich and over-privileged classes . . .

"Don't start that again," said Cathie. Douglas hadn't even realized he was talking out loud. "Remember what Jean Montrose told you—they're no different, really, from the rest of us."

"Oh yes," said Doug in a sneering tone he only used when the issue of social class arose, "and that was a bicycle his father came to the funeral on, not a Rolls-Royce, right? And being Lord Aviemore is just like being plain Mr. Aviemore, right? Not different, huh! Not half!"

Cathie didn't argue. When Douglas got started, it was hard to get him to stop, and it made him bad-tempered for the rest of the day.

The news of Dempster's whereabouts didn't lull Doug into thinking the case was solved; even if Dempster still had Magnus's blood on his hands when they found him, there were a number of disturbing loose ends that would have to be tied up at some point. Who was the vagrant who'd stayed in the empty house? He'd never appeared, although the pallet and the old army bag were still there. He'd have Jamieson stake it out for one more night, then he'd have to abandon the issue. And what about Graham Ross? He'd heard rumors about some big financial deal involving Dempster Lumsden and Graham's bank that had fallen through just before he disappeared. Could there be any connection?

And of course he couldn't ignore Keith Armstrong; that man certainly had it in him to be a babykiller. Doug had heard that his wife Danielle had been known to appear at the store with a black eye or other signs of physical abuse, and it was well known that he hated Dempster; he had frequently said so himself in front of witnesses. It would be a typical coward's crime, to get at the father by killing his baby son, especially if he could also get Dempster blamed for it. Keith's personality certainly matched the crime.

Still, the key thing was to find Dempster and talk to him. Doug was sure that would be the major step in solving the case, one way or another.

He felt cooped up and irritable, sitting at home; there was not much he could do until he heard more from Leith. He went upstairs to change into a pair of jeans.

"I'm going out to wash the car," he said when he clumped down the narrow stairs again. He took his old anorak from the hook by the door and pulled it on.

Cathie glanced up at the sky through the kitchen window. The clouds were billowing white and gray now, and had that heavy, water-laden look. She felt sure it was going to rain, but she held her peace; she could see that he needed to get out. There was nothing that relaxed Doug as much as washing his Sierra; all his energy and enthusiasm went into cleaning and polishing its already glowing surface. Sometimes Cathie could have wished he'd be as interested in changing the tired wallpaper in the front hall, or fixing the lighter on the gas stove. But she felt a kind of calm just watching him through the kitchen window, splashing away at his car with his bucket of warm suds, oblivious but close. Cathie and Douglas Niven understood and appreciated each other in a way neither of them could have explained very well; it was as if they'd settled all their major disagreements in a previous life.

* * *

"Do you think Mum knows what's going on?" Fiona sat on the end of her bed in her basement room.

"I'm not sure . . ." Lisbie sounded more upset about what her father might be up to than Fiona, who was merely curious. "I don't think so, but you never know with her. She doesn't miss much."

"Except for what's happening under her own nose," retorted Fiona. "While we're on the subject, do you think Doug's going to come over to see Mum tonight? He'll probably want to talk to her about the funeral." Her eyes gleamed.

"Why do you like him so much?" asked Lisbie, looking for her shoes under the bed. "He's not that attractive, and God, he's so *old!*"

"He may be old, but he's got something that gets to me right here." Fiona put a hand on her heart. "Anyway, I've always liked older men. They have more conversation, and they're not always just talking about themselves."

"He's not interested in you," said Lisbie loftily. "Anyway he's married."

"So?" asked Fiona, equally lofty. "What do you think that means, nowadays?"

"Is the horse coming with us tonight?" asked Lisbie.

"The *horse?*"

"You know, what's his name, the one who looks like Tam-o'-Shanter's . . ."

"You mean Alec? I doubt it. He's probably nursing his hand right now, and not thinking about the cinema."

"What happened to his hand?"

"Remember in the car when I said he breathes like a horse, as well as looks like one? Well, I didn't want to say anything in front of them, but last night when he was taking me home he was putting his hand where it shouldn't be, and he wouldn't stop, so I said in a real loving way, 'Give me your hand, just for a second,' as if I was going to kiss it, or something . . .''

"You *bit* him!" shrieked Lisbie, clapping her hands. "Wow, Fiona, you actually bit him! Good for you!"

"You should have heard him," said Fiona. "In fact, you could have heard him yelling all the way home. He almost drove right off the road."

Lisbie couldn't stop laughing. "I don't believe it," she said.

"Have you ever bitten anybody?" asked Fiona reflectively. "It feels really sexy. It makes you want to bite all the way through . . ."

Chapter Twelve

Willie Stranach climbed heavily down from the cab of his tar-laying machine, went round the front to be out of the wind and lit a cigarette in its lee, cupping the flame with his hand. When he wasn't smoking, he could taste the tar he worked with every day, even at meals. Everything tasted of tar. The other men had gathered in the canvas hut twenty yards up the road to eat their piece, their lunch sandwiches, but he needed to stretch his legs a bit after four solid hours up in the cramped cab.

It was a good job he had, even if his wife complained about never being able to get his clothes clean nowadays. The pay was good, most of the time he was sheltered from the weather and nobody bothered him much. He knew what he had to do, and the foreman didn't interfere. The laborers laid down the sand, covered that with gravel, then he would light the long petrol burner at the back of his vehicle and come after them, slowly, his machine belching hot, choking tarry vapors as it turned the rocky surface into a smooth black road.

Today they'd opened up a new section about a mile long. First thing that morning, as soon as they got to the site, he'd gone with the others in the lorry to set out the orange cones; the men in the lorry pulled the cones off the stack and passed them out to him as he walked along, six paces between each cone.

Willie dropped his cigarette and ground it out carefully under his boot. He was always careful with that; once, when he was a boy, he'd seen somebody drop a lit cigarette into the boiling tar . . .

He realized that his bladder was full. He looked around. There was a fair amount of traffic going past on the Edinburgh road, and it was slowed down by the fact that only one lane was functioning in each direction. Of course, the portaloos were at the other end of the work area, almost a mile down the road. There was a straggly beech hedge at the bottom of the embankment, set back a few yards into the field, so he half slid, half walked down through the long rain-wet grass to be out of sight behind a bush. He struggled with his thick waterproof work trousers, and finally made it. Sighing as he performed one of the small pleasures of his life, Willie looked along the hedge, and what he saw half-hidden by the long grass shut him off in midstream.

"Oh Jesus," he said. Deliberately he closed his fly, keeping his eyes fixed on the thing that had caught his attention, and stood still for a few moments. It was about ten feet from him, and looked like a heap of old clothes. He forced himself to walk over to it, and stood a couple of feet away, then stepped around it. Maybe it was a tramp, asleep . . . But he knew that it wasn't.

A shout from above startled him. "Hey, Willie! Are you coming up for yer piece?" It was Jamie Reed, his foreman.

Willie fought back the urge to leave, to scramble back up the embankment and join his mates as if nothing had happened. This thing at the foot of the hedge was none of his business.

"Jamie . . . you'd better come doon here," he shouted back, but the strength had gone out of his voice, and he had to call up at him again before Jamie understood what he was saying.

"I bet it's Doug," said Fiona when the doorbell rang. They had just finished supper and the girls were helping with the dishes. Sometimes Jean thought her daughter was fey, had second sight. She seemed to know when the phone was about to ring, and who would be calling. Fiona ran to the door and returned with Detective Inspector Niven, who was looking mild and almost defenseless in a brown suit and sloppily-knotted blue woollen tie.

"Mum, didn't I say it would be him?"

"Yes, you did." Jean smiled at Doug. "I think Fiona's in love with you, Doug, she talks about you all the time."

"Mum!" Fiona's face flushed a beetroot red, and she ran out of the hall. They heard her clatter down the basement stairs to her room. Douglas looked uncomfortable until he saw Jean's amused expression. "It was easier to do it that way," she said tranquilly, "otherwise she'd have been hanging around here listening to our conversation. Put your coat up and have a seat."

Douglas took off his coat and went back to the hall to put it on the peg. He always liked coming to this friendly, laughter-filled house; the Montroses always seemed glad to see him, but that wasn't why he was here. Right now, he was thoroughly confused.

"We found him," he said simply, coming back into the living room.

"I saw it on the news," replied Jean. She had finished the doilies and was now knitting a dark blue sweater for her mother; when finished it would have pegs rather than buttons, which were too difficult for her arthritic fingers to manage. She hoped to have it ready for Christmas.

"How long had he been there?" she asked, her brown eyes intent on the pattern.

"Can't tell yet, but from the look of him I'd say two or three days. Everything was soaked in rain. Do you want to go to the autopsy? Dr. Anderson'll be doing it, tomorrow morning, at the Infirmary."

Jean hesitated, then a thought seemed to strike her. "Perhaps I should. Do you think they'd call me when they're ready to start? I have a really busy day tomorrow."

"He'd been run over, by the look of him," said Douglas.

"Would you like a cup of tea?" asked Jean, putting her knitting on the low table beside her. "I'm ready for one." She got up with a little grunt. "I'm getting stiff in my old age." She smiled and went through to the kitchen to put on the kettle. Steven loved gadgets, and Jean had one of the latest square white plastic electric kettles. Doug came through and stood in the doorway of the kitchen while Jean took down a packet of chocolate biscuits and some slices of fruit cake and put them on a plate.

"Hit and run, do you think?" asked Jean.

"Looks like it . . . I think he was maybe trying to come back for Magnus's funeral, hitch-hiking, probably, and got hit by a car."

"Where was *his* car? I've never heard of him being so drunk he didn't use it."

"He probably left it in some car park in Leith and forgot where it was," said Douglas. "The Leith boys didn't find it either. Did I tell you they tracked him down to a bar there? Lost him, though . . . Yes, milk and one sugar, please."

"Was there a ticket in his pocket? I mean the kind they give you at those car parks. Let's go back into the living room. If you'll take the biscuits and your cup I'll take the tea."

Jean led the way slowly, balancing her teacup, which she had overfilled, and carrying the teapot in the other hand. "I should have used the tray. I'm not thinking too well these days."

"No, there wasn't a car park ticket. But there was a one-way ticket to Lisbon, and another from Lisbon to Rio de Janeiro."

"Well, isn't that interesting? When was he supposed to be going?"

"On the very day that Magnus was murdered. The plane to Lisbon was supposed to leave Heathrow at 6.15 p.m. He'd have had plenty of time to get down there."

"Was the ticket in his own name?"

"Yes, actually . . ."

"So, if you had alerted the airports . . ."

"Yes. We did, in fact, and we knew that he was booked on that Avianca flight."

Jean looked reproachfully at him for a moment.

"Well, there were some things I couldn't tell you, Jean."

"So I see. Why do you think he didn't take the flight?"

Doug shook his head.

"I've no idea. He must have changed his mind at the last minute."

"Seems odd, doesn't it, that he'd go to the trouble of booking himself on a flight, all the way, then not go."

"Maybe he suddenly realized he'd get picked up, so he went back to his favorite haunt in Leith, a place called Aladdin's Cave, which is where he was last seen."

"Was his wallet missing?"

"No it was there, in the pocket of his trousers. There was no cash, but he had money scattered around in various pockets and in the lining of his jacket."

"Enough to take the bus?"

Doug nodded. He was beginning to feel a bit despondent about the kind of questions Jean was asking.

"So he could have come to the funeral, right? He could even have called Stella to come and get him, don't you think, if he wanted to get back for it?"

"Maybe he thought she'd tell me, and wanted to come back incognito, sort of . . ."

Jean took another biscuit. "Where exactly did you find him?"

"About five miles from here, on the side of the Edinburgh road. They're resurfacing, and one of the workmen found him behind a hedge."

"Was he going or coming?"

Doug looked puzzled, so Jean said, "I mean which side of the road was he on?"

"Oh, yes. On the left side, so he'd have been coming from the Edinburgh direction."

"I thought . . . well, never mind. He must have

got there somehow, assuming he didn't walk all the way from wherever he was coming from.''

"You think someone could have brought him to where he was found, then he was run over, maybe trying to get another lift to take him the rest of the way?''

"That's not quite what I had in mind, but it certainly is a possibility.'' Jean refilled Doug's cup. She could see the signs of tiredness and frustration in his face.

"Could he have finished up by the hedge if he'd been hit by a hit and run driver?'' she asked gently.

"Yes, I think so,'' he said. "That was one of the first things we thought about. It's amazing how far a body can be thrown when it's hit by a fast-moving vehicle. Our theory is that he was hit really hard, maybe by a lorry, was thrown down the embankment and rolled down until he was stopped by the hedge.''

"Do you still think he killed his child?''

"Yes, Jean, I do.''

"So you think he killed Magnus, having decided to leave the country to escape the consequences, got sidetracked in the Leith bars, tried to come back for a glimpse of the funeral before taking off, and got himself killed trying to hitch a lift?''

Douglas hesitated. Put like that it didn't sound quite so convincing. But he said, "Yes, that's about it, pending the postmortem report, of course.'' He spoke with as much confidence as he could muster.

"Well, if you believe that,'' said Jean, picking up her knitting again, "let me tell you how Santa Claus lands on the roof with his reindeer at Christmas time.''

Douglas reddened. "Why, what's wrong with my theory?''

Jean hesitated, then guiltily took another biscuit off the plate. "It just doesn't hang together, Doug. He must have got the ticket to Rio at least a few days before Magnus was killed, right?"

"Three weeks before," said Doug, feeling nettled. "We traced it back to the travel agent."

"I bet it wasn't a local one," said Jean quickly.

"He got it by phone from Cook's actually," said Doug, puzzled. "The main Edinburgh branch. He put it on his Visa card. But what. . . ?"

"Do you really think Dempster would have *planned* to kill Magnus? Three weeks in advance?"

Douglas hesitated. "Why not?" He caught Jean's eye, then stared at the floor. "Okay, not likely, maybe. But still, Jean, you have to admit, the facts are more against him than anybody else. We know he didn't like the kid, we know that he had been drinking heavily, we can assume he was depressed about his financial affairs . . . And there's nobody else, Jean. There's not a single other person with the slightest reason to kill that child."

Jean watched his expression and felt sorry for him. "It's not that I have the answers," she said, more gently, "and you may well be right, which could be the best thing, all round . . ." Jean's eyes were troubled as she escorted Douglas back to the front door. Even if Dempster *had* murdered his child, she knew there was much more evil hovering around the Lossie Estate than had so far come near the surface. Slowly, the dimensions of that evil were beginning to take shape in her mind, and it made her physically ill to think about it.

"So how's Jimmy doing at the hospital? I talked to his doctor yesterday, and he said he's feeling much better since they took the fluid off his chest." Jimmy Castle's mother, Mary, was in again, and seemed more upset than usual, and Jean assumed it was because her son was still in hospital, being treated for his pleurisy.

"The doctor scared me," replied Mary. "I think he said something about tuberculosis, but he has that funny accent, so maybe I heard him wrong."

"No, that was quite right," said Jean gently, putting a hand on Mary's shoulder. Mary started to weep silently. "It can be taken care of very well nowadays, with streptomycin and a drug called Isoniazid . . ."

"My father had TB," sobbed Mary, "when he was young, like Jimmy. They put him away for over a year in a sanitorium, and he had an operation to collapse his lung, or something. He never really got over it."

"They don't do anything like that anymore," said Jean firmly. "That was before they had the antibiotics to cure it."

"When will he be home, do you think?"

"That's up to Dr. Ramasandra," replied Jean, "but usually it takes a week or two, maybe more. But thank goodness we caught it before it caused real trouble."

"Well, that's thanks to you, Dr. Montrose. I don't know what we'd all do without you. But it's hard, working while he's at the hospital, and the other kids are so little . . ."

A faint memory stirred in Jean's mind.

"Who is it you work for again?" she asked.

"Mrs. Armstrong, up on the Lossie Estate." Mary Castle looked restless, as if she were trying to say something but couldn't quite bring herself to do it. "That was a nasty business up there, now . . ."

Jean busied herself with her forms to give Mary time to say whatever she wanted to get off her chest.

"I thought maybe I should tell somebody, but I was scared . . ."

Oh my God, thought Jean, what could have happened now? Still she said nothing, but she could feel her heart beating faster. What could Mary Castle have seen or heard while she was working for the Armstrongs?

"I saw them . . . last week . . . I could never go up there again, Dr. Montrose, I'd be too frightened . . ." Mary clutched Jean's arm, and Jean stopped writing. Mary's face was now pinched and scared.

"What happened?" asked Jean, summoning up her most matter-of-fact voice. "Come on, Mary, I think you're building this into something more than it really is."

"I am certainly *not*," replied Mary with asperity. "He was holding her by the throat, I thought he was going to kill her."

"Who was holding who?"

"Mr. Armstrong, of course. He had that poor little Mrs. Armstrong up against the wall just outside the kitchen when I came in through the back door, and he didn't hear me. He said to her in that voice . . . Oh God, he is a bad man . . . He said that if she breathes one word, the same would happen to her."

Mary was sobbing quietly. Eleanor looked through the door; she indicated that there were other patients waiting. Jean shook her head and Eleanor disappeared.

"What did you do?"

"I crept out again, Dr. Montrose, I can tell you I was shaking, and I wanted to run, but then I thought of that poor little woman in there and how he might kill her if I just went off . . . So I went back in making a lot of noise, and he'd gone, but she could hardly talk. Sore throat, she said, but she was trembling all over so bad I thought she was going to fall down. Dr. Montrose, I've never seen anybody so scared in my life . . . Oh God, what should I do?"

"What do you think he meant by what he said?"

"About. . . ? Well, he meant the same as what happened to the baby, of course!"

"Now, come on, Mary Castle, that's not the only thing he could have meant, surely. Maybe he was talking about something quite different . . ." Even to Jean, her words didn't sound very convincing.

"I dare say you're right, Doctor Montrose," said Mary. "But you werena there, and you didna see his face the way I did."

"Did you think of telling all this to Inspector Niven?"

"And what way would I be going to the police?" she asked, now indignant. "I'd have a' the neighbors talking about me in a minute. They know that you only talk to them if you're guilty of something . . . No, I couldn't."

Jean sighed. People like Mrs. Castle never went to the police, whatever happened. Maybe it was cultural, but whatever the cause, even if wild horses dragged her into the police station, nothing could make her talk if she didn't want to.

Chapter Thirteen

With a sinking heart, Jean Montrose parked her car as close as she could get to the pathology department, at the back of the hospital near the kitchen entrance. Maybe it was tradition, she thought, or a feeling held by generations of hospital architects and planners that it was shameful to make a place for the dead within the precincts of an institution dedicated to life and health, but hospital pathology departments were usually relegated to the least desirable part of the hospital premises, often below ground level, near the incinerator of the laundry. The pathology department never had pride of place in any hospital Jean had ever seen.

The metal door was heavy, and Jean almost fell backward when someone pushed the door open from inside. It was her patient Mrs. Leuchars, who worked four days a week in the hospital laundry. Jean talked to her for a few minutes before going on toward the pathology department. The poor woman, she thought, it didn't seem as if she would ever really get over her son's death.

Dr. Anderson must have got used to seeing Jean Montrose slipping in during postmortems ordered by the Procurator Fiscal, because he didn't bat an eyelid when she appeared next to him. He was wearing thick red rubber gloves which came almost up to his elbows, and most of his heavy, jovial face was hidden behind a corrugated paper mask. He was already hard at work on the mortal remains of Dempster Lumsden. The place had the pervasive smell of carbolic and formaldehyde, together with the unmistakable stench of decomposition coming from the open body on the ancient white porcelain-coated autopsy table.

"Good morning," ventured Jean.

"Aye, and the top of it to you too, quine," he said, his voice loud and jovial enough to scatter any ghosts that might be lurking in this emporium of death. Jean smiled uncertainly; maybe it was the atmosphere, the presence of death that stimulated his grim camaraderie.

"Maybe we'll be needing you to take care of yon bobby, like the last time." He waved with his red glove in the direction of a young policeman who was standing opposite him, notebook at the ready.

"No, I'm all right, Dr. Montrose," grinned the young man rather self-consciously. "This doesn't bother me a bit. Actually, I'd rather be doing this than directing traffic up by Bell's distillery, which is what . . ."

"Crushing chest injury," said Anderson, not waiting to hear the end of the young policeman's words. He indicated the open chest. The lungs and heart had been removed, and Jean could see from the inside the bruising of the chest wall and the broken, splintered ribs.

"Did you find anything else?" Jean's voice sounded strained.

"There were haemorrhages in both lungs, and contusion of the heart," he went on. "The liver showed some fatty changes, early to moderate cirrhosis, I would say. Here, take a look for yourself.'' He had already cut portions of the liver and put them aside for further study in a yellow plastic container. Jean peered at the reddish-yellow pieces of tissue, but they didn't tell her much.

''You can tell by the feel when you're cutting it,'' he explained. ''It's stiffer than normal liver, grates a bit on the knife, but of course we'll have to wait for the microscopic slides before we have a definite diagnosis.''

Jean still appeared to be waiting.

''Were you expecting something else?''

''Yes, I was, as a matter of fact,'' she said slowly, as if the words were being dragged out of her. She spent the next few minutes telling Dr. Anderson what she was concerned about, and inquiring whether a certain type of analysis could be carried out. Dr. Anderson scratched his side with his elbow and shook his head, puzzled by her request.

''We're not equipped to do that kind of thing here,'' he said. ''As you very well ken. But if you think it's really necessary . . .'' Jean's expression told him that it was. ''The only place North of the border that does that kind of analysis is the mass spectroscopy lab in Edinburgh,'' he said finally. ''I'll send the specimen over there. But they won't like it,'' he warned. ''It's slow and expensive . . . Do you have something they can use as a control?''

Jean fished in her bag and held out a small envelope, but he wouldn't touch it with his gloves.

''Put it in my trouser pocket,'' he said, and turned sideways to make it easier for Jean.

''If they're able to do it, we should have the results back within a week, I should think. I'll get them to send you a copy." He pulled off his mask; it left a red mark down each side of his nose. Dr. Anderson smiled paternally at her; he was obviously fond of Jean, but then most people were.

"If the test's negative, I'll send you the bill," he said. Jean hoped he was joking.

Alexis had assembled his brother's papers and was going through them one by one; a methodical man, he put aside his distaste, and assembled all Dempster's business documents into a huge pile. Stella and he had found them stuffed into old cigar boxes and plastic shopping bags scattered in different places around the house. Stella was not much help to Alexis; she was still trying to get a grip on herself, and used to her new situation as a childless widow.

Understandably, she was having to deal with mixed feelings about Dempster's death; he had not been a particularly good husband to her, she reflected, with his drinking and inability to control his own financial affairs. If he hadn't always given in to that terrible urge to run when things were tough or going badly, her reaction might have been very different.

Stella had a better head for business and figures than Dempster had had; at least she was able to keep some kind of control, but that was limited to seeing that the tradesmen were paid with some regularity, that rents due to them were paid also. But there was only so much she could do, and when Dempster went off and lost hundreds, sometimes thousands of pounds gambling, or even more in some of his ill-advised financial ventures, she was helpless to prevent it.

"How is it going?" Stella asked Alexis. He was

seated at Dempster's old rosewood desk, the same one Doug had used as his operations center the day Magnus was killed. Stella had recovered much of her poise, and only the pallor of her face showed the strain she was under. And even that was well camouflaged by skillful make-up.

Alexis looked tired, worn by the events of the last few days.

"Slowly," he replied. "I can't believe Dempster could have got his affairs in such a mess."

"I told you."

"Yes, but still . . ." Alexis looked at the heap of papers in front of him and shook his head.

"Do you have any idea where it leaves me financially?" Stella's voice was strong, controlled.

"As far as I can tell so far, you won't starve." Alexis's bright white teeth flashed for an instant. "Luckily you had a joint bank account, so you can still draw from it. There's about three thousand pounds still in it."

"I know about that," replied Stella with a touch of asperity. "I do know how to balance a cheque book. I also know that the bank account doesn't reflect his financial position in the least."

Alexis nodded. "Again, it's early to tell, but the worst of it seems to be that factory he built on spec, the one he hoped the Hokkaido Corporation would buy. You do know about that, don't you?"

"Yes, he told me a bit about it. The last thing he ever said was 'That factory will be the death of me.' I wonder what he meant."

"Yes, I would wonder about that too . . ." Alexis paused for a moment, then grinned suddenly. "Well, I don't expect you to understand the financial entanglements of all this, but I finally found a purchaser for the factory. They're tough customers, those Japs, but they want it badly.''

"Oh Alexis, you are amazing! Does that mean Dempster won't have to go bankrupt?''

"My dear, you can't go bankrupt when you're dead. But the estate can, and will.''

"But Alexis, if you've found a buyer. . . ?''

Alexis shrugged, and some of his toughness showed through, just for a second.

"I look at this simply as a business opportunity, Stella. After the bankruptcy, the factory will be sold at auction by the bank, but they'll hardly get anything for it because it was built for a special purpose and isn't of any use to general industry. A group based in the Bahamas, which I happen to control, will buy it, and resell it at an agreed price to the Matsu Maru Corporation, Hokkaido's chief competitor.''

Stella put her hand on Alexis's shoulder and stared hard at him.

"Alexis, but that will mean that our neighbor, Graham Ross, will have lost his bank over a million pounds.''

Alexis smiled. "That, my dear, is the way the biscuit disintegrates, to paraphrase our American cousins. Their loss is our gain. They can afford it, we can't, and I assure you I'm not doing anything illegal.''

Stella thought about it for a minute.

"Well, Alexis, as you well know, I'm in your hands. Now it's time to think about dinner. Amanda should be home soon.''

"Yes . . . There was a funny look in your eye just now, when you mentioned Graham Ross. Is he . . . anything special to you?''

Stella laughed, a musical, confident laugh that somehow matched the way she looked.

"No, but I couldn't say the same for him. He's chased after me like a sick puppy ever since they came here. All very embarrassing, but not without some usefulness."

Alexis sounded suddenly cautious, and his blue eyes narrowed for a moment. "Do you imagine that . . . Well, would anybody think he had something to do with . . . certain recent events?"

Stella moved toward the kitchen as if she were shying away from the question.

"I wouldn't be surprised if that thought did occur to certain people, would you?"

They both smiled, she a little nervously. Alexis was certainly taking command of the situation; in a way it was a relief, but . . .

"Detective Inspector Niven asked me about Graham Ross, and also about the other fellow who lives in the house opposite him—what's his name? Keith Armstrong." Alexis had his head down over the papers again.

"What did you tell him?"

"All I could say was that Dempster owed Graham's bank a lot of money, and that he wasn't on the best of terms with Keith, but I didn't know why."

"*Do* you know why?"

"Well, sort of. Apparently he'd subsidized Keith quite heavily, set him up with his workshop and the house, and then it became clear to Dempster that Keith had some other kind of relationship in mind."

"Dempster never said anything about that to me, but if it's true, that would have sent him right through the roof. He detested any . . ."

"I know. And it's hard to believe, anyway. One

would hardly think so, to look at the chap. Look at the size of him, the muscles. He's built like a bull. And that big red beard . . .''

"You never can tell from appearances," said Stella, sounding prim, as if she had a lifetime's experience of dealing with such things.

"Did you say Amanda was due back now?" asked Alexis.

"She's down seeing Jean Montrose again, so she should be back any time."

"She's spending quite a bit of time down there, isn't she?"

"Well, she's still very upset . . . and her wrist got infected and needs treatment."

"What do you make of all that? Was she so close to Dempster, or the baby for that matter, and so depressed she'd cut her wrists? She's hardly spoken a word to me since then."

"She won't talk to me either, as you well know. To tell you the honest truth, Alexis, I think she feels guilty because she wasn't there when she was supposed to be. And somehow I get the feeling that she knows what happened, but won't or can't talk about it."

"As if she were trying to protect someone?"

There was a long silence.

"Something like that," said Stella. She turned and went across the hall into the kitchen, and Alexis pulled his chair in and started tapping away at the rather fancy desk calculator in front of him.

Amanda had come into Jean's office as usual at about 3:30, when most of the patients had been seen, and Jean would have more time to talk to her. Amanda was slender to the point of emaciation, wore long, flowing skirts and walked in an awkward, long-striding way, her slightly curved back giving her a bird-like look. She had a habit of standing with her weight on one foot, and Steven said she looked like a gray heron at the water's edge. Amanda had been rather pale as long as Jean had known her—something over a year—but since the episode of cutting her wrists, her face was porcelain-white, with high bony cheekbones and sunken cheeks. Her dark hair stood out like an untidy halo around her head. Nobody looking at her would have guessed that she was the older sister of the immaculate, desirable and beautiful Stella Lumsden. Amanda's marriage to a minor-league Swiss playboy had lasted less than a year before he dumped her and flew off with a richer and more glamorous bird; he had been taken in by her parents' apparently wealthy life-style.

"She doesn't have any money, can't dance, can't cook," he said to a close friend just before his final departure. "And you can see daylight between her thighs, even when her knees are together. Who could love a woman like that?"

"I have to go to an emergency call," said Jean, already halfway out of the door. "Dr. Inkster'll be seeing the rest of my patients this afternoon."

Amanda looked so upset that Jean took pity on her.

"If you want to, you can come with me and sit in the car."

Amanda accepted gratefully and Jean felt embarrassed, because she didn't really want to hear about Amanda's problems as they drove around town. That was the time she normally reserved for sorting things out inside her head, thinking about her family, listening to music and generally catching up with her life.

"Do you ever see life as a series of short, sharp, jerks?" asked Amanda suddenly, as Jean stopped at a traffic light.

"That's how I see some of the men I know," retorted Jean, without taking the time to think. Amanda looked at her without comprehending.

"I mean that life, well, goes on, then something happens and it stops, then you start again at a different level. Then the same thing happens again . . . I know I'm not explaining it very well, but do you see what I mean?"

"Sort of, Amanda," answered Jean cautiously. It really had been a mistake to bring her along.

Amanda tried again. "What I mean is, it would be really nice to start off afresh at each new level, without having to remember everything that happened at the level before."

Jean was thinking about Steven. Business had not been good at the glass works because of all the cheap glass coming in from Czechoslovakia and the Far East, and there was even talk about closing the factory down. That would be awful, because Steven was not a young man anymore, and who would want to employ somebody who'd spent his life manufacturing vases and glass paperweights?"

"But that's called experience, isn't it, Amanda?" she said, only half her mind paying attention to what her passenger was saying. "If you didn't remember what happened, you'd just fall into the same mistakes again and again, wouldn't you?"

At Bridgend Jean kept on the main Dundee road; the house she was going to was on Fairmount Road, about two miles beyond the bridge, on the other side of the river.

The traffic slowed as the lights changed. Jean got into the right hand lane to cross the bridge. She was so worried about Steven . . . Although both Helen Inkster and she worked hard, their practice was not that big, and the two of them only made around £14,000 each per year. If Steven wasn't working, they'd have trouble getting by on that, and certainly there wouldn't be enough for holidays or any kind of extras like that. Luckily the house was mostly paid for, but there were still two years of payment to go on her car and a year on Steven's Rover.

"But what happens if the memories just *paralyze* you, and you can't get on with your life?" Amanda was getting visibly agitated, and Jean forced herself to pay attention.

"What is it you're trying to forget, Amanda?"

"I can't get away from it, I can't! I try, but I can't sleep, it comes back all the time, the nightmares! I was supposed to have been there when it happened, you know . . . the baby, or maybe it's memories, I don't know, I'm starting to see things . . ." Amanda was shouting now, and her eyes were protruding. She banged the heel of her hands against the side of her head in an effort to drive away the demons.

"You see, I saw Keith . . . I know what happened . . . everything! And all the rest, with Dempster, God save his soul, flying to heaven. I can't live with the evil. Jean, did you ever stop to think that the Devil is just 'evil' with a 'D' in front of it? And nobody will ever know because it's all much too clever and I'm trapped inside it . . ."

Amanda was suddenly silent, staring at the road but obviously seeing nothing. She was wriggling on the seat with agitation, and her long, thin fingers picked at the material of her tights, pulling up little tents above her knees, then letting them go. Amanda's legs were so thin. . . . A muscle in her neck twitched, twitched again.

Oh God, she's going off her rocker, thought Jean. They were on the middle of the bridge and the traffic had almost stopped.

"You see, Jean, I'm trapped." Amanda started to sing, a high-pitched, tuneless crazy singing. "I'm the fly . . . in the middle of the amber . . ."

Suddenly she undid her seatbelt and before Jean realized what she was doing, Amanda opened the door and jumped out. Annoyed and concerned, Jean jammed on the handbrake and got out on her side, just in time to see Amanda clambering up on the stone parapet on the opposite side of the bridge.

Jean screamed, "No! Amanda!" but she never knew if Amanda heard her, because at that moment she jumped off and vanished from Jean's sight.

The traffic had stopped, and people got out of their cars as Jean ran across the bridge and looked over, dreading what she would see. Amanda was lying motionless, her arms and legs stretched out on the foot of one of the pillars, about forty feet below her. There was no way Amanda could have survived such a fall. Jean couldn't take her eyes off the broken body, and felt the warm tears coursing down her cheeks. Somebody had a carphone and called the police. There were no steps down, and Jean could only wait helplessly, looking and shouting down at Amanda, hoping she'd raise her head or move her arms, anything to show some sign of life.

Eventually, the fire department put an extension ladder over the side of the bridge and a burly fireman came back up with Amanda's slack, floppy body over his shoulder. Hoping against hope, Jean examined her, even tried mouth to mouth resuscitation, but all along she knew it was hopeless. Amanda was dead, her terrified eyes still open, as if the demons had chased her beyond the boundary of death.

Slowly and shaking in every limb, Jean went back to her car; both doors were still open. Behind her was a big Dutch articulated lorry. The driver had long since switched off his engine, and he watched her stolidly from his high cab as she slowly walked around to close the passenger door before getting into her car.

After the ambulance men had removed the body, Jean resisted the impulse to go home, lie down on her bed and cry. Instead she drove slowly out to see her patient, took care of the problem, and called Stella from the patient's house, saying she would be coming out there in twenty minutes, and that unfortunately she had some more bad news for her.

Poor Stella; she seemed to take the news of Amanda's death even worse than when baby Magnus and Dempster had died. Jean was really concerned about the effect this fresh tragedy would have on her. Her son, her husband, and now her sister had died the most violent of deaths. Was that all, or were there going to be more deaths, and if so, who was going to be next?

But it was Alexis's reaction that really confused Jean; he was sitting in the great front room on one of the leather easy chairs when she came in. After Jean sat down next to Amanda and told them what had happened, Alexis, who had shown exemplary fortitude with the other tragedies, put his head between his hands. His shoulders shook, and Jean was certain that he was weeping. But his eyes and hands were dry when he raised his head. If Jean didn't know what she knew, she would have sworn that his true feeling at that moment was one of relief.

Jean drove slowly home. She felt numb, unable to respond. Could she have prevented this latest tragedy? Shouldn't she have known that Amanda was on the verge of actual suicide? After all, she was just getting over a previous attempt. She put a tape in the cassette player but didn't hear the music.

The awful thing was that it wasn't over, Jean knew that. Not over by any means.

Chapter Fourteen

Detective Inspector Douglas Niven stood immobile on the doorstep of Jean Montrose's house. Glumly he looked at the few faded roses still hanging on in the little front garden, and ignored their neighbor's tabby cat, which wound herself around his legs, purring as if she'd been waiting there all day to see him.

When the bell rang, Fiona disappeared upstairs, still smarting from what her mother had said last time, about being in love with Doug; as often happened, Jean had come too close to the truth for comfort. Lisbie answered the door.

"Well, Lisbie, you're looking right pretty! Are ye awa' dancin' tonight?"

"Aye, in a while. D'you want to see my Mum?"

She led the way back to the dining room while Fiona, bright-eyed, peered over the banisters at the top of the stairs. Lisbie saw her out of the corner of her eye, and stifled a giggle. Doug looked at her suspiciously. He didn't like it when people laughed at him. The Montrose girls were too old to be fooling around like that, anyway.

Jean was sitting alone with her box of patient records. She was looking more tired than he had ever seen her.

"Hello, Jean." He looked around. "Is Steven no in?"

"He's late at the office. He's got a few problems down there."

"Aye, I've heard. That was a bad business this afternoon, with that Amanda; I spoke to the Procurator Fiscal about it, and he said to be sure to ask you if her seat belt was fastened. Can you imagine?" Douglas shook his head in disbelief. "I'll never know how that fool ivver got the job. Politics, I suppose."

"It was fastened, all right, until she unclipped it. It doesn't take a second, and of course I was hardly expecting her to jump out like that."

"Did you know she was one of the suspects for the Lumsden baby's murder?"

Jean raised her eyes. To Doug's compassionate astonishment, they were full of tears. She shook her head, trying to smile.

"Your suspects don't seem to live long enough for you to question them, do they? What about Dempster? I thought you were pretty sure he was the one who killed Magnus."

"Aye, I think he did at that, but there was an anonymous call that came in a couple of days ago, saying Amanda was the one who'd done it. We have to follow up a' these calls, you know, even if we're fairly convinced otherwise."

"Was it a woman or a man?"

"Who made the call? A woman, we think, but the voice quality wasna good, it was hard to be sure."

Jean got up. "Would you like a cup of tea? I could certainly use one. You know, Douglas, today for the first time in my life I thought I might treat myself to a wee breakdown . . ." She smiled, but her lip quivered, and Douglas could see that she was again on the verge of tears.

"Was it the accident? Amanda?"

"Before she jumped out, she said that she knew what happened. I'm sure she was talking about Magnus Lumsden. She said she'd seen Keith . . ."

Doug sat up. "Tell me exactly what she said. The exact words, if you can remember them, please."

Jean, who had a good memory, was pretty sure she'd got it right.

"What do you think she meant by being trapped, like a fly in the amber?" asked Douglas. The whole case was getting worse, more complicated each day that passed.

"I don't really know. What I don't understand is why she didn't tell you that she'd seen Keith. What could he have been doing there?"

"You mean at Lossie House? Maybe she just saw him in the distance when she was out walking. Which reminds me . . ."

"I don't think so. The way she spoke, I'm sure she saw him up close." Jean couldn't repress a shudder.

"But why didn't she *tell* anybody, then?" asked Douglas, echoing Jean's words. "Maybe she was the one who did it, and because she hated Keith for some reason, wanted to put the blame on him . . ." His words faded away, as they had a habit of doing when he was explaining one of his theories to Jean.

"There are so many wrong things, Douglas. None of it hangs together, and I can't think what's happening. There are now three people dead—it's like a plague that's struck the whole Lossie complex. Who's next? What's behind it all? Douglas, there *has* to be a logical explanation for those horrors, but it feels all wrong . . ."

Douglas followed her to the kitchen and watched as Jean switched on the kettle and put out the little tray, the milk, the sugar, and of course the biscuits. This time there were some chocolate-covered ones as well as digestives. She made two neat overlapping rows on a plate with a blue Chinese pattern.

Douglas said nothing, wondering what she meant by "wrong." The whole thing was wrong, as far as he was concerned, of course it was wrong. His job was to find the perpetrator, and bring him or her to justice. And a glimmer of light was beginning to shine through the darkness. He'd get his man, or woman, he thought grimly. You don't have to be a Mountie to do that.

"Wrong" . . . Douglas had a feeling that Jean meant something else, some kind of moral outrage when she used that word.

He followed her back to the living room, carefully balancing the tray, and they sat down. There was the sound of a car outside, and Steven came in. Jean could tell he was not delighted to see Doug, although he was polite enough. It was obvious from the tension in his face that the meeting at the glass-works hadn't gone well. Jean forgot her own worries and bustled about, getting Steven his dinner out of the oven while he made himself a stiff drink at the sideboard.

"Are you having one?" he asked Doug, holding up the bottle.

"No, thanks, Steven, I have to go back to work tonight, and I canna risk a drunk driving charge." His faint witticism passed without comment, and he sighed. He didn't feel too comfortable when Steven

was around, whereas Jean had a way of making him
feel easy and at home.

Jean came back into the room with Steven's pud-
ding, and put it on the table beside him. She looked
anxiously into his eyes, but she knew he wouldn't
say a word about the meeting as long as Doug was
there. And of course, he didn't even know about
Amanda, unless he'd heard it on the car radio.

She sat down again, and the awful feeling about
the Lumsdens came back to her. Steven opened the
newspaper with one hand while he tucked into the
beef stew with the other. Jean jumped up; she'd forgotten his potatoes, but she popped them into the
microwave for a minute and the situation was saved.
Doug grinned, wishing that Cathie would fuss
around him the way Jean did around Steven, making
sure that everything was just right, just the way he
wanted it.

"It says here the police are baffled," said Steven
through a mouthful of stew, poking a finger at a col-
umn on the second page.

"Aye, we're baffled a lot of the time, with one
thing or another, I suppose," said Douglas grimly.
"And they like to point that fact out occasionally."

Steven relapsed into silence.

Jean picked up her knitting. She'd have to get a
move on if it was going to be finished by Christmas.
Then in her mind's eye she saw Amanda hitching her
dress up over her long, skinny legs and getting up
on that parapet . . . Why hadn't she been able to
predict that she might do something like that? Here
she was, Amanda's doctor, and the poor woman had
obviously been crying for help, and she'd failed her,
right up to and including the very last moment of
her life.

"I wanted to ask you about Amanda," said Douglas, sounding more diffident than baffled. "Did she say anything else that might . . . throw more light on the case?"

Jean paused before answering. "Maybe . . . She seemed to want to forget something that had happened, and it was driving her mad, but I don't know whether it was the baby, or Dempster Lumsden, or something to do with her divorce. God, Douglas, I wish I could forget about it all myself . . ."

Steven looked up from the table in surprise; for a second Jean's voice had cracked. She explained briefly to him about Amanda's suicide. Without a word, Steven got up from the table, went over and put his arms around her. He held her close for a few moments, and with an unexpected jab of envy, Douglas could see how Jean relaxed in his arms and felt protected by him. It seemed to be a much better marriage than he would have guessed.

"Do you think Amanda could have killed the baby, maybe in a rage because he wouldn't stop crying, something like that, and jumped because she couldn't handle the guilt?" Douglas wanted Jean's attention back on the case.

Jean, still holding on to Steven, shook her head.

"I don't think so. She'd have said so, I'm sure of it, even at the last second if she had done it. No, it sounded more as if she was being forced to protect someone, maybe Keith. Doug, I don't know, and it's going round and round my head until I'm dizzy."

Jean sat back in her armchair again, looking much more composed.

"What about the fellow you caught in the empty house next door?" asked Steven, going back to the table. He pulled the top off a pot of raspberry yogurt. "There was just one mention in the paper, then nothing."

"Red herring, I'm sorry to say. He came in two days after the Doctor here had looked in . . ." He gave Steven a quick glance to see if Jean had told him about it, and Steven's momentary smile told him she had. She'd probably also told him about the embarrassing injury she'd caused Constable Jamieson. Doug smiled suddenly.

"At first we thought he was just a tramp," he said, "but actually he was wanted for a car theft in Dalgleish, so we didn't entirely waste our time."

"If you're pretty sure that it was Dempster who killed the baby, then got himself killed by a hit and run driver, are you going to close the case?" Jean looked levelly at Douglas, and he could feel the challenge in her voice. This was a tough, uncompromising lady, he recognized, a contradictory mixture of tough and soft.

"I'm not quite ready to do that yet," he said, although until a moment ago he had been.

"I agree with you," said Jean quietly. "And maybe those murders are not even the worst things that are going on up there in the Lossie Estate."

Evelyn Ross stood at the window of her upstairs bedroom and stared out over the dark rhododendrons at the lights of the big house fifty yards away. Somewhere inside that house was Stella Lumsden. Evelyn visualized her, sitting in that huge living room, reading under the white standard lamp, and the hatred swelled in her soul. She'd been unconsciously picking at a fold of skin on the back of her hand, but now her fists clenched until the long nails bit into her palms. She had detested people in her time, oh yes, but never with the kind of obsessive hatred she felt for Stella. Stella, who had just about everything, why did she want what *she* had too? Not that Graham was much of a prize, but still . . . And they had been such friends, at first; it had been like a new life starting here in Perth, in the Lossie Estate, after the disastrous time in Aberdeen, and before that at home in Edinburgh. Of course life was like that, she supposed, with ups and downs, but it seemed to be a constant factor in her life that the people she liked, adored even, always finished up savagely turning on her, for no reason at all.

Even at school, Marika, the Greek girl who'd come to live next door with her parents was a good example. Marika had been the same age as Evelyn, fifteen, with long, glossy, straight black hair that hung down her back and great big flashing eyes, but Marika was more developed than the Scots girls. A lot more. What a family the Konstantins were! The father was big, fat, and jolly; he liked to go around wearing only a vest and trousers, and didn't shave on Sunday when the restaurant was closed, and sometimes not even when it was open. Evelyn still shuddered at the thought of him, with his fat belly sticking out over his trousers, laughing so loudly at some incomprehensible Greek joke. He was too fat for a belt, and wore great wide red braces which he liked to snap against his chest with his thumb. It made a loud cracking noise, and the first time Evelyn heard it she was right next to him and gave a little yelp of surprise, and they all roared, thinking it was very funny. They were always laughing, that family, even Mrs. Konstantin. With a blush of retrospective embarrassment Evelyn remembered seeing Marika's father coming quietly up behind his wife while she was working busily in the kitchen. Mrs. Konstantin was a big, hearty woman, ample in all her proportions, with more than a suspicion of a mustache on her upper lip. He suddenly pulled up her skirt with one hand and gave her bottom a great big smack with the other. She turned round with a wet sponge in her hand and got him in the face, and they chased and hugged and laughed and fell about with mirth, but to Evelyn, the worst thing about it was that Mrs. Konstantin had been wearing *no underwear!*

Anyway, Evelyn had made friends with Marika, who seemed very grateful at first, especially as her English was not good. The other kids laughed at Marika's accent, and sometimes Evelyn joined in, teasing her with the others, just in fun, certainly not to hurt her feelings. But Marika had a really fiery temper, and the last time that happened she slapped Evelyn hard on the face, shouted something at her about being supposed to be her friend, and stormed off. Evelyn had been very upset, because after that Marika made another best friend, and wouldn't talk to her anymore. Evelyn's father told her that all foreigners were like that, treacherous and unreliable, and she should take it as a lesson. But all the other girls seemed to be more or less like that too, would slip away from her just when she thought she had a nice friendship going with them, and it always hurt her terribly. And she tried so hard, would give them presents, sometimes much bigger ones than she could really afford, and that didn't help. Sometimes it even seemed to make things worse, because she knew they spent a lot of time talking and laughing about her behind her back.

When boys started to come into her life things

changed, at least for a while, because they flocked around her, wanting to take her out. They told her how beautiful she was, brought her flowers . . . But even that didn't last, and after Tom, it was as if she had the plague. And it really hadn't been her fault. Tom had appeared more or less out of the blue. They had been in the same class at school, and although he was very popular she'd never paid any attention to him, nor he to her. Then one day, soon after her sixteenth birthday, he'd invited her to the cinema to see a rerun of *Gone with the Wind*. Her father had been doubtful about it, but had finally agreed that she could go, with stern warnings about when she should be home. Tom had bought a half-pound box of Black Magic chocolates, and while the lights were out there was a moderate amount of touching and groping around, enough so that Evelyn never had a very clear idea of what happened to Scarlett in the end. Afterward they had gone for a drink in a pub, where they both looked old enough to get served, then he drove her to a quiet, dark place under the big chestnut trees behind Grayfriars cemetery. What happened after that remained a confused blur although some moments stood out clearly from the others, but she came home quite late, and what she told her father sent him to the telephone and the police were there within half an hour.

Evelyn was frightened; things had got out of control, far beyond what had at first simply been an excuse for coming home late, but the attention and understanding of the two female police officers somehow inflamed her histrionic talent, and she told them a story which was entirely worthy of their sympathy. At the time, Evelyn was only concerned at the effect on the officers; every tightening of the lips, each indrawn breath was a small triumph, and it was only when they finally left with siren wailing to interview Tom that she realized that she had not only got him into trouble, but was in real trouble herself.

The results of the police investigation were equivocal; it was noted that Evelyn's allegations were identical to those made in a recent and much-publicized rape case in the town only a few weeks before, so there were no court proceedings, but Evelyn's life at school was made miserable from that day on. Tom was a popular boy, and almost everybody believed his story. Evelyn was shouted at, treated like an outcast by both boys and girls and even the teachers until she left the school at the end of the term. Much later, a hospital psychiatrist said the whole episode had been a major determining factor in her aberrant psychological development, whatever that meant.

A shadow passed in front of one of the upstairs windows of Lossie House; Evelyn quickly switched the lights out in the bedroom and returned to the window. The shadow moved again; it wasn't Stella, so it must be that brother-in-law of hers. He seemed nicer, more of a gentleman than that pig Dempster, Dimster, Duster, Pigster, Swinester . . . Stop! she shrieked silently at herself, but her mind skated wildly and ran obscenely on for a few moments like a motor that couldn't be turned off.

Dempster Lumsden, who'd fooled Graham so completely, and got him to finance that factory of his. Graham would never recover from that, it would be the end of his career. The bank people, those nasty little men with their round glasses and black hair combed over to hide their white, shiny baldness, they would never forgive him. Graham was finished at the bank, there was no doubt about that, and rightly so. Justice. It moved in mysterious ways. Graham certainly deserved all he was in for, and more, but they would be the payments for his *real* crimes—adultery, deceit, mental cruelty, all the tortures he had put her through. But he didn't know who he was dealing with. She wasn't just one of those poor, ignorant floosies he liked to twist around his little finger. Oh no. And she'd learned a few tricks in her time. Witchcraft, they called it, but he'd never believe in that. Superstitious nonsense, he'd say. Well, maybe not now, not anymore, now the results were so clear. Look what happened to Dempster Lumsden, who'd pretended to be so nice to both of them, and had chatted her up nicely too . . . He'd got what he deserved, as had that misbegotten bastard baby. She saw again in her mind the round smear on the wall, the crooked, sightless head . . . Evelyn opened the window and leaned out, beaming her hatred across to the big house, so that Stella would feel the heat of it against her skin and shudder with fear. Evelyn had learned how to do that from a woman at the Royal Mental Hospital in Aberdeen, the very first time she was admitted there. Stella, she beamed across the cold air, a beam to penetrate into the innermost cracks and interstices of the big house, Stella, you're next . . .

"Why have you got the window open?" The light went on, and Graham's sour voice startled her. Evelyn just managed to regain her balance and prevent herself from falling out. She backed against the wall like an animal at bay, and bared her teeth at him.

Chapter Fifteen

Douglas Niven knew quite well that at this stage he could make out a report which would effectively dispose of the Lumsden case, at least as far as his superiors and the press were concerned. In fact he'd gone so far as to write out a draft which would have impressed even him, had someone else on the force sent it in for his approval. In it he showed that the Hon. Dempster Lumsden, late of Lossie House, Perth, had been under increasing stress due to business and personal problems, had been drinking heavily, had said in front of witnesses that he would like to dispose of his epileptic and chronically ill child, that he had been seen in the vicinity of the house at the time the child's murder had occurred. Careful investigation had revealed no other possible motive for the killing. The aforementioned Lumsden had then gone back to his drinking in another city and had eluded all efforts to find him. On learning that his infant's funeral was about to take place, he headed for home but was struck by a hit and run driver when only a few miles from home, and was killed instantly . . .

Doug pulled the typed report out of his aged Olivetti and stared at it. It was a report he could be proud of; well typed, properly centered heading, no spelling mistakes that he knew of. And it succinctly covered all the salient points of the case, in their appropriate order. Best of all, once he sent it in, the waters would close over it as over a sinking ship; a week or two from now, everybody would have forgotten about the whole episode.

Doug slowly tore up the report before dropping the pieces in the wastepaper basket. He wished with all his heart he could have sent it in; he knew that many of his colleagues would have done so without a second thought. And all the facts there were true enough . . . But it simply wasn't a correct interpretation of what happened, and his professional pride wouldn't allow him to pass it off as such.

But what *had* happened? His mind was a violently confused muddle of impressions, feelings that certain people had lied to him, or that they had told the truth in a way designed to mask what had really occurred. In the tangled jumble of theories that swirled around in his brain, he even lay in bed one night next to his warm, gently snoring wife, wondering whether Jean Montrose herself might have done it; maybe Amanda had realized it was her, had confronted Jean, and got herself pushed over the parapet as a result . . .

Doug looked at the luminous dial on his watch; it was 5:30 A.M. He lay there for a few more minutes, then his increasing restlessness took hold of him and he slid out of bed. His wife moaned, rolled over and grabbed his pillow, but didn't wake up. Doug got dressed, put on a parka and a pair of trainers and went out into the cold gray early morning. He shivered as the last of his night-warmth left him. There was nobody in the street; the only sound was his own rubbershod footsteps on the wet pavement.

He walked down Barossa Place toward North Inch, the big tree-lined park and public golf course which ran for a mile or so along the bank of the river Tay. It was his favorite walk, and he had resolved more than one difficult case while thinking and trudging around its grassy, windswept perimeter.

The streetlights were still on, although it was almost light now, and their cold glow accentuated the stillness of the early morning.

He stopped when he got on to the path. Should he go around to his right, or the other way? The last time, when he was puzzling about the warder who was killed leaving his car in the prison car park, he'd gone anticlockwise, and after the first circuit he'd already worked out how it had been done and who had done it . . . Resolutely, Douglas turned right. Anticlockwise it would be.

His mind was usually at its clearest at this time of day, so he decided to go through each of the suspects in his mind, and review the possible case against each one. Of course, it might have been someone quite different, someone he hadn't even considered, but he had an instinct that the killer was located somewhere in or around the Lossie Estate.

Dempster. He'd pretty well disposed of him as a suspect for the baby's killing. For one thing, he was not at all convinced that Dempster had come back on the day of the murder. In the first place, he probably would have been too drunk to drive, and secondly, only Keith Armstrong thought he'd seen him, and Doug had his reservations about that. And if he *had* come back and smashed his son against the wall in a drunken rage, would he have put him back tidily in his cot before leaving as invisibly as he had come? Thirdly, and more telling, whoever did the deed was almost certainly right-handed, and Dempster, he had ascertained, was left-handed. Again Douglas visualized a big, shadowy figure, standing feet astride like a golfer, picking up the child by the legs and swinging it in the same direction he would swing a golf club.

Stella Lumsden. She would have the strength to do it, and she was right-handed. But why would she kill her own baby? Douglas's mind almost stopped him there, but he went on. He was determined to consider everybody. All these people were suspects, every one. Back to Stella. She was there, at the time and at the scene of the crime, and therefore, on the face of it, the most likely suspect. She could have killed the child either before or after going shopping. According to the pathologist, it would have been before, and of course Jean had been the first to see the baby and would have known instantly from his body temperature if he had been killed just moments before. Jean had said, and Dr. Anderson had backed her up, that it was within a couple of hours, probably around one, maybe a little less. And it fitted. Doug had checked with the tradespeople in the shops Stella had visited, and they had confirmed exactly what she'd said. Of course they all knew her, she was the great lady, the châtelaine of the area. With distaste, Doug had noted the slavish, feudal respect they obviously had for her. But then they did the same kind of unthinking cap-in-hand grovelling with Dempster Lumsden, although Doug was sure they all knew about his little exploits and his unreliability.

But if Stella had done it, why? That was the question he couldn't answer. She had always taken good care of the baby, and seemed to be as fond of him as anyone could expect. And from what Jean Montrose had said, Stella had been totally devastated when she came home to find his little body dead in the cot. But why had she left him alone? Amanda was supposed to have been there to look after Magnus while Stella was out shopping, so Stella seemed to have taken reasonable precautions for the care of the child. She couldn't have been expected to know that Amanda would take it into her head to go for a walk as soon as she, Stella, had left the house.

Doug shook his head. When there were so many variables, he usually made an effort to put it all down on paper. He'd done that, but this time it hadn't helped at all, it had just made the confusion and complexity worse. Still, it had given him the feeling that he was at least doing something.

How about Dempster's death? If there had been foul play there, could Stella have had a hand in it? Again Douglas's mind rebelled against the thought. Dempster was big, strong, and it simply didn't seem possible that Stella could have in some way lured him to his death, even if he was blind drunk. Not willing to give up a suspect completely, he made a mental note to compare the tire marks found on Dempster's clothing with the tires on her car. They had already checked Graham Ross's Jaguar and Keith Armstrong's Vauxhall with negative results. Wait a minute, he said to himself, the tests on the Jag were not negative but inconclusive. He'd need to push the lab for a more definitive result.

Alexis Lumsden, Dempster's younger brother. Douglas didn't know too much about him, but there wasn't any point thinking in terms of his being a suspect, because at the time of Magnus's death, Alexis had been in Inverness, a hundred miles away. Careful as always, Doug had the Inverness police check him out, and there was no doubt about it; Alexis had been there when the call came through from Lossie House. Reluctantly, and with the proviso that he was certainly not closing the door if some new information were to come in, he decided to eliminate Dempster, Stella and Alexis from the list of prime suspects.

Amanda. She had been living in the house, her manner had been very strange when she came home and the baby was dead, she had attempted suicide once, and then had been successful on a second try. Was it the feeling of guilt that she couldn't stand? She'd said something about wanting to forget; was it the sound of the baby's cracking skull she wanted to get out of her memory? But when he'd interrogated her after the murder, he had the feeling that she could never have done such a deed—she was too shocked, too upset. Somehow she seemed too gentle, too vague to perpetrate such a brutal crime. And apparently she had really loved Magnus, and competed with Stella in caring for him. But still, he couldn't rule her out. And there was also the matter of the anonymous phone call, pointing the finger squarely at Amanda. In his frustration, Doug picked up a piece of dead wood and flung it as far as he could. It slithered for a few feet on the wet grass. He had never been on a case like this one, where the people who could have best helped him in his inquiries had died off one by one. It was like those stories from America you read about in the newspapers, where witnesses in Mafia cases were killed to prevent them from testifying. "Rubbed out," Doug said aloud, scraping his shoes along the path. "That's what they were, rubbed out."

With an effort, he brought his mind back to bear

on the case. He had a lot of unresolved problems, and he was already a quarter of the way around the North Inch.

Next on the list was Tim O'Bannion, the man they had caught in the deserted house. He was an Irish layabout, a vagrant, who said he knew nothing about the murder and on the morning of that day was in Dundee. Douglas grinned, thinking of Constable Jamieson, who had used more than necessary force while arresting O'Bannion. Maybe it helped him to forget his own humiliation at the hands of the Wee Doc.

And having disposed of these five, thought Douglas, let's get down to the meat of the matter. The Rosses and the Armstrongs. The killer was one of that quartet, he now felt quite sure of it, and whoever had killed Magnus had probably killed Dempster also, which would most likely rule out Evelyn and Danielle, unless of course there had been some collusion between two or more of them.

Keith Armstrong. Doug had trouble working him out, and always put him at the end of his lists because he was the most difficult. When he'd talked to him, he got a bad impression of the man. He displayed a Uriah Heepish servility, which was completely at odds with his imposing physical presence. He knew that Keith was a bully, occasionally maltreated his wife, and owed Dempster Lumsden a considerable amount of money. The two of them had been good friends until something happened. Some said he'd made a pass at Stella, others said he'd made a pass at Dempster. Whichever way it went, did Keith Armstrong have any reason to kill Magnus and then Dempster? Money, said the small cynical voice which had been getting louder recently. With

Dempster out of the way, he would have a better chance of charming or terrifying Stella into being less financially demanding than the unpredictable Dempster had been. But of course, if he had somehow developed a serious liaison with Stella, he might well have wanted to get the sick baby out of the way too. As to whether he *would* do it—what Douglas knew about his flaring tempers, his vicious treatment of Danielle certainly would suggest that yes, he could, easily.

Douglas walked around the playing fields with their lonely goalposts, past the pigeon-whitened statue of Albert, which had been raised around the turn of the century by a grateful populace—although exactly what the Prince Consort had done for the citizens of Perth was not clear. Beyond that he passed the memorial below the end of the old bridge, dedicated to the local troops raised for foreign wars, then Douglas turned into the path that followed the river bank upstream. It was now the coldest part of the day, just as dawn was beginning to break, and long strands of high cirrus stretched across the eastern sky, which was now lightening in a faint, sickly gray behind the low hills across the river. Doug shivered inside his parka. Wisps of mist rose from the water and made a blanket across the river from bank to bank. On the far side, the outlines of rooftops and chimneys stood out against the pale sky like black paper cutouts.

It was a peaceful scene, and Douglas appreciated it immensely. Brought up near the center of Glasgow, he had never experienced silence until he was ten years old, when his parents rented a caravan to take a holiday by the side of Lochnagar. He remembered how he couldn't sleep, and how his ears and mind scrabbled for the sound of traffic, police sirens, trains, the people upstairs, and he had filled the silence with all kinds of imagined horrors.

Doug put his mind back to work. Keith Armstrong, he'd dealt with him, but Doug realized with a familiar sense of frustration that Keith remained a suspect, high on the list, perhaps, but the way things were now, there was nothing firm, nothing definite, just a feeling. Maybe he'd be less careful when the next body appeared. Which raised the point; should he be putting the Lumsden house under some sort of protective surveillance? Alexis would presumably be going home to Inverness at some point, and Stella would be left alone. The answer was yes. He'd get that under way as soon as he got home.

Two large crows flapped untidily down from a low branch of a sycamore tree, landed on the crossbar of one of the goalposts, and cawed raucously at each other. For some reason, fragments of an old Scots poem came into Douglas's mind, and he spoke them aloud, watching the crows stepping stiffly along the crossbar, their beaks turning from side to side with an inquisitive, predatory arrogance.

> "As I was walking all alane
> I heard twa corbies making a mane . . ."

Douglas couldn't remember all of it, but the words about the new-slain knight came back into his mind like a ghostly vision:

> "And naebody kens that he lies there,
> But his hawk, his hound and his lady fair.
> His hound is to the hunting gane,
> His hawk to fetch the wild-fowl hame,

His lady's ta'en another mate,
So we may make our dinner sweet . . ."

The two crows cawed hoarsely, and watched
Douglas with their coal-hard eyes as he trudged
along. The morning wind was picking up a little,
coming from the North, which probably meant there
would be some rain later in the day.

"Ye'll sit on his white hause-bane,
And I'll pick out his bonny blue een:
Wi'ae lock o' his gowden hair
We'll theek our nest when it grows bare . . ."

As if on a prearranged signal, the two birds flew
off, and a sharp gust of sudden wind made Douglas
shiver and pull his parka tighter around him. The
last stanza came back into his mind, and he spoke
it aloud as if to ward off the evil eye.

"Mony a one for him makes mane
But nane sall ken where he is gane;
O'er his white banes, when they are bare,
The wind sall blaw for evermair."

Douglas put the vision of the dead knight out of
his mind. The Rosses. Now that was an odd pair if
ever there was one, although Douglas was honest
enough to acknowledge that three weeks ago, before
the Lumsden business had started, he would have
said they were a perfectly happy, normal couple.

Graham Ross. He was in more than a little trouble
over Dempster Lumsden, according to his sources.
Dempster had left him carrying the can on a major
investment that had gone sour, and Lord Aviemore,

to whom Doug had spoken briefly before the funeral, had been totally unsympathetic.

Lord Aviemore had decided to stay at the Gleneagles Hotel, about twenty miles from Perth, and received Douglas in his luxurious suite, which looked across the golf course. Bloody playground of the rich, grumbled Doug to himself as he climbed the wide, thickly carpeted stairs to the third floor, you could feed every hungry person in Scotland on what's spent in this place.

But Lord Aviemore was easy enough to talk to; tall, imposing, immaculately dressed, he was nevertheless direct and straightforward.

"He was a wastrel," he replied curtly to Doug's question. "We thought marriage would straighten him out, but it made him worse. Irresponsible. Spendthrift. Nice enough, otherwise. Fond of Stella and all that."

"You know there was some question about the possibility . . ."

Doug raged inwardly at his inability to talk normally to people like Lord Aviemore. He used long words he never normally employed, and he could hear the falsity of his "cultivated" accent.

Aviemore mercifully interrupted him. "You mean could Dempster have killed his baby? I think it unlikely, but I suppose he could, yes. I know of at least one occasion when he got into a bit of a fight."

"Can you tell me a bit about that?" asked Doug. Outside the window, he could see a group of very well-dressed golfers approaching the green. Americans, he felt pretty sure. Probably millionaires.

Lord Aviemore flicked his hand to brush the subject away, obviously regretting he'd brought it up.

"I imagine the next thing you're going to ask concerns his investments, and whether I'm going to underwrite his losses. The answer is no. I don't see why I should have to pay for his stupidity and incompetence. There is no legal reason why I should, so, no, I won't, and that's that.''

He must have been a terror as a father, thought Doug. Didn't give an inch, probably never had.

After a few more equally inflexible comments, Lord Aviemore got up. The interview was over. Doug couldn't think of anything more to ask him.

''Sorry I couldn't help you more,'' said Aviemore rather gruffly at the door. *''De mortuis nil nisi bonum,* right?''

''Yes, sir,'' said Doug, wondering what the old man was talking about.

What he learned from that interview was that Graham Ross was up the creek without a paddle. Not only that, but his boat was sinking. Douglas knew that the big bank people from the head office in Edinburgh were going to descend on the Perth branch any minute now, and Graham would not survive. Could he have killed the baby and then Dempster in a vengeful fury? Or as a desperate bid to get Aviemore to come up with the money?

And then Evelyn. A nut case, without a doubt. After talking to Jean, Doug had carried out some investigations of his own. He found out about her stays in mental hospitals and some of the problems in her early life. It was amazing that Graham hadn't twigged before he married her. There was no doubt he was fully aware of it now.

A particularly disturbing aspect of the case was that Evelyn, who had been so full of hate for Stella, had recently been making every effort to be reconciled with her. Why? What secret reason could she have? To gain access again to the Lumsdens' house? So that she could wreak her vengeance?

Doug was not a particularly sensitive man, but a shiver passed through him which had nothing to do with the wind in the North Inch, and he was glad to step back inside his own home. He postponed thinking anymore about the Rosses or the Armstrongs; there were so many things that needed clearing up he'd have to interview them all again. He sighed at the thought, and opened his front door. His wife was long since out of bed, and was bustling around the house singing one of her lilting Hebridean songs. The kettle was boiling, and he could smell the bracing aroma of frying eggs and bacon. The ''twa corbies'' disappeared from his mind without trace.

Almost every day Jean went to see her mother in the nursing home. The old lady was very frail since breaking her hip a few months back, and was frightened for the other one, although Mr. Imrie, the orthopedic surgeon, had given her an injection of Vitamin D and told her it would recalcify her bones.

Nevertheless, Mrs. Findlay wasn't about to take any chances. She didn't trust doctors much anyway, especially since she had one in the family. If Jean could do that doctoring business, then it couldn't be too complicated, or do that much good. So Mrs. Findlay spent most of her time in bed, although she was healthy enough and was in full possession of all her faculties. She kept up with the news, was upset if she couldn't finish the *Telegraph* crossword, and maintained a watching brief over Jean's family. She particularly looked out for Steven, whom she felt had carelessly stumbled into a marriage with a professional woman instead of selecting the kind of woman he really needed, someone to take full-time care of the house, the children, the cooking and the entertainment.

"What's this about a young woman jumping out of your car and going over the bridge, Jean?" she asked, looking up from her paper. "I might have understood if it had been a young man."

"Not funny, Mother," said Jean, whose sense of humor was beginning to fray around the edges. "That's just what happened, she jumped out. It was horrible."

"You must have said something to make her do it," said Mrs. Findlay sharply. "Young women don't just jump out of cars and commit suicide for no reason."

Jean looked round the room. The lilies she'd brought a couple of days ago were already fading. Her mother liked the temperature stifling hot, and the heat must have been too much for them.

"Do you need anything? The *Radio Times?*"

"You could get me some grapes," answered the old lady. "I think the nurses creep in here at night and gorge themselves on what little food I have here . . . And bring Proust. Volume one of *A la recherche du temps perdu.* I'm not sleeping well and I won't take their pills, because as likely as not they'd poison me with medicine ordered for somebody else. Proust does the job just as well, and an overdose is rarely fatal." She sat up and looked complacent.

"Would you like to get up and go for a wee walk?" asked Jean. "It's a fine day, and we could go out a bit."

"And break the other hip? Jean! And you a doctor! You should know better. Is that what you tell your patients, to go dancing and gallivanting around just after breaking a hip? Phew, I'm glad I have a real doctor looking after me. Mr. Imrie wouldn't make foolish suggestions like that.''

''Please yourself, Mother.''

''I intend to. Have they found out who killed that baby yet? It's a disgrace, we spend all that money on police protection and look what happens. I think it was his father.''

Jean glanced around, hoping that the other patients were out of range of her mother's penetrating voice.

''Mr. Lumsden's dead, Mother.''

''I know that,'' snapped the old lady, staring Jean down with her pinkish, rheumy eyes. ''The family had him killed for doing it. Omerta, you know.''

''Omerta?''

''A Sicilian term,'' Mrs. Findlay answered vaguely. ''Means godfather, or something.''

Jean understood. One of the features of her mother's aging process was that she could go from complete lucidity to some strange state where fragments of book plots, television plays and newspaper articles came together in a bewildering stew, to be stirred and served with enough of a sprinkling of reality to confuse the unwary.

''Right,'' she said. ''I'll tell Douglas Niven. He's the one who needs to know about it.'' However, with all the things that were going on in her life and in her practice, she forgot to mention it when she saw him later that day.

Chapter Sixteen

Detective Inspector Niven sat in his office on the second floor of Police Headquarters. It wasn't much of an office, with its graying white walls and flaking radiator under the window; there was barely room for his desk, a visitor's chair and a couple of filing cabinets. Doug had learned to ignore the draught from under the door, except when the wind came from across the river; then it could be strong enough to blow the match out when he was lighting a cigarette.

He stared thoughtfully over the head of his visitor; the focus of his vision was on the wall, at the faded official picture of the Queen, but he didn't see the familiar smile or the jewelled diadem. He was seeing Graham Ross, but in a new light, and the reflections were not pretty.

"When did it first occur to you that Graham was having an affair with Stella?" He spoke gently; he could see the distress in Evelyn's face.

"It was just over a year ago." Evelyn was holding a small embroidered handkerchief and her long thin fingers were twisting it into knots. Her normally pale face was stark white, and the cheekbones stood high and prominent under her great dark eyes. She was the kind of woman most men would turn around to look at, especially as she sometimes dressed in a rather bizarre way, some days wearing a dark skirt with a hem that trailed around her feet, other times a very short leather skirt and fishnet stockings that scandalized the older ladies of Perth. Today she was wearing a dark woollen dress with a *décolletage* which could easily have taken Doug's mind off his work if he hadn't studiously avoided looking at it.

Douglas sat very still so as not to disturb her train of thought, but he needn't have bothered; her eyes were clouded, distant, reliving the scene at the Lumsdens' house fifteen months ago. She had been looking forward so much to that party; the Lumsdens always gave one around Christmas, and they pulled out all the stops, with a band, a butler, waiters and bartenders hired for the occasion. At that time, Evelyn couldn't decide if the Lumsdens were rich or poor; they seemed to have the best of everything, but they had no staff except for a woman who came to clean three times a week.

Although it had been drizzling on and off, Graham and she had come up the drive on foot; it would have been silly to take the car as it was barely a couple of minutes' walk along the Lumsdens' drive. Graham had his big black umbrella, but they didn't need it. The big house was floodlit and looked baronial and splendid; cars lined the drive, and they recognized a few of them. There were also a couple of Rolls-Royces, a few Jags and a bright red Ferrari, which looked almost black in the reflected light.

"Your old heap would look a bit silly in this lot," she remarked acidly. She hadn't meant her voice to sound so contemptuous, but it came out that way. Graham hadn't answered, but she'd hit home. Graham was at the stage when he knew he would never number a Rolls-Royce among his possessions, probably not even a Jaguar less than five years old.

The door was opened by an elderly, white-haired butler with shaking hands, who helped them off with their coats before hanging them up on the coatstand at the end of the long hall. The living room was all decorated, with a tall, glittering Christmas tree at the far end, and a welcoming log fire crackled in the fireplace. There must have been two dozen people there, all chattering brightly and looking very elegant. Everybody was in evening dress, there was a faint haze of Havana smoke, and it was very apparent from the clothes, the jewelry and the accents that there were two distinct groups, the aristocrats and wealthy county people, and a sprinkling of more plebeian neighbors and local folk like themselves.

But everybody was friendly, and the Rosses separated and mingled with the guests. After talking briefly to Steven Montrose, Graham made a beeline for their hostess, Stella, who was talking animatedly by the fire with Keith Armstrong, and Evelyn had an instinctive feeling that there was something going on between Stella and her husband. Then she found herself talking to Dempster, and he was so charming and attentive that she didn't bother watching Graham anymore, but a great anger at him welled up inside her.

At dinner, Evelyn was put between an elderly deaf gentleman who paid attention only to the food, and a hawk-nosed young man with a rather loud public-school voice. Evelyn took one of her instant, lethal dislikes to him.

He pulled back her chair and Evelyn sat down, her shoulder touching his arm for a second. She shuddered and her hand went instantly up to the place he had touched, as if he'd applied a hot poker to her arm. He didn't notice.

"Splendid place here, what?" he said, sitting down beside her. He looked around the crowded dining room. In fact, Evelyn had to admit, it *was* splendid, with its elegant silver centerpiece and crystal glittering in the candlelight from the huge candelabra, but Evelyn didn't answer. There was no law that said she had to talk to people she didn't like.

"Not too much hunting around here, is there?" he went on, poking at his crab salad, unconscious of her reaction. "That's the only real drawback. It's a nice area otherwise."

"So you're one of them?" asked Evelyn loudly. "One of those swine who hunt foxes to their death?"

He flushed, and the other guests at that end of the table heard her and stopped talking.

"If that sport offends you, perhaps we can talk about something else," he said politely. Evelyn was too striking a woman simply to ignore.

But Evelyn was well away, and made enough of a scene to mortify the young man, and the dinner turned into a disaster, although as she said later, she was only standing up for the rights of dumb animals who had nobody to defend them.

Douglas Niven watched her carefully as she told him the story; her tale was rambling, with quick flashes of emotion and apparent anger. She waved her hands as she talked, and kept wandering off the subject. Suddenly he found himself speculating about her present state of sanity. His wife Cathie had more than once mentioned that Evelyn Ross was weird, but he'd assumed that she had completely recovered from her psychiatric problems.

Finally he had to interrupt. "Evelyn, you said Graham was having an affair with Stella."

Evelyn stopped and looked at him as if he'd just appeared in the room.

"Yes. At the end of the party, when most of the people had already gone home, I went to fetch my coat in the hall." Evelyn paused dramatically and passed a hand over her forehead. "They were coming down the stairs. Both of them, Graham and Stella. They were laughing, laughing . . ."

Evelyn stood up, fists clenched, then slowly sat down again.

Douglas paused, waiting, then looked at her in amazement.

"That was it?"

"No, that was not it." Evelyn was suddenly calm, secure in her knowledge. "I know what you're saying—'this woman's jumping to wild conclusions, just because she saw her husband coming downstairs with another woman.' " She gave Doug a quick smile of startling insight and sanity, and Doug sat back in his chair, astonished. This was really a remarkable woman; as soon as he'd decided she was mad, she came up with something that proved her sanity beyond any reasonable doubt.

"Soon after the baby was born," went on Evelyn serenely, "he developed epilepsy, did you know that?" Doug nodded. "Do you know that epilepsy's a hereditary problem? Did you know that Graham has been epileptic from birth, and he still has a couple of mild attacks a year, in spite of the medicine he takes? No? I'm not surprised." Evelyn crossed her legs and Doug bit his lip. He was all attention; he wrote on his notepad, mostly to take his eyes off her legs.

"There's no epilepsy in the Lumsdens' family,"
went on Evelyn, conscious of the effect she was having. "So that proves it. Graham fathered that child
Magnus, there's no doubt in my mind about it."

Douglas was shaken. Graham Ross and Stella
Lumsden! Until that moment, he'd never heard any
kind of gossip about her, any suggestion that she had
an improper liaison.

"But still," he said gently, "even if everything
you've just said is true, that's a long way from what
you were saying when you came here, that Graham
first killed the baby and then Dempster Lumsden."

"Graham came home the morning the kid was
killed. To take me out to lunch, or so he said . . ."
A sneer crossed her face. "He must have stopped
first at the Lumsdens' on his way home."

"But why?"

"So it would seem that Dempster had done it;
everybody knew that he was a drunk and didn't like
the baby."

Douglas sighed under his breath.

"But why, Evelyn?" he repeated. "Why would
he want it to look as if Dempster had done it?"

"Because it was the only way that he could get
old Lord Aviemore to pay Dempster's debts to the
bank," explained Evelyn, talking as if to a child.
"Lord Aviemore is a lovely gentleman. He wouldn't
leave Stella with such a problem." Her eyes flashed
again for a second, and Douglas saw the frightening
burden of hatred she was carrying. "Of course he
doesn't know what a slut and whore his daughter-in-
law is."

A faint throbbing started up between Douglas's
temples, but after another half an hour of gentle
questioning he felt he had the whole story; Evelyn

told him about the factory built with the bank's money, Dempster's imminent bankruptcy, the plan Graham and Dempster had cooked up between them, whereby Dempster would leave the country for South America, and finally his last minute cancellation and disappearance.

"So you see," she said finally, "the only way Graham could keep Dempster away was to make it look as if he'd killed his child, then he wouldn't be able to come home. Then Aviemore would come in with the money to pay back the bank, and Stella could eventually join him in Argentina or wherever it was."

Douglas stood up. "Thank you, Mrs. Ross, I really appreciate your taking the time to tell me all this. I'll do some checking, but to be quite honest with you, it doesn't sound a very likely story." Evelyn stared at him, her eyes seeming to get blacker and deeper as he spoke. "I think we'll find that someone else was responsible for the murder," he went on, "so I wouldn't go around repeating what you told me, for your own sake."

She picked up her handbag and left without a word, leaving a faint trace of her perfume behind her.

Douglas sat quietly for a moment. Constable Jamieson came in with a steaming mug of tea and put it on the desk in front of him. Absently, Douglas picked up the hot mug and rolled it slowly between his hands, warming them. Evelyn Ross was really a head case, he thought. It had been very uncomfortable, sitting there, listening to her rambling tale and seeing the strange, haunted look on her face. She was probably quite capable of dreadful things on her

own account, he thought, particularly if she felt her
husband had betrayed her.

Jean was having a busy morning at the surgery; normally she allotted about five minutes to each patient,
which was enough to hear the story, listen to a chest
or look down a throat and write out a prescription,
but she'd had two more difficult cases, one of which
had forced her to consult Helen Inkster.

She poked her head into the waiting room to apologize to the people waiting, and to her astonishment
saw the slight figure of Danielle Armstrong sitting
there, her eyes downcast, with a long gray scarf tied
around her throat.

"Send Mrs. Armstrong in after the next one,
please," she told Eleanor.

Eleanor looked at the list.

"There's six other folk in afore her," she said, a
touch aggressively. Arranging the order of admission
to the doctors was one of the few responsibilities of
the surgery that truly belonged to her, and she felt
very protective of her rights. "They don't like it
when . . ." She caught the look in Jean's eye.
"A'right," she said resignedly. "You're the boss."

And don't you forget it, said Jean to herself, returning to her examining room. It was three o'clock,
time for her afternoon tea and biscuits, and she often
felt a bit irritated around that time.

She took a quick look at Danielle when Eleanor
ushered her in, at the same time bringing in her tea.

"Would you bring in another cup for Mrs. Armstrong, please?" Jean asked her. Poor Danielle
looked as if she could use one. Eleanor's eyes registered surprise. A second breach of surgery proto-

col within two minutes; her lips compressed and she left the room without replying.

Danielle sat, looking like a whipped dog, her eyes averted and red, as though she had been crying.

"What's the matter, Danielle?" asked Jean gently.

Danielle raised her head but didn't look at Jean.

"Nothing much," she croaked. "I've just got a sore throat."

Jean was about to say something when Eleanor returned with an overfull cup of tea. She put it down in front of Danielle and some slopped into the saucer.

"Let's have a look." Jean picked up her penlight, and held Danielle's tongue out of the way with a wooden spatula.

"Looks all right," she murmured. "Take off your scarf a second."

Danielle hesitated, then unwound it. The marks on her neck were obvious.

Helen Inkster opened the door.

"I'm about done, and you have about eight waiting," she said, eyeing Danielle's neck. "Shall I take a few of them?"

"Yes, thanks, Helen," replied Jean. "Much obliged." The door closed.

"Tell me about it, Danielle," said Jean, but when she saw the way Danielle's eyes flickered, she went on. "Just don't bother telling me you ran into the clothesline or anything like that, okay?"

Danielle hesitated, then made a noise which sounded halfway between a hiss and a whistle before she found her voice again.

"It happened the day before yesterday," she said. "He was yelling at me, then . . . he caught me around the neck . . .'' Danielle's shoulders hunched up protectively at the recollection.

"Has he ever done anything like that before?"

Danielle looked at Jean with a painful little smile.

"Not for a while. This time I really thought he was going to kill me. Luckily Mrs. Castle, the cleaning woman, came in just at that moment."

Jean was indignant. "Why do you stay with him? Isn't there anywhere you could go, your parents or somewhere?"

"My parents are dead, and my brother lives in Australia. I don't have any money, and the children . . . No, I can't leave, although I wish I could." She coughed, and put a hand up to her throat. It was obviously hurting her to speak.

"What happened? I mean why did he do this?" persisted Jean.

Danielle's eyes went to the floor again. "No real reason. He thought his dinner was cold, something like that."

Jean shook her head. "Have you thought of talking to Douglas Niven?" she asked. Danielle's head came up as if she'd been slapped.

"Oh, no," she said, her agitation plain. "He'd be sure to think . . ." She caught herself. "I couldn't do that. It would just cause more trouble for me and the kids in the long run. If they arrested him and put him away, what would we live on?"

"Did it have anything to do with little Magnus Lumsden?" asked Jean suddenly, her eyes on Danielle.

"Oh God," said Danielle, putting her hand up to her mouth and watching Jean with big, scared eyes. "No, of course not!"

Jean shook her head and pulled a prescription pad

in front of her. "I'll give you some lozenges," she said, writing. "They'll numb your throat . . . And you should put some warm compresses on your neck." She sat back. "I'll tell you one more thing, Danielle. I'm going to call Keith in here and give him a good talking to. If he ever touches you again, you're to let me know, immediately. All right?"

"Please don't," begged Danielle. She really looked terrified now. "If he thought I'd asked you to . . ."

"Don't worry," answered Jean. "You didn't have to tell me how you got those bruises. I'm going to talk to him and that's all there is to it."

After Danielle had gone and Jean had seen the last of her patients, she reached for the phone to call Keith Armstrong. He was still at the store, and said brusquely he was too busy to come over.

"I'm not asking you to come over," Jean snapped, "I'm telling you." She had a sudden, fearful vision of his bulk, looming over her. "I've just examined your wife." There was a moment's silence.

"I'll be there in ten minutes," he said grudgingly. "But I've got nothing to tell you."

Jean tapped on Helen's door, then went in. Helen had a pile of NHS forms in front of her.

"This is the part I really hate," she said. "If they'd told me in medical school that most of my job would be filling in forms, I'd have gone in for something else."

Jean told her about Danielle, and Keith Armstrong's impending visit.

"I saw her neck," said Helen. "Did you know he was violent like that?"

"Well, Mary Castle told me this had happened . . . but before that, no, although I should have guessed. Whenever she looks at him, there's a kind of fear on her face. Well, it's easy to see that in retrospect, I suppose." Jean felt terrible. She seemed to be missing everything that went on around her, and her lack of attention to the realities of people and situations verged on the criminal.

"I'd better stay around while he's here," said Helen. She smiled suddenly, and her rather homely features lit up with the light of battle. "If he gives you any trouble I'll come through and smack him over the head with my old hockey stick."

They laughed, but a little nervously. Very occasionally they had problems with obstreperous patients; it was the only identifiable disadvantage of not having a male doctor in the practice.

Eleanor decided to stay too, more because she didn't want to miss anything than out of solidarity with her doctors.

When Keith arrived he slammed through the door like a whirlwind and went straight through into Jean's room, glowered at her and sat down. The chair creaked alarmingly under his weight.

Jean wasted no time on civilities.

"Danielle was here. If she hadn't begged me not to, I'd have called the police."

"The police! If you called them, you'd have done a really foolish thing, woman." Keith's little eyes were fixed on Jean, and she could feel the violence in the air. "You've just heard her side of the story . . ."

"Yes, I suppose you were only defending yourself against her," said Jean contemptuously. "I've written my clinical findings in my notes here, and if it ever comes to pass that you hurt her again, I'll make sure you get arrested. Now get out of here."

Keith stood up, and put his huge hands on the

desk in front of her. In spite of herself, Jean shrank
away from him.

"You think she's just a little victim, don't you?"
he said. "Well, let me tell you something. She's not
the person you think she is, not by any means. You
think she wouldn't hurt a fly, don't you?" He gave
a short laugh. "Maybe you'll find out some day, or
somebody else will. Meanwhile, a very good day to
you, m'lady."

He left the room, and Jean heard the outer door
bang as he went out. Within seconds, Helen and
Eleanor were in Jean's room.

"Well?" said Helen. "What did he say?"

"Not much," confessed Jean. "I told him I'd call
the police if he touched his wife again, and he said
. . . well, he indicated that Danielle wasn't quite the
timorous wee thing I thought she was."

"Cowardly pig that he is," said Eleanor. Jean and
Helen looked coldly at her and she went quickly back
to her outer office to finish up.

"It seems to be getting more and more complicated," said Helen thoughtfully. "Do you think
maybe Keith . . . ?"

"You mean could he have killed the baby and then
Dempster Lumsden? It's possible, I suppose, but
why on earth would he? What possible motive would
he have for doing such dreadful things?"

Helen thoughtfully rubbed a finger along her nose.
She always had a surprisingly good knowledge about
local events and the people involved in them. "Well,
I heard that Dempster had turned against him because he was getting too interested in Stella. Do you
think there's anything to that?"

"I don't know." Jean started to put her papers in
order on her desk. "She certainly seems to have

bowled over a lot of the local male talent, although I'm sure she didn't encourage them.''

''And apparently he owes Dempster a lot of money and Dempster was trying to get it back. He was about to start legal proceedings, and Keith would have been forced to sell out. He'd have lost everything.''

Jean looked up. ''You seem to know a lot of classified information, my dear.'' She grinned. ''Where did you hear all that?''

Helen blushed. ''I have my own sources,'' she said. ''Remember, I've lived in this town a lot longer than you have.''

Helen clumped out of the office. Jean felt such a sense of solidity and comfort from her. She could never have found a better partner, she was quite sure of that.

Chapter Seventeen

When Jean left the surgery it was dark, and the wind was picking up again. She went carefully around the puddle at the bottom of the steps, thinking for the hundredth time that she should do something about that, because not all the patients knew to look out for it. The ones who got their shoes full of water didn't appreciate it, particularly if they'd come in with a cold or bronchitis.

She opened the car door, put her handbag on the passenger seat and got in. It wasn't getting any easier, climbing in and out of her car these days; she would really have to go on a diet. Maybe Steven would do it with her, it would be a help, but then he wasn't really overweight. The windscreen was fogged up, and she turned on the demister and waited for it to clear.

She felt so ineffective, she could have cried. Why was it that she never really understood why people did what they did? In her job as a family doctor, people came to her every day to explain their troubles, and really at this point she had quite a lot of experience with all kinds of different people and the difficulties they were apt to run into. Then why was it she had so much trouble understanding their motivations, the real thoughts that went on behind the mask of their faces? It wasn't that she didn't try . . .

Had Keith Armstrong attacked his wife in an ungovernable fury, and if so, what had precipitated it? Or, as he hinted, was there much more to the story than that? Could he have killed the Lumsden father and son? And given that he was physically capable, why? And growling like a ground bass in the back of her mind was the question—could she, the frail-looking Danielle, could she have played any part in this horror? Toying with that idea, Keith's attack on her became almost understandable, if he knew or even suspected that she'd killed that child . . .

The traffic was slow, and it had started to rain again. The drops sparkled on the glass, then vanished with the whining stroke of the wipers, as Jean strained to see ahead of her. South Street was a blaze of lights, and for the first time Jean felt the Christmas spirit moving in her, although it was still six weeks away. She started to think about what she would get for her family. Steven was always difficult, he bought every kitchen gadget and electrical device known to man, and he already had enough leather gloves, ties and scarves to restock Marks and Spencer. Something for his car . . . A weekend's break for both of them . . . No, that would look as if she were really getting it for herself. She stopped at the lights, and on her left she saw the windows of Kelso Gents Outfitters, and although she couldn't see what they had in the window, she suddenly knew what she would get him. One of those nice Astrakhan hats, a real one made of curly lambswool . . . That was it. He'd really like that. Steven was always very conscious of his appearance, and she encouraged him to dress well. He was in the public eye a lot, being the manager of such a big company, and it was important for him to look good, more important than for most people. Jean smiled to herself, visualizing how distinguished Steven would look in it. She'd get him a black one, like the one Gorbachev wore at the last May Day parade.

By the time she pulled into the drive of her home, her confidence had come back and she was feeling more like her usual cheerful self. The clock on the dashboard said six-thirty, and she hoped that one of the girls would have made the dinner. Steven didn't appreciate being kept waiting too long.

"Hello!" she called from the hall. She always did that, and whoever was within hearing distance would answer, so she knew who was home and who wasn't. There was a long pause, and then Lisbie's voice came down the stairs. "Mum?" Jean's heart missed a beat. Lisbie sounded as if she were crying. She came down the stairs, and Fiona appeared from the living room, looking white.

"Whatever's the matter with the two of you?" She stared at them; it couldn't be too bad, whatever it was, because they were both there and apparently in good health.

"There's a letter there for you, Mum," said Fiona quietly, pointing at the hall table, still watching her mother. Jean picked it up. There was no stamp, and it looked like Steven's handwriting on the envelope.

"What's all this about?" she asked, good-naturedly, tearing open the envelope. "Did your father win the pools or something?"

The two girls stood very still while she read it. Jean felt all the blood draining out of her face, and she sat down suddenly on the hall chair.

"Do you girls know about this?" she asked, very

quietly, still holding the piece of paper and the envelope. Her voice sounded as if it belonged to someone else, and Jean felt that she had climbed into some kind of bad dream, because it was quite impossible that this could really be happening to her.

"Mum, didn't you *know?*" asked Fiona. Lisbie was now sobbing unrestrainedly, and she buried her head on Jean's shoulder. Jean shook her head. No, she didn't know, she didn't know anything.

Jean got up slowly. "Well, I suppose we'd better have some dinner, or have the two of you eaten?"

"No, of course not," said Fiona stoutly. "We wouldn't start without you."

Fiona went and got a small glass of sherry for each of them. They needed it, she said.

Lisbie had made a shepherd's pie, and they all sat down to eat it. The dining room table seemed huge with only the three of them around it, and Steven's empty chair spoke as eloquently as the ghost of Banquo.

"Did you know?" asked Jean in a humble voice, looking at each of the girls in turn. Once again, she told herself, she hadn't seen what was going on, not even an inkling.

"I heard about it at work," said Lisbie, and she started to cry again.

"When he was having all those meetings at night, Mum, didn't it occur to you. . . ?" Fiona had a puzzled expression. "We thought you knew, but weren't saying anything about it."

Jean cast her mind back for some tell-tale hints and found that she had ignored everything, all the signs . . . Poor Steven, he must have been trying to tell her . . . The faint odor of perfume she'd noticed once or twice on his clothes, and shrugged off, the lipstick she'd seen on his collar when she was going through the wash, the late-night phone calls, the hang-ups, the long meetings at the office . . . Poor Steven, she couldn't help thinking, it must have been very difficult for him.

"Do you think he'll ever come back?" asked Lisbie, then burst into redoubled tears.

"I don't really know, dear," answered Jean. "I'm sure he'll want to see the two of you from time to time, and according to his note, he won't be living that far away."

"But why did he do this to us?" asked Fiona. She seemed more angry than upset. "We never did anything bad to him, did we?"

"I think it's a mid-life crisis," said Lisbie, having difficulty talking through her tears.

"Oh come on," said Fiona crossly. "You read that in *Woman's Own.* "

"Sometimes even the most sensible people do irrational things," said Jean after a pause. "I just hope she takes proper care of him." She thought of all the little things that Steven insisted on, the way his shirts had to be ironed, how he liked his breakfast toast just very lightly browned . . . On reflection, Steven had quite a lot of small foibles, and it would take a new woman a while to learn them.

It wasn't until Jean crept into her cold and unwelcoming bed that she fully began to realize what had happened, and it was well into the small hours before she finally cried herself to sleep, blaming herself bitterly for her own inadequacies.

There was an air of expectancy around Perth; the word, disseminated through shops and offices and by friends stopping to talk while doing the day's shopping, was that an arrest was expected any minute for the murder of Dempster Lumsden and his son Magnus.

Even around the police station there was a feeling that the case had finally been broken, and the sneers from the press and the public would soon be silenced. Detective Inspector Niven was looking his old self again; the spring was back in his walk, and he had regained the jaunty look he wore when things were going well. His colleagues hoped he would say something when he passed them in the corridors of the headquarters building but were too polite or too intimidated to ask. So, like everybody else, they speculated.

Opinion was divided as to who the guilty persons might be; most went along with the official police theory that Dempster Lumsden had killed his child in a drunken fury, and was in turn killed in a hit and run accident, probably by a lorry, while trying to hitch a ride into Perth.

Constable Jamieson had worked out the trajectory which resulted in Dempster's body being found at the foot of the embankment.

"It's quite clear," he said, pointing to his meticulously drawn diagrams. "He was hit by the side of a lorry going at about sixty-five, driving near the verge. The poor bugger was probably just too drunk to get out of the way. Anyway, being hit on the side like that would give him an angular momentum that would project him to the side, and the slope of the bank would do the rest."

"Come off it," said his friend Archie Webster, the despatcher. "Just 'cos you go to night school and learn about angular whatever it was, doesn't alter the facts. When you get hit on the road, you finish up on the road or right next to it. You must have seen enough dead dogs on the side of the road to realize that.''

The people in Lisbie's office were also pretty sure that Dempster had killed Magnus, but that his own demise was at the hands of his family, who had him killed because of the disgrace he had brought to his ancient lineage. As Lisbie pointed out, most of the people in her office were lawyers, so they should know.

It was the sudden flurry of new interviews which had sparked off all this new speculation.

Although he'd interviewed all the suspects immediately after the murder of Magnus Lumsden, and some of them again after the discovery of Dempster's body, Doug felt that the knowledge he had gained since that time made it advisable to see them all over again, but this time he restricted his interviews to only a few people, and he saw them all separately in his office, and recorded the conversations.

He used a common technique for getting them scared and on the defensive; rather than visiting them at home or making an appointment, he sent, unannounced, two uniformed policemen to bring them to Headquarters from their place of work.

Keith was furious. Business was bad enough without this, he shouted, while the girl who helped in the shop watched with round eyes. The two policemen were wary because of his size, but he quickly calmed down and clumped down the stairs and into the back of their car.

Douglas was waiting for him.

''Mr. Armstrong,'' he said after listening to Keith's rantings for a few moments, ''this is a murder investigation. If you don't feel you can help us voluntarily I have enough evidence here to arrest you on suspicion.'' After that, Keith suddenly became much more tractable.

"I'm going to record this conversation, so please speak clearly. If the answer to a question is yes or no, please answer, don't just nod your head, all right?"

Keith shrugged his massive shoulders.

"Tell me exactly where you were and what you were doing on the morning of Magnus Lumsden's death.''

"I've told you all that already. Why don't you just look at your old notes?''

Douglas ignored the comment and repeated the question.

"I got up late, showered, had breakfast . . .''

"What time was that?''

Keith hesitated. "About ten, maybe ten-fifteen.''

Douglas nodded. "Then what?''

"I went down to the basement and worked out.''

"Worked out?''

"Lifted weights, did exercises, press-ups . . .''

"For how long?''

"About an hour. You asked me all that last time . . .''

"Right. So this brings us up to when?''

"I came up from the basement about eleven, I suppose.''

"Then what did you do?''

"I went into the kitchen to get something to eat.''

"What did you eat?''

"A loaf of bread, some cold lamb . . . Let's see, a jar of pickles . . .''

"Then what did you do?''

"I went into the garage.''

"What did you do there?" Douglas sounded bored, ready to go on forever, but he was very wide awake, looking for inconsistencies and quite prepared to annoy Keith into making them.

"I worked on my car, changed the plugs, adjusted the headlights . . ."

"You take pretty good care of your car?" Douglas's voice was deceptively off-hand.

"Yes, I suppose so."

"While you were doing this, do you know what was going on at the Lumsden house?"

"That must have been about the time when the baby was killed, I suppose."

"Right." Douglas poised for the kill, earlier than he had expected. "Do you know Frank Kinnear?"

"The garage man?" Keith looked surprised at the question.

"He says he's never known you to do any work on your car. He also told me you don't know a gasket from a hole in the ground, and—" Douglas's voice hardened—"also that he changed the plugs on your car a month ago."

"I got a manual," replied Keith, without a flicker. "I'm learning how to do all that myself. Kinnear charges an arm and a leg, and he's not that great."

"Now, Mr. Armstrong . . ." Doug stopped writing and looked directly at him. "I am going to ask you a new question. One I haven't asked you before. Think very carefully before you answer, all right?"

Keith nodded. There were beads of sweat on his forehead.

"Who was your visitor that morning?"

Keith looked startled. "Who said I had a visitor?"

Doug repeated the question. Keith started to fidget, opening and closing his great hands. Douglas looked cautiously over toward the door; Jamieson was there, his hand ready on the handle of his truncheon.

"All right. I suppose you know, otherwise you wouldn't ask. It was Amanda Delincourt. Who told you?"

"How long did she stay with you?"

"I dunno. We didn't look at the clock . . ." Keith essayed a leer, which made Doug want to smash him over the head with a blunt instrument.

"Try to remember, Mr. Armstrong. Five minutes? Ten? Longer?"

"Maybe a quarter of an hour, not much longer than that. Stella had only gone down to buy a few things in the shops, so Amanda couldn't stay too long."

"Did you go back to Lossie House with her?"

"No. She . . ."

"And having gone to the house, did the two of you not go into Magnus Lumsden's room and smash his head against the wall?" Doug stood up; he found he was almost shouting.

"No, I didn't go back with her." Keith, for all his size, backed away from Doug. He was obviously shaken. "But I think Amanda did it," he stammered, "before Stella got home, then after she did it she went out of the house again . . ."

"Why didn't you tell us all this before?" asked Doug coldly. "It's called withholding information, and may be the basis of a separate charge against you."

"You never asked," replied Keith with a trace of his old cockiness. "But I'm telling you now. I knew that girl pretty well, and I'm damn sure she had something to do with it.''

"I have somebody at your house right now check-ing your shoes and boots,'' said Douglas heavily. "I'll know if you were down there at Lossie House before tomorrow.'' Douglas switched off the tape re-corder for a moment, and leaned toward Keith, his face twisted with disgust. "And I hope you were, Keith, I really hope you were.''

Keith looked at him with fear in his eyes. Doug switched the tape recorder on again, and went on in his normal voice.

"Did you see anybody else around the Lumsdens' house about that time? Did you see Dempster Lums-den, for instance?''

"How could I? I just told you, I stayed at home.''

"Why did you commit an assault on your wife last Thursday, at which time you injured her neck?''

"I'm not saying I did, and nor is anybody else,'' said Keith threateningly. "I know my rights, and that's a slanderous statement you just made.''

"Was it because she threatened to turn you in, inform the police about what you had done?''

"Do you really see *her* threatening *me?*'' Keith postured, flexing his biceps for Douglas to see.

"Very impressive,'' murmured Douglas. "Have you ever heard of the Aladdin's Cave?''

"In kids' books, yes,'' replied Keith. "Why?''

"I'm talking about a bar in Glasgow called the Aladdin's Cave.''

"In Glasgow? It's . . .'' Keith caught himself. "Personally I don't drink anymore,'' he said. "It interferes with my exercise program.''

Douglas was watching him closely.

"You're quite right, Mr. Armstrong, the Aladdin's

Cave isn't in Glasgow. It's in Leith, as you were about to point out. Careless of me, wasn't it?''

Keith stared at him, his jaw hanging open. ''I don't know what you're talking about,'' he muttered.

Doug decided that this was the time to let him go so he could remember all the questions he'd been asked, and what he'd replied. He stood up.

''That will be all for now, thank you, Mr. Armstrong.''

Keith looked surprised. ''Will you send a car to take me back to my shop?'' His voice sounded relieved, more relieved than he wanted to appear.

''A man of your physique? No, I'm sure you'd want to walk, just for the additional exercise,'' said Douglas smoothly. ''Oh, Mr. Armstrong, just one more thing,'' he said when Keith reached the door. Keith turned. ''Has it occurred to you what they'll do to you in jail? The other prisoners, I mean? To a man who killed a baby in cold blood . . .''

''I didn't . . . I swear I didn't . . .'' Keith's face was white with fear. He swayed and leaned heavily against the door for a moment.

Doug grinned at him.

''By the way, Mr. Armstrong, I am formally warning you not to leave Perth without my written permission, until further notice. Do you understand?''

Keith nodded, then went out, making a big effort to look and sound carefree and debonair.

He's maybe feeling relieved now, thought Douglas, because I didn't arrest him, but when he's had a chance to think it all over he may not feel quite so confident. Meanwhile . . . Doug picked up his raincoat and went down the back stairs to the garage.

There were now enough things he needed to talk to Mrs. Stella Lumsden about to warrant an unannounced visit to Lossie House. The thought of sending somebody out to pick her up and bring her in didn't even occur to him.

I'm really getting allergic to those fancy folk, he said to himself as he turned the sharp corner into the Lossie Estate. Because Dempster was an Honorable, did that mean she was one too? The Honorable Mrs. Stella Lumsden. Or would it be the Honorable Mrs. Dempster Lumsden? Doug shrugged his shoulders in a familiar attitude of annoyance. Sometimes he wished the guillotine had been invented on this side of the Channel; each year he would have celebrated the British equivalent of Bastille day with the greatest of relish.

Stella was at home, and so was Alexis. As he came through the door, he wondered suddenly if the two of them were starting to develop something more than an innocent in-law kind of relationship.

Alexis was in the hall, managing to look elegant even in his baggy country tweeds. He was cleaning a double-barrelled shotgun. Doug knew a bit about guns, but although he'd heard of them, he had never actually seen a Purdey before. Even as he admired it, and felt the perfect balance of the weapon, he was thinking it must have cost as much as he made in six months, and the mere thought made his bowels tighten.

"Mrs. Lumsden," he said. Stella was standing beside Alexis. She seemed to know quite a bit about guns too. "There are a few things that have arisen, and that I would like to discuss if you have a few moments . . ." There he went again, he thought furiously, tongue-tied as if he was a mental case.

"Why don't we go into the living room?" said Stella. "Alexis, join us when you're done, please . . ."

"No, if you don't mind," said Douglas, stiffly. "There are certain things I would prefer to ask you in private."

Alexis raised his eyebrows, and Stella gave a tiny shrug. She led the way into the huge living room, and she sat on the sofa by the fire. Doug sat down on the edge of the big leather armchair next to her.

"Mrs. Lumsden, there are certain things that have come up in the last period of time . . ." Stella's beautiful eyes were on him. Look as he might, he couldn't find any trace of disdain or condescension in her expression, and he eased off a little. "It was reported to me that you had had an affair with Mr. Graham Ross. I'm not looking for scandal, you understand. You people can do whatever you like . . ." He paused to check the effect of his words on Stella. She was smiling, an angry, tight-lipped smile. "It's only insofar as it connects to our investigation of the death of the deceased."

Stella's voice was even and controlled. "Well, the mere idea of having an affair with that . . . man revolts me. Of course he did try . . . and on a couple of occasions he put me in an embarrassing position as hostess when he was here." She paused. "Dempster had a business relationship with him, so I couldn't exactly tell him what I thought of him." Looking at Stella, Doug could hardly blame Graham Ross. She was enough to turn any man's head, especially if she was going out of her way to be agreeable.

Doug took out his notebook and wrote laboriously in it. If what Jean Montrose said was true, and these people weren't so different from normal ones, the wait would make her edgy, if she had anything to hide.

Stella sat stock-still.

Doug looked up. "Why didn't you tell me that your sister Amanda was supposed to be looking after the baby?" His voice had returned, thankfully, to its normal Scots accent.

Again Stella's lips tightened. Doug could see that she really didn't like her sister, even now that she was dead.

"It wouldn't have helped. It wouldn't have brought Magnus back." Her lip curled. "She was . . . involved with that creature Keith Armstrong . . ." Stella shuddered. "I knew where she'd gone. I even thought that the two of them . . ."

"Yes, Mrs. Lumsden?"

"Might have done it. Keith was angry enough with Dempster to do something like that."

"But do you think Amanda. . . ?"

Stella looked pensive, then shook her head. "No. Absolutely not. She hated me enough, I'll tell you that much, but she wouldn't have had it in her heart to kill Magnus, I'm quite sure of it."

"Could Amanda have prevented Armstrong from killing Magnus, if he'd . . ."

"Yes, I'm sure she could." Stella's voice was emphatic, but Doug watched her eyes as they looked around for support from Alexis, who at that moment came in, although Doug had asked him to leave them alone. Remembering Keith's size and his known potential for violence, Doug wasn't nearly as sure as she seemed to be.

He decided to try another tack. "Mrs. Lumsden, there are still a number of aspects of this case that are not entirely clear to me." He stood up suddenly and leaned toward Stella in an almost menacing way. "When Magnus was found dead, he had been carefully put back in his cot. Who but a mother, Mrs. Lumsden, would take the trouble to do that?"

Stella's jaw dropped. "Are you suggesting. . . ?"

"I asked you a question, Mrs. Lumsden, and I'd like an answer, please."

Stella's voice was low and very shaky. "Inspector Niven, I don't know much about the psychology of child killers, so I can't answer your question. If you're suggesting that I killed Magnus . . ."

"I already told you I wasn't suggesting anything," replied Doug gruffly, but the fire was out of him. Doggedly, he tried once more. "When I was talking to you after Magnus's death, I asked you if you knew where Dempster might be, and you answered that he usually went to Glasgow on his binges."

Alexis was standing with his back to the fire, several feet away, but Doug could see that he was watching and listening to every word that was being said. Alexis's eyes moved to Stella with a curious expression, as if he had been the one who'd asked the question.

"Well?" Stella didn't appear to attach any significance to Doug's query.

Doug took a deep breath. If anything was going to break Stella, this was it. His voice was quiet, but the accusation was evident in the tone.

"The barman at the Aladdin's Cave told me that during one of Dempster's binges about four months ago you personally went there to fetch him. So you knew that when he went off he was going to Leith, not Glasgow." Douglas, watching her, couldn't keep the triumphant note out of his voice. He knew that he had Stella by the throat.

But Stella didn't look or sound at all defeated.

"I've picked him up in bars in Glasgow, and Dundee, and Stirling," she snapped, apparently at the end of her patience with what she considered Douglas's outrageous questioning. "When he went off this last time, he said he was going to Glasgow, and that's what I told you. Now, unless you have some more intelligent questions, or can tell us something that will make us feel you're conscientiously doing your job, I'll bid you good afternoon, Inspector!"

To his own surprise, Douglas was not intimidated; he was merely disappointed that his own intimidating tactics hadn't worked.

He got up, as if he had shot his last bolt. At the door, just after saying goodbye to a rather distant Alexis and an angry Stella, he threw his final grenade.

"It's the timing, Mrs. Lumsden," he said. "Who else knew that morning that you had left home, and that it would be safe to come into the house? Who else could have known the house would be empty, just for that short time?" Doug glared at her. "Mrs. Lumsden, do you have a passport?"

"Yes, I do. But what . . ."

"Is it here, in this house?"

"Yes, it's in the wall safe, with . . ."

"I am formally requesting you to turn it in to me now," said Doug grimly. "I shall give you a receipt, and it will be returned to you in due course when the investigation is completed."

"Does that mean that you suspect me?" asked Stella with an incredulous look at Alexis. "Of killing my baby? Or killing Dempster?'' She took a deep breath. ''Or both?''

Doug had a sinking feeling that he might be in the process of making a grave mistake, but he went on. ''This is just a precaution until these questions are fully clarified,'' he said.

''You'd better give it to him,'' said Alexis quietly, without taking his eyes off Douglas. Obviously angry, Stella silently turned and went back into the living room. While they waited, Alexis and Douglas stood uncomfortably silent, avoiding each other's eyes.

Stella reappeared with the dark blue passport. Doug wrote out a receipt, as usual taking his time. And maybe this time he was rewarded. The glances Stella and Alexis exchanged seemed more intimate than was usual between a brother-in-law and a sister-in-law. But then Douglas's upbringing and code of behavior was so different from theirs. He would really have to discuss the matter with Jean Montrose.

As he drove back into Perth, Doug considered the technique he was employing. Those people should understand what I'm doing, he thought, better than anybody. It's like shooting grouse; you surprise them, flush them into the air, and wait for one to make a wrong move, to fly in the wrong direction. Well, all the likely ones were in the air now; all except for Graham Ross. He was next.

Doug suddenly felt more cheerful. He wound the car window down and enjoyed the clear air and the sunlit view over the Perthshire countryside.

He didn't believe much in intuition or that kind of stuff. Hard work, painstaking effort, unrelenting attention to details, that's what solved cases, and nobody knew that better than he did.

Nevertheless, Douglas felt a kind of lightness in his spirit that wasn't all due to the fine weather; he could feel in his bones that the Lumsden case was nearing a climax. Something had to happen; somebody had to break, and his police sense told him it was going to be soon.

Chapter Eighteen

The first breakfast after Steven's departure was a strange, sad meal. Although Steven rarely came down before Jean and the girls left for work, and in fact often had breakfast in bed brought up by one of them, his absence was felt sharply and cruelly by all.

Jean bustled about as usual, trying hard to give the girls a feeling of security and continuity; there was no point in letting them see how badly hurt she was.

"Fiona, pass the milk, please . . ." Lisbie's words faded into tears. Her face was a mess; she looked as if she'd been crying all night.

"For God's sake, Lisbie!" said Fiona, passing the milk jug. "To listen to you, you'd think he was dead, or something." Fiona herself was turned out as carefully as always. What Fiona felt didn't show; it never had.

"He might as well be . . ." Lisbie put her head down between her arms and her shoulders shook.

"Now, Lisbie," said Jean. "You don't want Gordon to see you like that." She went over and put her arm around the girl. "After all," she said, trying to make a joke out of it, "remember I've lost a husband. You've only lost a father."

"You can always get another husband," said Lisbie, her voice muffled. "We can never have another father."

"Lisbie, for God's sake!" said Fiona again. "We're tired of all this whingeing. It's the same for everybody, so just stop it, okay?" Fiona looked at her watch, then got up from the table. "Come on, girl, you have to move your car before I can get mine out. It's time we left."

After the girls had gone to work, Jean picked up the phone to get her calls from the surgery. What was she going to tell Helen and Eleanor? A hot blush of embarrassment came to her cheeks as she thought about it. She would have to say something; when Steven started to be seen in town with Pearl Blaikie the word would get round so fast . . .

Helen would be wonderful; there was no problem there. Helen knew plenty about broken homes, because she came from one. Tears started to course down Jean's cheeks. A broken home! Hers!

Once again, she hadn't seen it coming; another smack in the face from an unexpected source. It was like fighting in a dark room, against an opponent equipped with radar. Jean was not looking forward to telling Eleanor; she was another story altogether. Eleanor did her job well enough, but she was known to be a great gossip. She had been warned at different times by both Helen and herself not to discuss patients with people outside the surgery, but they were pretty sure she did. But now . . . She'd be on the phone as soon as she had a free moment, and she'd have the news all round town in no time flat.

Jean forced herself to dial the number. Eleanor gave her the messages, and Jean told her she'd be coming in shortly. She decided that she would tell them simply that Steven had gone, and she didn't know when he would be back. Later, in private, she would tell Helen the whole story.

She went upstairs to get dressed, but she simply could not decide what to put on. She had some brightly colored blouses and dresses hanging in the cupboard, and the mere sight of them made her feel shaky and nauseated. Finally she pulled out a dark blue blouse with a matching skirt. On, they made her look even paler than before.

Jean felt numb, and grateful to have a routine which didn't allow her the time to brood. Thank God, she wasn't one of those people who, when something went wrong, could stop doing their job and feel sorry for themselves; it wasn't a luxury, it was more of a trap.

At the surgery, she duly delivered her message. Eleanor got up from her desk and put an arm around her.

"Men are all pigs," she said.

Jean looked at her in astonishment.

"Oh, no," she said. "It wasn't his fault. It was mine. It's just taken me until now to realize it, that's all."

Helen took her arm and led Jean into her office and sat her down in the patients' chair. She went behind her desk and pulled a bottle of single-malt Scotch out of the bottom drawer.

"Here," she said, putting two small glasses on the desk, "it won't heal the cut," she said, "but it will take away the pain."

"I couldn't," said Jean, smiling at her friend. "It's only nine-thirty in the morning, and I have patients to see . . ."

Unperturbed, Helen poured out two stiff drinks.

"It'll all work out," she said confidently, clinking glasses with Jean. "You'll see."

Jean smiled uncertainly, and downed the burning liquid with a gasp.

"That's right," said Helen, watching her. "Just think of it as medicine."

Graham Ross was working in his office when the two police officers were announced. He barely had time to collect his thoughts before they were shown in. He got up from his desk, unnaturally pale.

"Yes, gentlemen?" he asked. His voice had a slight tremor, and that annoyed him, but they didn't seem to notice.

They showed him their credentials, and the little ceremony made Graham feel sick. It was like the first step of a long journey which would ultimately land him in jail.

"Inspector Niven would like to see you at Headquarters, Mr. Ross," said the older of the two. His voice was cultured, polite. The other one was young, chubby, red-faced, with short red hair and looked embarrassed. Graham recognized his name; his father worked in the bank downstairs as a teller.

"Concerning what, do you know?" Graham clasped his hands to keep them from shaking.

"The Lumsden case, I believe, sir," said the older one. To his surprise, he saw a flicker of something like relief in Graham's eyes, but it just lasted a second, and he could have been mistaken.

They had left their car parked outside with the blue light flashing, and a few curious passers-by saw Graham get into the back of the car, escorted by the younger policeman. The other one jumped into the driver's seat and the car roared off as if they were going to a fire. It took only three minutes for them to get to the Headquarters building.

Doug was waiting in his cramped office. Graham compared it to his own panelled, carpeted sanctum and wondered whether he would ever see it again.

Doug held out his hand, and Graham shook it rather limply.

"Please sit down, Mr. Ross." Graham's eyebrows went up for a second at the formality of the address, but he understood. In this kind of case, pre-existing acquaintances were invalidated.

Doug explained to him that the interview was to be recorded, and made the usual warning and notification of his rights. He did it all slowly, thoroughly, and noted with satisfaction that Graham was getting irritated at the ponderous way he was proceeding. Graham looked at his watch, but said nothing.

"Now," said Doug finally, leaning back in his chair. "There are a few routine questions I have to ask you concerning the Lumsden case." He spoke in a relaxed, slow kind of way, as if time meant nothing to him. Watching Graham, he decided to hit him fast and hard.

"Your wife was in here a couple of days ago." Suddenly his voice was accusing. "She told me about your business dealings with Dempster Lumsden, and your suggestion that he leave the country. Is that correct?"

Graham's eyes narrowed. That treacherous bitch!

"She has a vivid imagination, does Evelyn," he said calmly after a brief pause. "She also thinks I had an affair with Stella Lumsden." He knew that would be coming next. He smiled, but it was a pale travesty of a smile, because he knew that his real danger was not here in the police station, but back at the bank, when the examiners came.

"Did you?" asked Doug sharply, a little disconcerted that he'd lost an arrow from his quiver.

Graham sat back and stretched his legs out. The man's really put on weight, thought Doug, watching him. His belly hangs out over his belt now; only a year ago, he looked stocky but still quite trim.

"You know that Evelyn's had mental problems on and off for years, don't you?"

Doug didn't answer.

"She's paranoid. So the doctors tell me anyway. She imagines that everybody's talking about her, that they want to kill her . . . And she thinks I'm having an affair with every woman I talk to."

"Did you have an affair with Stella Lumsden?" Doug repeated, but for some reason Graham didn't seem concerned anymore, as if he'd passed some unseen crisis.

"No, as a matter of fact, I didn't." Graham hesitated, then smiled again, but his smile had some of his old assurance back in it. "But to tell you the truth, I would have been very happy to have had a liaison with Stella." He shrugged. "I guess I'm just not her type."

"Evelyn says you're an epileptic." Doug made it sound as brutal as he could, and Graham flinched.

"True," he said levelly. "But I haven't had an attack in several years. I take phenobarb . . ."

"Evelyn said you get two or three attacks every year."

"I can only refer you to my doctor. I will authorize her to tell you anything you need to know."

Douglas was getting perplexing vibrations from this interview; he'd expected Graham to collapse under his aggressive questioning, or at least show his resentment, but on the contrary, Graham was displaying a strange kind of calm. He'd probably developed that ability through living with Evelyn. Douglas had a moment's sympathy for him. But still, it was odd. Being a prime suspect in a murder case usually made people very nervous, but with Graham . . . He was behaving almost as if he *had* committed the crime, but was being charged with a minor traffic offense.

Douglas tried another tack. "Does the name Aladdin's Cave mean anything to you?"

"That was the place Dempster used to go to, over in Leith. It was far enough from home for him not to worry about who he'd see there. I went with him a couple of times, about a year ago, before he started his binges."

"Do you know if he ever went there with anybody else?"

"Probably. At that time he didn't like to drink alone . . ."

"Are you saying that he did drink alone more recently?"

"I don't really know."

"It's an out of the way place, down a back street by the docks, as you know. Would you be able to find it again, do you think?"

Graham hesitated. "Yes, I think so. I might have to stop and get directions a couple of times, but yes, I think I could find it again, assuming it's still there."

"It's still there all right," said Doug grimly. "That's where Dempster Lumsden was last seen before his body was found on the Edinburgh road."

There was little if any reaction from Graham, almost as if his mind was elsewhere. Doug, hoist by his own petard, was the one who was now getting irritated.

"Somebody came to fetch Dempster and took him away. The barman saw it happen."

"Good," said Graham equably. "Then he'll be able to tell you it wasn't me."

Douglas bit his lip. There was no point in telling Graham that Arthur, the barman, had only seen the man from behind for a split second as the two of them left the bar.

The rest of the interview was just as unsatisfactory, from Doug's point of view. When he finally switched the recorder off and stood up, he suddenly became benign, almost apologetic, and offered to drive Graham back to the bank. Graham refused politely; it was just a couple of minutes' walk, and it was a fine morning.

Douglas considered himself a pretty good judge of people's expressions; he would have been shocked to discover the seething hatred behind Graham's calm, almost dignified countenance.

When Fiona and Lisbie got home that afternoon, Jean was still working. Fiona phoned the surgery to make sure she was all right, then made a cup of tea for both of them. While she was in the kitchen, she heard Lisbie rattling around in the dining room sideboard before coming back in the kitchen. She looked agitated, and watched Fiona pour the hot water into the pot.

"Did you know Dad has taken the vodka with him? And the rest of the drinks?"

Fiona turned to face her squarely. "No he didn't. I did. You're going to become an alcoholic if you don't watch out. And it's not just me. Dave and Carole both mentioned it last week.''

"How dare you say that? Where did you put it?''

"Here, have some tea instead." Fiona filled a cup for her sister.

"I'm not an alcoholic, Fiona . . . God, I never thought you'd turn against me like that, my own sister!''

"Listen, I know you're not. I just don't want you to become one. I can knock it back too, you know.''

"I was just going to say," Lisbie started indignantly. "You drink . . .''

"I tell you what," said Fiona. "Let's both of us stop. I mean stop. No more, not even wine, nothing. Okay? Starting today, now.''

Lisbie hesitated. She really needed a drink now; she'd been looking forward to it since she left work.

"How about one last one, then we can stop? Where did you put it?''

"Lisbie, listen to yourself! It's really got a hold on you. No, we're stopping right now. That's it, make up your mind. No more. We've had our last drink.''

"God, Fiona, you mean forever?''

"Let's say six months. Then we can re-evaluate, okay?" Lisbie bit her lip. It was probably a good idea, but really she needed one now . . .

"Okay," she said. "I'll go along with that. If you can do it, so can I.''

About an hour later, Jean still hadn't come home, and Lisbie was getting very restless.

"I need to go to the chemist," she said. "The curse starts tomorrow.''

Lisbie and Jean got back at almost the same time.

Fiona had made dinner; nothing special, some baked fish and potatoes, but it was good.

They talked about their day, and tried to ignore the empty place at the head of the table. As a gesture, Fiona had removed the chair and put it against the wall.

"What were you getting at Strachan's, Lisbie?" asked Jean as she gathered up the plates. "I was going past when you came out. Isn't there any wine left in the sideboard?"

Fiona glowered at her sister, who turned scarlet and mumbled something under her breath.

Later, when Fiona challenged her, she said angrily, "You do what you want. And I'm going to do whatever the fuck I like, so there!"

Normally, Fiona would have turned the problem over to her father, but of course he wasn't there. He was having a jolly old time with that slut from the office. And she couldn't tell her mother; for one thing she would be so shocked . . . and anyway, this was hardly the time to be breaking that kind of news to her. Fiona suddenly felt very tired. She went upstairs into the living room to say goodnight.

Jean was sitting upright in her chair, the box of medical records on her lap as usual. The room was dark; the only light was a splash from the anglepoise lamp set on the table beside her. She was writing on the cards and looked up when Fiona came in. She seemed so small, so alone, and so woebegone in the quiet of that big room that Fiona couldn't stand it. Choking back a sob, and with a feeling of overpowering sadness in her heart she ran to her mother's chair. They hugged silently for a long time, holding on to each other as if for dear life, and their tears mixed unheeded on their cheeks.

Chapter Nineteen

"But Dad, what can you possibly see in her? She's not even pretty!"

It was Saturday morning, and Fiona and Lisbie sat opposite Steven Montrose at a table in Kennaways restaurant on South Street. The tension was high; Fiona had demanded to see him, and at the last minute she decided to bring Lisbie with her, mostly so that she could keep an eye on her, but also to exert some additional pressure on Steven. Lisbie had lost some weight over the last week, and kept on bursting into tears without any apparent provocation.

Steven felt seriously embarrassed, but felt he owed it to the girls to explain his position.

"Pretty? Well, Fiona, that's in the eye of the beholder, isn't it? She looks pretty to me."

"But why did you leave us like that, so suddenly?" asked Lisbie. Her eyes were brimming; she couldn't help it. "Why couldn't you . . . Why couldn't you have just seen her from time to time, and stayed at home?"

Steven was about to answer when Fiona cut in.

"That would have been *much* worse, Lisbie, don't you see? Anyway, Dad, I think we should all try to be grown up about this."

Normally Steven would have smiled at that, said something funny, but he didn't feel funny at all to-day. Things weren't working out at all the way he'd foreseen.

Fiona was the most profoundly angry of all of them; she felt her father's leaving was a direct slap in her face, an unwarranted, undeserved slap. Her immediate instinct was to slap back.

"Nobody I've talked to is on your side," she said. Her voice was hard, unyielding. "Everybody thinks it's a disgrace, and you don't deserve the nice family you have."

The waitress came, and they ordered coffee and cakes. Lisbie was about to say she didn't want any-thing, but Fiona threw her a warning look and or-dered for her.

"Do you want to hear what I have to say, or are we just wasting our time here?" Steven pushed back his chair, and tried to regain the initiative. It was an unusual and unpleasant experience for him to feel on the defensive with his own children.

The girls glanced at each other.

"I'm sorry, Daddy," said Lisbie, contritely. Fiona could have smacked her for being so spineless.

"I assume you know that I've been having prob-lems at the office," said Steven rather stiffly.

"You mean aside from Miss Blaikie?" asked Fiona sarcastically.

Steven finished his coffee. "Okay, Fiona," he said, "if you're just going to be sarcastic, there's no point in continuing the discussion. We can all just go home."

"Oh please, Daddy! And you shut up, Fiona," said Lisbie, turning on her sister with a sudden, uncharacteristic fury. "We're here to find out what *he* has to say, not you!"

She reached out and found Steven's hand. She held it tight and bit her lip in an attempt to stop her emotions getting the better of her again. He smiled at her, trying to look comforting; he was feeling almost as tearful himself. He hated to upset people, especially his own children. In that case, said his small inner voice, why hadn't he thought of that before?

"I'll try again to explain things," he said. "Look, I'm just as uncomfortable about all this as you are . . ." He shrugged helplessly. "Things are going badly at the glassworks. I may lose my job." Lisbie drew in her breath audibly and tightened her hold on his hand. Fiona looked up at the ceiling.

"I've been trying to tell your mother about it for weeks and weeks, but she's either too busy, or else she just doesn't hear what I'm telling her. I can't discuss things with her because she's never at home. And I've just had enough of it. I've found somebody who's concerned about me, who takes the time to talk things over with me . . ."

"Me, me, me, me," said Fiona. She banged her hand on the table and made the cups and saucers jump. The people at the next table stopped talking and stared at them. Unable to control her anger, Fiona stood up and shouted at him.

"That's all you think about, just yourself. Don't you ever think of us? Don't you think we all have our own problems?" She picked up her purse and stormed out of the restaurant.

Lisbie's tears overflowed. Steven put an arm around her, and tried to comfort her.

"It's a bad time for everybody, sweetheart," he

said. "But things will get better, eventually . . . I suppose." He didn't sound too sure about it.

"Do you like being there as much as being at home?" asked Lisbie, drying her tears. "Are you happy with her?"

"It's very different," replied Steven, avoiding her eye. "How's your mother keeping?"

"She's doing all right," said Lisbie. "She's sort of gone very quiet, though."

"Still as busy, I suppose?"

"The usual. She tries to come home earlier to spend more time with us, but it's really been hard on her."

Steven's lip trembled for a second. "You and I are still friends?"

"Of course, Daddy. You know that. But it's all just so awful . . ."

"I know, sweetheart. I miss you . . . I miss all of you."

"Mummy too?"

Steven hesitated, then remembered Pearl Blaikie's lithe young body and the exciting things she did with it. No, of course he didn't miss Jean. Not at all.

He stood up. "I have to go back to the office," he said. "Would you like me to drop you off?"

"No thanks. I'm going to do some shopping. Can we do this again next week?"

Steven hugged her. "Of course. Phone me any time you want, okay?"

"Okay, but I don't want to talk to *her,*" said Lisbie. She was beginning to look a little more cheerful. "I might say something really nasty to her."

Steven raised his eyebrows. "Why would you? She's actually quite a nice person," he went on lamely. "Under more normal circumstances, I'm sure you'd like her."

"Yes, maybe," said Lisbie. "But if I got to like her Fiona would kill me."

"Tell your mother I said hello."

"All right, Daddy, take care of yourself."

At the door, she kissed him on the cheek, then they went their separate ways. Steven went to the car park at the back of the restaurant to get his car. He wanted to sit down and weep, because in reality nothing was going well for him, but instead he got in the car and went off to the glassworks. At least working kept his mind occupied.

"I want to suggest a truce," said Keith. "With everything that's been going on around here . . . There's enough misery all round without us adding to it."

Danielle was in the kitchen with the children, and he'd just come in from the shop.

"You must have had a good day," she said warily. The children grabbed him around the knees and he put a hand on each small head.

"Good day! Good day isn't in it," he said.

My God, thought Danielle, that's how he sounded after he'd first met Dempster Lumsden. Full of joy, anxious to spread it around. Like manure.

"What happened? Go on, kids, go into the playroom. We'll come through in a minute." The aside to the children had no effect; they wanted to be with their Big Daddy, and they would stay with him until *he* said "no more." Then they would go, without argument or discussion.

"The buyer from Harrods was in this afternoon." Keith tried to sound casual, but he couldn't keep the excitement out of his voice. "She liked the stuff, and they want it for a new fabrics boutique they're opening. Danielle, she *really* liked everything I showed her."

Danielle was never sure nowadays how much she should participate in Keith's joys and triumphs. Not that there had been many recently, far from it. But this time she couldn't help feeling a trace, just a whisper of his elation. If it was true, if it wasn't some new crazy idea or some awful misunderstanding, maybe it *would* make her life a bit more bearable. She decided to let a bubble of her growing enthusiasm come up to the surface.

"Keith, that's terrific! What did she say? How much do they want? Which patterns?"

Keith laughed. He stepped forward and picked her up, as easily as lifting a feather duster. Danielle's heart missed a beat; was he going to crush her, or do one of his dangerous and painful tricks? Sometimes Danielle thought he had no idea of the pain he inflicted on her. But the children were laughing excitedly—they could feel that something unusual and good was happening.

"One question at a time," he said, and put her down gently.

That evening was the best either of them could remember, although it turned out that the order from Harrods was a small one. They had ordered a dozen shawls, the same number of scarves, and some lengths of material to be made into skirts, but with a promise of a much bigger order if the sales were at the level they expected.

That night, after they had made love and he had been gentle with her, she lay awake, listening to his breathing. Night-time was when the terrors always came to her, and tonight they came back with a vengeance. What had brought about this sudden change in Keith's attitude? What had made him so joyful and happy? Was it really the Harrods lady buyer, or had something else happened that Danielle didn't know about? In spite of herself, she shivered. Up to now, her experience of Keith's periods of elation was that they eventually turned him angry and brutal. It was a long time before she finally fell asleep, and if Danielle had believed in the predictive power of dreams, she would not have found her own reassuring.

Chapter Twenty

Graham Ross sat at his desk at the bank. It was a spacious, well-appointed office, as befitted the manager of this prosperous branch, with oak panelling on the walls and a large portrait of the founder looking benignly down from behind an impressive set of muttonchop whiskers. Graham's desk was a solid, wide, glass-topped affair, overlooking a white leather-covered sofa and matching armchairs set around a low table for more informal conferences.

Graham leaned back in his padded chair and reviewed his position. It was desperate, he knew it, from every point of view, but the strange thing was that nobody else seemed to be aware of that fact, or if they were, they didn't make it obvious. The bank personnel treated him with the same respect, although for some days now he had been watching for any sign, any flicker in their eyes that might show they knew what was happening, and were just watching and waiting for the big crash. Even after his trip to the police station the day before, there had been nothing. They probably assumed that the police wanted to consult him about something, ask for his opinion about some new information they'd gathered. But anyhow all these people were stupid, like the rest of them born in this stupid town; they

didn't have the experience or the mental equipment
to know any better.

There was one good thing about his perilous situation; it gave him a kind of freedom he'd never had
before. He could now think, plan and do things he'd
never have conceived of when he was a good, law-
abiding banker, firmly ensconced in the establish-
ment.

There was a knock at the door, and Graham braced
himself, but it was only Ted Crowley, his assistant
manager.

"I'll be off now, Mr. Ross," he said, "unless
there's anything you'd like me to do."

"No, thanks, Ted." Graham couldn't believe that
his guilt wasn't somehow written across his forehead
for all to see, especially by Ted, who was quite per-
ceptive, at least by local standards. "Have a good
weekend, now. See you on Monday."

See you on Monday . . . The words rang in his
head like a peal of bells long after Ted had closed
the door and gone.

Graham had less time than he thought. Doug
Niven had scared him, with all those questions and
all that stuff Evelyn had told him. He clenched his
fists. She would have to be taken care of too, but
that would be a pleasure . . .

Graham got up and locked the office door before
going to the combination safe set in the wall behind
his desk. It was an old, black-lacquered antique, but
still quite functional, and Graham liked its solid,
stuffy character. The name of the manufacturer, Jos
Kruger, St. Louis, Missouri, was written in green
letters outlined in gold on the heavy front door. Graham twisted the heavy combination several times,
then turned the handle and pulled. The door slowly

swung open like the door of a cavern, like an Aladdin's cave . . .

The papers were in a pile, tied together with a pink document tape, and he put them on the desk, leaving the safe door open, which was contrary to one of his own immutable bank rules. "Always close the vault or safe the moment cash or documents are removed, even if it's only for a minute." He enforced that rule strictly, and woe betide the employee who didn't remember. The safe door yawning open behind him was a measure of Graham Ross's own personal separation from the system that had nurtured him and which he had stoutly upheld for so many years.

But Graham was not in the best of shape, emotionally or physically, at this time; for weeks he had been sleeping poorly, and found himself occasionally verging on the irrational; he couldn't go on like this, he knew it, but then of course he didn't plan to. Graham untied the knot in the document tape and spread the papers out over his desk. Many of the papers bore Dempster Lumsden's flamboyant signature. The swine! Graham felt the bile rise in his throat. That signature had never been worth anything. The bastard had lied, produced forged documents, and in the process had smilingly ruined him, all with that careless disdain and aristocratic disregard for other people's lives and fortunes.

There, at the top of the pile of papers was the bank's undertaking to deliver, let's see . . . Graham glanced at the figure. One million, one hundred and forty-three thousand pounds sterling, at a compound annual interest which worked out at sixteen point four percent. Normally that would have been a nice little piece of business, had it been well secured and made with an honest client. Clipped neatly to the document were the property deeds which backed the loan. They were genuine enough, the bank's lawyer had made sure of that; the problem was that they didn't belong to Dempster, but to his father, Lord Aviemore. Even so, all would have been well had the sale of the factory gone through; the loan would have been repaid on schedule, and old Aviemore would probably never have known that these property deeds had been put to such illicit use. Now, of course, he'd be told about it in a matter of days. Graham could imagine two senior officers of the bank driving up to Inverness to see the old man, cap in hand, hoping that he would pay up what Dempster owed them. What a hope!

It was quite clear to Graham that there was no legal way out of the trap he was in. No amount of talk or promises, none of the debts he was owed, not all his friendships in the banking world would save him. His career was over, and in addition he would almost certainly be sent to prison. He had not only aided and abetted the performance of a felony, but had conspired to conceal the fraud and assist in the escape of Dempster Lumsden . . . As he listed each crime in his mind, the prison sentence lengthened, and the police and bank lawyers would be sure to find more charges that he hadn't even thought of. And Graham was well aware that white-collar crime of this kind was now being dealt with very harshly in the Scottish courts.

Graham took a deep breath. And all that was quite apart from what they might do to him because of what happened to the males of the Lumsden line . . .

Evelyn . . . His mouth hardened as he thought of her. She had shopped him, Douglas Niven had told him so. And now for the last couple of days, she'd been wearing this triumphant look, this serene smile, every time she spoke to or looked at him.

An ugly grimace twisted his face. Dear Evelyn; she was the one who should have died, there had been a great miscalculation there, but one which could be corrected. A tidal wave of hatred washed over him as he thought of her. Between her and Dempster Lumsden, they'd really done a job on him. She had totally ruined his life; she had alienated all the people who were important in his career—the board members, the influential local people who used the bank. And domestically his marriage had been a disaster, even worse after she thought he was having an affair with Stella. Graham allowed himself a small, lopsided grin at that thought. It had been stupid of him to be seen coming down the stairs with her at that Christmas party at the Lumsdens', and he should have known it would cause trouble, but only a person with a profoundly paranoid mentality such as herself could have come to the conclusions she reached.

It had been carelessness, sheer carelessness on his part, the very fault he always warned his subordinates against, and he had committed that sin again when he unwittingly allowed Evelyn to hear the plans for Dempster's escape to Rio de Janiero that evening when Dempster had come over, and he thought she was too drunk to notice anything.

Well, in for a penny, in for a pound. His course was pretty well set now, and he'd had enough time to finalize his plans and check every detail in that methodical way his superiors at the bank so appreciated.

Graham had no intention of spending the best part

of his life behind bars, and the plan he'd worked out over the last few days seemed pretty well foolproof. It was rather neat. Unlike the great majority of criminals, he had the worldwide facilities of a major bank behind him. His bank account was already opened for him in the Rio subsidiary, not in his own name, of course. An electronic transfer of funds would be made from one of his large corporate accounts over the weekend, hidden amongst thousands of other legal ones. Graham knew how to work the system; it would take weeks for them to find out what had happened, by which time the funds would have been moved repeatedly, converted into stocks and bearer bonds, resold, transferred, until the money was quite untraceable.

Already Graham felt himself on the other side of the fence, the side where the forces of law and order were the enemy to be circumvented and eluded. At this moment, he was still on the threshold, the final steps which placed him beyond the pale were yet to come. He had decided also to take some cash from the bank away with him; the theft would be obvious as soon as the vault was checked on Monday morning, but by that time he would already be in South America. And the missing cash would distract their attention from the big electronic transfers.

Graham glanced at the clock; soon he would be the only person in the bank. He turned to the safe and took out the two keys and the electronic passcard for the vaults. There was only one person who could override the time locks, and that was himself, the manager. That would be just one of the procedures they would change, he thought grimly. They'd make sure two people were needed, as they did in most banks. In the end, he'd be responsible for great improvements in the bank's security systems, but he needn't expect a letter of thanks from the chairman. At that thought, he started to laugh, at first quietly, then without any restraint. He stopped suddenly, frightened at his own reactions. He put his hands on the desk in front of him and spread his fingers out. The little muscles on the back of his hands were twitching, twitching . . .

Graham planned to go home and take care of Evelyn as soon as he had the cash from the vault in his briefcase. Then he would drive to Edinburgh, leave his car in the car park and buy a ticket for the shuttle flight to Heathrow. He would then drive a rented car to Glasgow, fly to Gatwick from Glasgow, then on to Paris for his flight to Rio.

But first, Evelyn. At that thought he felt the crazy laughter bubbling up again inside him. He would feel much, much better knowing that she was dead, knowing that she had paid for all the misery she had caused him over the years they had been married, and for her final treachery, which had brought him down.

When the girls got home after seeing Steven, Jean sensed immediately that something was wrong between the two of them. It was really strange; she had become sensitized to how the people around her felt, and it was not always a comfortable experience. Before, she would have either just ignored it, or not even realized that anything was the matter. But now, it was like wind blowing on raw skin; it hurt.

She waited for one of them to say something, but all she got was that they had had coffee in Kennaways with their father, and he had asked Lisbie to say "hi" to her.

"Was that all he said?" she asked, trying to sound nonchalant. "How did he look?"

Lisbie said he was having a difficult time and didn't need anymore problems than he already had. She looked pointedly at Fiona as she spoke.

Jean wanted to hear every word that had been spoken, a report of each glance, every movement; did his shirts look clean or rumpled, did he look as if he were being cared for properly . . . but she didn't dare ask. Fiona, particularly, would have had a fit.

Jean went back to her surgery that afternoon feeling vaguely dissatisfied. It was as if she herself had been with Steven, but couldn't remember anything of what had been said.

The rest of the day passed by in a trance; she saw patients, did her visits, but she felt that she was on automatic pilot, functioning on reflexes rather than on normal reactions and responses.

Even the arrest of Graham Ross at his home didn't really break through the barrier, though Douglas Niven called at the house that evening to give her a rather self-satisfied blow by blow account of what had happened the day before.

Evelyn had called Douglas at his office on Friday morning, saying that she feared for her life, and would he please send somebody to guard her. Douglas was sorely tempted to put her off, reassure her over the telephone and forget about it, but as she'd already virtually accused her husband of being the killer of the two Lumsdens, and Doug wasn't in a position to deny it, he sent Constable Jamieson with orders to keep out of sight and to return as soon as he felt that the situation was under control.

What happened at the Rosses' house aged the poor constable by at least ten years. He arrived to find Evelyn in a state of considerable agitation. First she shouted at him for leaving his car outside the door, allowing everybody to know that he was there. Obediently he went out and moved it round the back of the empty house next door. Walking back along the weed-ridden path alongside the house, he unconsciously rubbed the muscles of his midriff; they were still bruised from the Wee Doc's elbow jab when he'd tried to arrest her . . . Even now, he blushed at the memory; he'd suffered agonies for a few days, not from the blow, but waiting for the jibes of his colleagues, but to his grateful astonishment Doug Niven had said nothing about it, and neither, apparently, had Dr. Montrose.

"He'll be coming home a few minutes before five," said Evelyn after the lunch hour had come and gone without a sign of Graham. She seemed unnaturally excited, and moved restlessly around the house wearing a loose housecoat of some thin material which blew around her when she walked, to the great distraction of Constable Jamieson.

"Where do you think I should wait, ma'am?" he asked respectfully. "Perhaps I should go in the coat cupboard when we hear him coming?"

"Of course not," snapped Evelyn. "Where d'you think he hangs up his coat when he comes in? He'd see you, and you'd just look even more like a fool."

Jamieson moved his weight to his other foot. He wasn't used to dealing with this kind of woman; he felt comfortable enough dealing with domestic disputes over in the housing estates, where arguments tended to be settled with kitchen knives and broken bottles, but here he was completely out of his normal environment.

"Maybe I should go behind the curtains when we

hear the car, then?'' Jamieson frowned portentously to add weight to his suggestion.

Evelyn made a gesture of disgust. ''He'd see you as soon as he walked up the path to the door. No, you're going to wait in the study, and I'll leave the door open a crack so you can see what's going on. He never goes in there when he comes back from work.''

''What is it exactly that you're expecting him to do, ma'am?''

Evelyn had a febrile excitement about her.

''I'm sure he's going to try to kill me, that's all I can tell you.''

''But why, Mrs. Ross?'' Constable Jamieson had a dogged persistence about him. ''Why would he want to kill you?''

''Because I'm the last witness,'' she said, and refused to say another word.

When Graham arrived, Constable Jamieson was almost caught napping, and just had time to get himself in position behind the door. They heard his hurried footsteps coming up the path, the noise of the key scraping in the lock, and then the thud of his briefcase on the hall table. At this point Jamieson could see nothing, and was starting to sweat. What would he do if Mr. Ross came into the study and found him there? A dreadful thought came into his mind. Oh God, maybe Mr. Ross would think *he* was having an affair with his wife . . .

He didn't have much time for such speculation, because Graham started shouting at Evelyn almost from the moment he stepped inside the house. He called her the foulest names imaginable, and when Jamieson finally pushed the door open enough to see him clearly, she was backed into a corner of the living room, cowering behind a small cane chair. Then to Jamieson's horror, he saw Graham take an automatic pistol out of his pocket and brandish it in her face, telling him she'd better enjoy her last moments; he wanted her to experience what it was like to look into the face of death.

To his everlasting credit, Jamieson unhitched his truncheon, almost dropped it, then crept into the room behind him and struck Ross a smart crack over the head. Graham never saw what hit him, and collapsed in a heap on the floor.

Douglas told Jean that they'd found two hundred thousand pounds of the bank's money in his briefcase. Graham woke up on the floor to find himself in handcuffs, and was taken to Headquarters, while Douglas hastily called a press conference. The prisoner was charged with a multiplicity of offenses, including embezzlement, attempted murder of his wife Evelyn, and the murders of Magnus and Dempster Lumsden, which, according to the papers, were part of a panic-stricken attempt by Graham to save his name and professional reputation.

Jean listened to all this quite placidly; she felt totally removed from all these events, as if they were happening in another country to people she'd never seen or heard of. While Doug was talking she was wondering how Steven was managing. She suspected that Pearl didn't own a washing machine, and he was so particular about the way his shirts were ironed . . . Maybe it would be better if he brought them home to her; after all she'd been doing his shirts for long enough, and maybe Pearl wouldn't mind . . .

"Congratulations," she said to Doug when he'd finished. "That was a very able piece of work. And you might compliment Constable Jamieson for me, too.''

Doug glanced at Jean, but he could see there was no irony intended. There was a strange, flat look about her face, and her eyes didn't crinkle up the way they usually did when she spoke.

''Are you all right, Jean?'' he asked. Somehow he didn't seem to know about Steven, or maybe he was just being kind. ''You look as if you've been overworking.''

''No, I'm fine,'' she answered, still in that strange voice without inflection. ''How's Cathie? She must be very proud of you . . . I hope you're taking good care of her, Douglas.''

''Sure, aye, of course,'' Doug laughed. ''I always take good care of her.'' But he found Jean's gaze disquieting, and wondered if she'd meant anything in particular by her comment.

At home, the girls did their best to keep things going; they kept their own private argument about Lisbie's drinking to themselves and made sure Jean remained unaware of it. They went out a lot less and spent more time with their mother, but the place still seemed empty, hollow without Steven's voice and shrunken without his presence. Luckily Jean was very busy at work, and that provided a distraction. She started to diet, and that became a joke among the three of them.

One of the things that disturbed her more than anything was Steven's visits when there was nobody at home. She would come back and find a batch of his jackets removed from the cupboard in the bedroom, or a pile of his records and tapes gone. For some reason, this piecemeal removal of his things really hurt Jean, and one day when she came home and found a whole section of books taken out of the bookcase in the living room, she sat down and wept inconsolably. She felt as if she herself was being eaten away, bite by bite.

Gradually she came back to life. Everybody complimented her on the new slim figure she was achieving, and Fiona and Lisbie got together and took Jean one Saturday to Edinburgh for a hairdo and a manicure at one of the better establishments in that city. It was just to cheer her up, they said, but it had a greater effect than any of them expected. Jean had never paid much attention to her appearance because she didn't have time for it, but now she didn't have Steven to look after, she used the hairdo as a starting point for a general overhaul of her wardrobe, and the effect was quite startling. The Wee Doc was getting to look almost slim, was dressing with more care, and paid more attention to her appearance, but she knew that it was all on the surface. The hurt of Steven's disappearance was like a toothache that didn't ease, and it was slowly sapping at her reserves of vital energy.

Her partner Helen had taken the news with more anger than Jean expected, and much more than she felt herself. Helen wanted her to take a week off and go somewhere to enjoy herself and forget about the bastard, but Jean couldn't do that. And she didn't feel comfortable at the use of the word "bastard"; she pointed out that it had been her fault, not his, because she hadn't taken proper care of him, and hadn't always bothered to wear make-up and make more of an effort to look nice and dress attractively. Helen was speechless, and could only shake her head in disbelief.

Jean saw Danielle and Keith Armstrong at a fundraising party for the hospital about a week after Graham's arrest. There was home-made food along a trestle table, and a small band played Scottish country dance music. Keith was dressed in a kilt and the angry look he'd had for so long seemed to have evaporated. He came over and asked Jean to dance the Gay Gordons. She glanced at Danielle, who waved happily at her. Jean had trouble remembering the steps, but after a short time she got the hang of it and enjoyed it enormously. When it was over, she was panting with the exertion, and they went and sat down with Danielle.

"Well, I'm glad it was you and not me doing that one," said Danielle to Jean, smiling. "You must have been practicing."

"One more turn, and I'd have died," said Jean between gasps of air. "I'd better start lifting weights like you."

"Not me," said Danielle. "I'm happy if I can just lift a glass from time to time."

"I'm glad the two of you are getting on now," said Jean quietly once she'd got her breath back.

Keith and Danielle looked at each other.

"That whole business with the Lumsdens really messed us up," said Keith. "There was a lot of suspicion, a lot of ill will. Until Graham was arrested, even Danielle thought that maybe . . ." He glanced at his wife.

"And the business is doing well, finally," Danielle interrupted proudly. She told Jean about the Harrods order.

"Is Stella going to move, do you think?" asked Jean, after complimenting Keith. "It's an awfully big house for just one person."

"I don't know, really," answered Danielle. "I

know Alexis is helping her to straighten things out. Apparently Dempster left his affairs in a terrible mess, and it'll take ages.''

"When is Graham's trial supposed to start?" asked Jean. "I imagine she'll have to stay until that's over."

"I read in the paper that it should begin in a couple of weeks," said Keith. "I feel sorry for Graham; a lot of people think Evelyn should be in the dock with him.''

Jean shrugged. "I'm sure justice will prevail," she said.

After Jean left, Keith remarked how changed she seemed.

"It's her husband leaving her like that," said Danielle sagely. "She doesn't really care anymore."

Chapter Twenty-one

Many of Jean's friends and the people she worked with felt that Jean had lost the spark which had made her the busy, happy, competent and bustling person everybody turned to in time of trouble. To Jean herself it felt more like a quietness, a settling down into a kind of gray routine, where she worked less for the sake of the work itself than for its anodyne quality; when she had to concentrate on a medical problem she couldn't, at the same time, reflect on her own unhappiness.

So she went about her daily work without noticing any major change; maybe the people around her laughed less, or chatted less often to her, but it didn't bother her; in fact she barely noticed.

At home, though, she paid more attention to the girls. Until Steven left, she had always thought of Fiona and Lisbie as following roughly parallel courses with her, needing no more additional attention than she did herself. In her mind, her present sense of isolation, the feeling of walking in a barren land, extended to her children, and they now seemed to her as vulnerable and spiritually destitute as herself.

She found herself taking much more real interest in their activities, and found out more than she had ever known about them. Fiona, the elder, who went faithfully every morning to her job as trainee manager was engaged in a strange tug-of-war with her sister. Ever since they were small, the first one home in the afternoon had set the table for dinner. Now, when Lisbie set it, she put out a place for her father, although she knew he wouldn't be there, whereas Fiona angrily and pointedly set out places only for herself, her mother and her sister. This was only the surface of their conflict; Lisbie persisted in acting as if her father were still living at home as an active, participating part of the family, and it infuriated Fiona, who put framed photos of him face down, or hid them away in the attic. She wanted all visible traces of her father removed from the house.

Jean mentioned this conflict to Helen Inkster one day; Helen had never married but retained a very sound outlook on life. She had a solid, Scots reality to her mind, unclouded by emotion and sentiment. She thought carefully about what Jean had said.

"Well, Jean, I know both your girls pretty well, I think. Fiona is the one who reacts more strongly, and right now she's overreacting. She loves her father but feels he's abandoned her, and it hurts her even to think about him . . ."

"I'm afraid he has, in a way," murmured Jean. "Although he does call them quite often to talk."

"And Lisbie's more emotional, more romantic. I can see her when she's married, remembering every anniversary, every birthday. She'll have photos and mementoes of all the trips she ever takes, and I'm sure she'll be one for candlelight dinners and soft music . . ." They both laughed; Helen had put her finger very accurately on the differences in the two girls' personalities.

Up to that time Lisbie had generally stayed away from serious involvements with boys, but within a week of her father's leaving, she had found a boyfriend and brought him back to the house on the following Saturday. Fiona said Lisbie was like a cat bringing home a dead bird, and the simile was cruelly apt, because with his beaky nose and long, black bedraggled hair Michael did have something fluttering and birdlike about him. He was never heard to utter a word in anybody's presence although Lisbie stoutly maintained that he was very interesting and totally beautiful.

Fiona focused more on her mother, and became fiercely protective of her. She understood better than anybody what Steven's disappearance had meant to Jean, how it had shattered the whole fabric of her life, and extinguished the fuelling spark of her existence. As Christmas was approaching, Fiona decided they would all go to Edinburgh to see a play, and they set off, with Michael in tow, all packed neatly into Jean's Renault. On the way, they stopped at Jean's surgery to pick up some lab reports she was expecting in the post.

She ran in, picked up the pile of envelopes tied with a rubber band and hurried out again, putting the letters in her coat pocket. After the show, they went to eat fish and chips near the theater. In spite of everybody's efforts, Michael could not be persuaded to utter more than the occasional monosyllable, and even Lisbie seemed to be getting a little weary of him.

"You'll have to do better than that to replace Dad," Fiona whispered acidly to her as they went back to the car. Lisbie's eyes filled with tears. He *wasn't* replacing Dad, nobody could. And why did Fiona have to be so mean to her all the time?

They dropped Michael off at his home, and the rest of the trip home was spent with Fiona attacking and Lisbie defending the boy, who had probably never had so much concentrated attention lavished on him in his entire life. Jean half-listened, almost dreading the thought of coming home to that empty house, but finally had to tell the girls to stop squabbling, after Lisbie suggested that Fiona was just jealous because she didn't have a steady boyfriend of her own.

It was very late, and they all went quickly to bed. Fiona had taken on the responsibility of checking the doors, making sure the cat was out, putting out lights and turning down the central heating.

Jean felt very fragile; she couldn't remember a time when she had been to the theater without Steven, and she missed him a lot tonight. They used to chat about the day's events after they'd gone to bed . . .

She got into her pyjamas, slid between the cold sheets and shivered. She always forgot to turn on the electric blanket until she was already in bed. Again and again she went over the questions in her mind. Where had she gone wrong? What did he get from Pearl Blaikie that he didn't get at home? Excitement, probably, a new face, a new body, more time, different things to talk about.

Just as she was beginning to get warm, she remembered the lab results she'd been waiting for, still downstairs in the pocket of her coat. Do it tomorrow, her body said, it can wait, and anyway, what does it matter now? For a few moments, her body seemed to be winning, then her conscience took over and she got out of bed, pulled her nice new terry-cloth dressing-gown around herself and went downstairs. The steps creaked in the darkened house. She knew where her coat was, so she didn't need to put the lights on. She pulled the packet of letters out of the pocket and crept upstairs again. Back in bed, she put on her reading glasses and riffled through the envelopes until she found the one she was looking for. It had a government stamp on it, and came from the Central Pathology Laboratory in Edinburgh.

She tore the envelope open, careful not to damage the contents. It was a single sheet of paper with perforations at one end. In computer type was the name, Dempster Lumsden, a long set of reference numbers, and then two separate numbers, one a normal value, and the other the reported value of the test which she had requested. Jean took a deep breath. The test was unequivocally positive; she could now forget about Dr. Anderson's threat of sending her the bill.

Jean's hand tightened around the flimsy piece of paper. It seemed like years since she'd thought about the Lumsden affair, and it was now like a bad memory compounded by a worse reality. Maybe she should forget about the whole thing, let the past rest in peace. If she acted on the information she had in her hand, she would just be ruining more lives.

For a good part of the night she heard the hours chiming away across the river from the church of St. John's, as each part of the puzzle swam around in her mind for a while before coming snugly to rest in its appointed place. Only when the last piece gently clicked into position and the entire picture was complete did she close her eyes and go to sleep. And it was only then that she was able to decide how she would deal with the situation.

When she woke, Fiona was shaking her.

"Mum, it's eight o'clock and I have to go now. There's coffee made, and toast in the rack . . . Bye!"

Jean got up, and as all her midnight thoughts came back to her, she quailed, unwilling to be burdened by such a load of unhappy and poisonous knowledge.

She washed, dressed, and went downstairs, the knot in her stomach getting tighter and heavier. She drank a cup of coffee, and two minutes later needed the evidence of the cup in the sink to prove to her that she had drunk it. Normally, this was the time when she organized her day, checked to see if there were any new calls to be made, worked out the route she would take to see her patients, and decided where she would fit in any other appointments she needed to make. Today, all she could think of was the whole sad and frightening complex of the Lossie Estate and the strange and devious people who inhabited it.

With a deepening sense of foreboding, she picked up the phone and called Police Headquarters, but Doug Niven wasn't there yet. She looked up his home number and tried that.

"Cathie? Jean Montrose here. Is your guid man there, by any chance?"

Jean heard her calling for Doug. Even on the telephone she could hear Cathie's lovely lilting voice. She came back on the phone.

"He's doon in the basement . . . The washing machine's nae working right, Jeannie. He'll be up in just a wee while."

Jean held the phone, wondering what *she* would

do if her washing machine broke now. Steven had always taken care of that kind of problem.

Douglas came to the phone and Jean told him what she had to say. There was a long silence, finally broken by Doug.

"I can't argue with that, Jean," he said. "But I think *we* should take it from here."

"I don't want to do anything I'm not supposed to do," replied Jean quite humbly, wishing that she could free herself of the responsibility, "but otherwise I think it could end in bloodshed. Just let me do it my way. I'm planning on getting up there about ten this morning."

"Okay . . . I don't want you to take any unnecessary risks," he said hesitantly. "But I have complete faith in your judgment. Now, this is what I want you to do first . . ."

There were a number of things Jean needed to do before going up to the Lossie Estate; she hurried down to the surgery, partly to make sure that Helen would cover for her. She explained briefly what she was about to do and Helen paled.

"You can't go out there by yourself! I'm calling Douglas Niven this minute!" and she reached for the phone.

"Don't bother," said Jean quietly. "I told him myself. He wasn't too happy, I must say, but he finally agreed it was the best way."

"That's insane!" exclaimed Helen. "You might get killed, and then where would I be? I can't handle this practice alone!"

Jean had to laugh. "I'm sure it won't come to that, Helen. Basically they're reasonable people. They just took a course of action . . ." Jean shuddered. Maybe she *was* putting her head in a noose; after all, the complexity, the planning that had gone into this whole series of crimes showed how ruthless and clever they had been. A thought struck her; she suddenly realized that she had no fear of dying now, maybe because she didn't have very much to live for anymore. The girls were grown up, and the principal effect she'd had on their development was over now; they would live their lives according to what was already inside their heads, their spirits and their consciences.

On the way out, Jean automatically put a tape into the player, and thought about that dreadful time she'd been called out to see the Lumsden baby. It seemed so long ago . . . Her entire life had changed in that time, as had the lives of all the people connected with the case. Poor Dempster—no wonder he turned into a drunk. Maybe he knew that he was going to die, and just didn't care anymore. Jean thought about the baby Magnus; she didn't feel exactly sorry for him because he hadn't really had a life, he had just been extinguished, never knowing what was happening to him. To think, though, that one day he might well have been the twelfth Lord Aviemore . . . And of course there was no question about his paternity; Evelyn Ross's hysterical association between Graham's and Magnus's epilepsy had no foundation in fact. Jean knew perfectly well that this type of epilepsy was not hereditary, and had occurred in the two of them by pure chance. Not that Jean hadn't had her doubts at one time, but it wasn't in Graham's direction that her suspicion had lain. The blood and tissue typing tests she'd asked for proved conclusively that Dempster was Magnus's father. Of course, in retrospect that hadn't really helped her to solve the crime at all, it had just been one of the several red herrings carefully put in the path.

Jean's head and mind were clearing like fog burning off in the sunshine; from the car she could see the sheep-studded fields and the long fences stretching away to the hills in the west. The morning air had a pure clarity to it which made her feel happy to be alive, and it was the first time she'd felt that way for weeks. There was no heather left on the hillsides now, and the higher ones had a dusting of snow, leaving black streaks where the lines of rock projected above the surface. Beyond the low hills the higher mountain tops were pure white, making the elongated shreds of cloud around the peaks look like gray remora, the scavenger fish that tag along with great white sharks.

Jean had come along this way so many times, she felt that if she took her hands off the wheel the car would be able to find its own way. She turned off the main road, and a large Bell's distillery lorry in front of her gave her a shiver of *déjà vu*—it could easily have been the same one she'd seen on that first fateful visit . . . The vegetable market was open, although it was too cold to have any produce outside, and a cloud of steam was escaping from a pipe above the launderette next door. Suddenly feeling tense again, Jean slowed for the corner into the Lossie Estate. It seemed such a calm, normal, prosperous place, with elegant, spacious houses on each side of the road. There was a removal van outside the first house on the left, the one that had been empty for so long. God, thought Jean, what kind of people are moving in there? Do they have strange and frightening pasts like all the present inhabitants? Is this entire Estate doomed to have liars, perjurers, adul-

terers and killers as a permanent part of its life? Jean
slowed as she passed, and saw two children, a boy
and a girl aged about nine and ten, laughing and
sliding down the ramp at the back of the moving
van. It all looked so normal, so happy and full of
hope and life . . .

Setting her lips, she stopped outside the Armstrongs' house, braced herself for a moment,
stepped out of the car and started to walk briskly
up to the door.

Chapter Twenty-two

Jean rang the doorbell. There was no answer, so she tried the door. It was unlocked. She hesitated for a second, took a deep breath and went in. She could hear a faint, dull, thumping noise which seemed to be coming from the bowels of the earth, then there was a thud which shook the floor.

"Jean? Is that you?" Doug's voice came from upstairs.

"Yes it is. Shall I come up?"

"Yes. We're all upstairs."

Jean went up. The stairs were much easier now that she'd lost some weight. Doug was waiting on the landing. There were sounds coming from the room at the end of the short corridor.

"Is it Keith making all that noise in the basement?" she asked.

"Yes. He said nothing was going to interrupt his workout, not even this."

"When does he work? He seems to spend most of his time pushing weights up into the air."

"It's Danielle's day at the shop," replied Douglas as they walked into the bedroom. From the window, Jean could see the upper floor of the Rosses' house. A curtain moved, and Douglas gently pulled her back.

"No point letting everybody know we're here," he said. Over to the left, over the top of the rhododendron-lined drive was the Lumsdens' stately home, seen clearly through the bare branches. It had a bleak, forbidding look, and Jean wondered if houses really took on the character of the events and happenings that occur within their walls. Certainly Lossie House didn't look like a happy home from the outside, but of course that was just her imagination.

"This is Dr. Montrose," said Doug. The two men setting up equipment near the window turned and nodded. Both were young, and although they wore dark blue police parkas, neither looked like a policeman; one was short, with a stubbly beard, and the other looked like a lanky schoolboy, with a thick strand of long blond hair falling over his face.

"Morning," grinned the bearded one. "Are you the hit squad?"

"Set up that microphone and don't annoy the grown-ups," growled Doug. He turned back to Jean. "We'll be ready in about ten minutes," he said, pointing to the long, telescope-like instrument mounted on a tripod and pointing out of the window.

"What is that?" asked Jean. She'd never seen anything like it before.

"It's a directional microphone," he said. "And that over there is the recording equipment." He indicated the stack of electronic gear in the corner. A single red light glowed on the console. Doug smiled proudly. "Jed, tell Dr. Montrose how sensitive your machine is."

"It'll pick up a mouse farting at a hundred yards," said the blond boy. The bearded one snorted with laughter, and they exchanged a delighted grin at the witticism. Doug reddened, opened his mouth to say something but changed his mind. Jean smiled absently. She was thinking of what she was about to do and say after she left the Armstrongs' house; she did feel a tingling sense of excitement, but that was overwhelmed by fear. Not fear for herself, only for the people she was about to confront.

"While you're over there we'll monitor what's being said, and come in at the appropriate time," said Doug. "Just in case, we're going to send you in wired; I'm going to put this radio transmitter in your bag. The high-tech here looks good, but it doesn't always work."

He looked grimly at the two young men. The bearded one looked around from calibrating his instrument and winked at Jean.

"Doesn't always work, huh?" he said. "Okay, listen to this." He walked over to the amplifier and turned up the gain control. There was a hissing noise followed by a deafening series of explosive crackling sounds then a clearly recognizable voice said, "Would you turn off the kettle, Alexis, please?" Jean gasped, and glanced again at the long mike. The window it was aimed at was almost a hundred yards away.

"Not bad, eh?" said the blond boy, grinning. Jean was astonished and impressed.

"Very good," she said. She had no idea that such equipment existed; it was amazing that they could pick up voices at that distance, and even through a window.

"Well, I'd better be on my way." Jean tried to sound calm, but her stomach was turning somersaults, and she had the feeling that she was about to do something terrible, that she was going to destroy lives which could have gone on quite happily if she hadn't been so nosy and interfering.

The boys stopped working and looked at her with a strange, almost respectful expression.

"Good luck, Doc," said the bearded one, and Doug scowled. In a sense, Jean was now his protégée, and he didn't like her to be addressed in such a flippant way.

"A little less of your cheek, young fellow," he barked.

Jean went back into her car, the butterflies in her stomach performing a tribal dance. She wasn't afraid of being hurt, it wasn't that, it was the thought that she was about to perpetuate and extend the evil in which he had unwittingly become caught up. She heartily wished that she could start all over again, and simply not get involved in this dreadful business. Except, a small voice said to her, except that you're in a privileged position, permitted to see and understand things that others cannot, and as a concerned citizen you have to take the responsibility. And a louder, harder voice said, These are dangerous killers who have put themselves beyond the pale of humanity, and you have to do whatever you can to help bring them to book.

Jean drove off slowly and, with a sinking heart, turned into the drive leading up to Lossie House. The wind blew the dead brown leaves in spirals around the car and whistled a warning to her to turn round and leave, get out while she had the chance, but she gritted her teeth and went on, ignoring the alarms that rang and howled inside her head.

She pulled up behind Stella's Volvo, just beyond the great portico. In front of the Volvo was Alexis's green Mercedes. Thinking about it, Jean was faintly surprised that he was still here; maybe he'd gone home to Inverness, then come back. After all, he had work to do on the family estates, and he couldn't stay away indefinitely.

She rang the doorbell and heard it echoing through the vast hall. A few moments later there was the sound of a bolt being pulled back, and Stella opened the door, first just a crack, then, when she saw Jean, she opened it wide. She was wearing a simple but expensive black dress and a pearl necklace which accentuated her splendid figure and the delicate, doe-like curve of her neck. The fact that she was not made up and obviously not expecting guests only accentuated her patrician beauty, which as always left Jean feeling plain, dumpy and plebeian.

"Jean Montrose! What a surprise! Don't stand there, do come in!" She stood aside and Jean stepped past her.

"We're in the living room," she said, and pushed the door open.

With every fiber of her body screaming at her to get out, Jean meekly followed Stella into the huge room. Even from the door she could feel the heat from the fireplace, where two great pine logs were crackling merrily.

Alexis looked over from a table at the far end of the room. In front of him was a computer terminal which looked strangely out of place in the old baronial setting.

"Alexis is putting my accounts on the computer," she said. "He's terribly clever; I don't understand a thing about it." Stella smiled. "Do sit down." She indicated the couch in front of the fire. Jean sat down on the edge of the luxurious cushions, nervously pulling the hem of her plain gray skirt over he knees. She should never have come here dressed the way she was; Steven would never have allowed it . . .

Alexis got up and came over. God, he was handsome, like a film star, Jean thought admiringly. He was tanned, slim, with an elegantly cut suit that must have cost the earth. No wonder that Stella . . .

Jean put her handbag down by her feet, where Doug had told her to put it. She felt as if it were hot, radioactive, beaming a message to announce its presence. Jean expected Stella or Alexis to grab the bag, rip it open, pull out the little black box and start shouting accusations at her.

"Well," said Alexis, smiling. "I hope you don't know of anybody sick in this house." There was a polite question in his voice, and Jean felt her mouth going dry. How on earth was she going to say what she had to say? Stella saved her.

"Would you like a cup of tea?" she asked. "Alexis just made some."

In her nervousness, Jean almost said, yes, I know, I heard you tell him the kettle was boiling, but instead she smiled and said, "Yes, please, I'd love some." Stella went out of the room. Alexis asked how she was, how Steven and the children were. Jean was surprised he remembered Seven's name; they'd only met once, at Magnus's funeral, and then only for a moment.

Stella came through carrying a tray with a lovely Georgian silver teapot and creamer, Meissen cups and saucers and a plateful of chocolate biscuits. They were Penguins, her favorite brand. She eyed them while Stella poured, but decided she wouldn't be able to swallow it if she took one. After they all had a cup of tea in their hands, Jean decided it was time to take the bull by the horns.

"How do you both feel about Graham Ross's arrest?" she asked. The words came out awkwardly because her mouth was so dry. She could sense the sudden chilling of the atmosphere.

"It's very sad," said Stella, rather too quickly. "But he killed my baby, and possibly my husband, and he's obviously totally insane, so I suppose I'm happy he's in prison and not still living there . . ." she gestured in the direction of the Rosses' house.

Jean sat silently for a moment, stirring the sugar in the cup. She could feel their eyes on her, waiting for her to say something.

"Yes," she said. "I agree with you. I think he probably is insane.'

Alexis smiled. Jean looked at her cup. It had a delightful pattern of handpainted flowers and birds, and a delicate gold stripe along the handle. It was old Meissen, quite priceless if the set was intact.

"But, as we all know, he didn't actually kill anybody, although he certainly tried to kill Evelyn."

Jean looked up. Both Alexis and Stella had a frozen expression on their faces. There was a rattling noise from Stella's cup, and she put it down hastily, trying to control the shaking in her hand.

Jean put down her cup too. "Why don't we speak quite frankly," she said, "and get everything out in the open. It'll be much easier for everybody that way. If we do that, I think I may be able to help you."

Stella started to say something, but Alexis put a firm restraining hand on her shoulder.

"Let's just hear what Dr. Montrose has to say." He spoke very calmly, as if they were talking abou something quite unimportant, like the latest show at the theater.

"All right," said Jean, sitting back and folding her hands in her lap. "I'll tell you." Suddenly she didn't feel nervous anymore, she just wanted to get this over and done with, then she could go back to the surgery. Helen was covering for her once again, and Jean was uncomfortable about that; she felt she was really imposing on her partner.

"First," she said, looking at Stella. "Let's talk about Magnus. Let's talk about the people who could have killed Magnus. Dempster. He was the obvious first choice. But we know from the barman at the bar he was at, I forget its name . . ."

"Aladdin's Cave," said Alexis. His voice was flat, and his eyes watchful.

"Right, Aladdin's Cave. The barman said he was there at the time Magnus was killed, and others confirmed it. So Dempster couldn't have done it." Jean's voice became slightly indignant. "Not that he ever would have, the poor man, he couldn't have killed a fly, the condition he was in . . ."

"More tea?" asked Stella. Her eyes were bright, and her voice had the overtones of early hysteria.

"No thanks . . . And of course Graham didn't do it. He was at home with Evelyn, planning to take her out to lunch . . ." Jean shook her head. "Poor Graham . . . Anyway you probably know he was released this morning for lack of evidence."

She looked at Stella and then at Alexis for confirmation, but they were staring at her as if they had been hypnotized.

"Amanda. Now for a while I thought she had done it, for various reasons . . ." Jean looked at Stella, who had her hand up to her mouth and was biting her index finger. "Of course, that morning she'd gone over to see her friend Keith, and by the time she came back the baby was already dead."

Alexis moved restlessly. "Dr. Montrose, this is all very interesting, but really, if you'd like to get to the point of this discussion we'd appreciate it." He looked at his watch; it was gold, with a square face like the Cartier watches Jean had seen in the advertisements.

"I'm sorry," she said contritely. "You're quite right, I was just rambling on . . . You see, once I had the proof, everything fell into place. There was nobody else who could have killed Magnus, except Stella."

She turned to Stella apologetically. "It wasn't your fault that you didn't love Magnus. Bonding between a baby and its mother normally takes place in the first few days after birth, and of course during that critical period you were still ill, Magnus was on a respirator, so you couldn't even see the baby, let alone touch and hold him . . ."

"I didn't just not love him," whispered Stella. "I *hated* him. He messed up my whole body even before he was born. He almost killed me . . ." Alexis put a hand on her thigh for a moment. Jean didn't know what message was transmitted, but Stella sat back quickly and was silent.

"Yes, I can understand that," said Jean gently. "And because he got in the way more than anybody, even more than Dempster. I mean got between you and Alexis."

Alexis put his hand back on Stella's thigh, but this time the message was protective, comforting.

Jean looked from Alexis to Stella. "I suppose the two of you were in love long before you married

Dempster.'' Her tone was mild, with an implied question.

"Well, just between the three of us here, yes, we were,'' said Alexis. "But my father decided she would marry Dempster and carry on the family name.''

"That must have been when you fought with Dempster, up in Aberdeen. You certainly got a very good plastic surgeon.''

Alexis touched the scar on the side of his nose. "Not too many people notice,'' he murmured.

"Lord Aviemore must have applied a lot of pressure,'' said Jean wonderingly. Things must be very different in those aristocratic circles.

"No, not much,'' said Alexis, trying to hide his bitterness. "Just the threat of disinheritance, minor things like that . . .''

He paused for a second, staring into the fire. "You don't know my father. What he wants, he gets, and God help anybody who stands in his way.''

"So you just had to go along with it, I suppose.''

"Yes. And Stella liked Dempster at the time, and she also liked the idea of becoming the Countess Aviemore when the old man died . . .''

"Come on, Alexis, that's not fair!'' protested Stella. "You know exactly how it was.''

Jean caught the glance that passed between the two of them. Poor Stella, she thought, it must have been very difficult for her, having to marry somebody she didn't love, a man who turned out to be a spendthrift, a drunk, and a maker of enemies.

"If you really must proceed with this . . . imaginative tale, Dr. Montrose, I wish you'd get on with it,'' cut in Alexis. He was impeccably polite, but there was a chilling undertone to his voice.

"Yes, of course." Jean spoke rapidly, licking her dry lips every few moments. "To come back to Magnus. Apart from you, Stella, there was nobody at home. Dempster was in Leith, as you knew, and Amanda had slipped off to visit Keith Armstrong. You got back from your shopping before Amanda, and the baby was alone, probably screaming his head off . . ."

Jean could feel the pressure of their eyes on her, but she went on in her calm, matter-of-fact voice. "And it was the right moment, so your head and your heart worked together . . ." Jean could not help shuddering at the recollection of that dreadful round stain on the wall.

Stella made a quiet moaning sound, and her dark eyes showed how close she was to panic.

Jean waited for her to say something, but Stella just kept staring, a mute plead in her eye, like an animal knowing it was being led to the slaughter. Jean's voice shook with compassion for a second.

"When Amanda came back from seeing Keith, she knew you'd done it, and also knew that if she'd stayed at home it wouldn't have happened. She couldn't handle the guilt, and that's why she cut her wrists and finally jumped."

Stella flashed a panicky glance at Alexis, but his eyes were as hard as marble, fixed on Jean.

"Don't think I don't blame myself for Amanda's death," said Jean, almost in a whisper. "I'll never forgive myself . . ."

"Can you prove all this?" asked Alexis. His voice was quite different from before; soft, each word clearly enunciated, and quite frightening.

Jean ignored his question and went on addressing Stella. "You proved that Alexis was in Inverness by getting me to phone him. That way he couldn't be implicated in the baby's death, and everybody would assume the killer was also responsible for Dempster's death.''

Jean took a deep breath, marshaling her thoughts the way they had come together last night as the sleepless hours went by.

''Go on,'' commanded Alexis, stirring the fire with the heavy iron poker. Jean tried to ignore the weapon; there was no way that Douglas and his people could see the danger she was in, unless she screamed for help.

''When you told Inspector Niven that Dempster went drinking in Glasgow, you knew perfectly well that he always went to a pub in Leith called the Aladdin's Cave. Two days later, Alexis went there, put the sleeping pills in Dempster's drink, drove him to within a couple of miles of Perth, took him out of the car, ran him over, then rolled his body down the embankment.''

Alexis's pale eyes glowed like the coals of the fire, and Jean's mouth went dry again. She cleared her throat, and went doggedly on. She had to convince them that there was no point trying to deny their guilt.

''You see, I know about the pills,'' she said quietly, ''because those were the sleeping pills I gave Stella and Amanda. They're a brand new Swiss product, a sample given to us to test in our practice. They are not commercially available, and I hadn't given them to anybody else. We did a special analysis of Dempster's blood to confirm it. It showed that he'd been given a large dose, enough to knock him out, especially with all the alcohol he must have had on board.''

"Very convincing," said Alexis, in a sneering tone, "but you haven't said anything about a motive. Why should Stella and I . . ." His hand tightened warningly on Stella's thigh. "What reason would we have to do such a dreadful thing?"

"Well, Alexis, first you and Stella were in love and wanted to be openly together. When Dempster started to drink so heavily, because he knew what was going on between you, you concocted this plan . . . And of course, on your father's death you'll become Lord Aviemore, and inherit all the money and the estates that go with the title, instead of it all going to Dempster and then Magnus . . ."

Suddenly Jean had a terrible feeling that something was going wrong; Alexis's mouth opened, showing his white teeth, and Stella stood up, pale as death. Alexis started to make a rattling noise in the back of his throat, and it took Jean a moment to realize that he was laughing, a ghastly, incongruous laugh that sent shivers down her spine.

With an effort, Alexis regained control of himself. "It's an interesting theory," he said. "Have you had the chance to discuss it with . . . anyone? You said the pieces all fell together last night."

Jean eyed the poker in his hand; it was the same one she'd picked up the day Magnus was killed, thinking the killer might still be in the house.

Stella was shaking. "No," she said to Alexis. "Don't do anything . . ." Her voice was high-pitched, cracked. Jean would not have recognized it. Alexis didn't take his eyes off Jean.

"We can't let her . . . She'll destroy us when she tells the police. We can't just let her go."

With a fatalistic horror Jean watched him raise the heavy poker. Everything seemed to be happening in slow motion. She saw his expression change and a look of pure hatred came on to his face. He must have looked like that when he ran over Dempster, he must look like that whenever anyone tries to foil him . . .

Alexis was much stronger than she was; she would be dead before she got out of her chair, so there was no point in struggling. Anyway she'd asked for it, she was trying to destroy them. Standing over her, Alexis could see that she was paralyzed with fear and wasn't going to move, so he adjusted his grip, holding the poker with both hands behind his head, then it started on its final, fatal swing . . .

Both of Jean's feet came up at the same time and hit their target with almost mathematical precision. After all, in medical school, Jean had spent an entire year learning the most minute details of human anatomy.

Alexis doubled up just as Douglas Niven, closely followed by Constable Jamieson, erupted into the room. The rest of it was just a blur to Jean; Alexis had stopped breathing from the kick in the groin, and Jean spent several minutes resuscitating him. For one ghastly moment she thought she might have killed him.

Doug and Constable Jamieson quickly handcuffed both Stella and Alexis, although Jean couldn't imagine that poor Stella would be able to do anybody any harm at this point. Jamieson called on his radio, and a few moments later two female officers came in and took charge of Stella. Jean knew both of them, but was upset by everything that had happened that she was barely able to return their greeting.

They all waited for a while until Alexis could stand up, then they led the pair outside. Jean slipped out behind them, got into her car and drove quietly off, feeling terrible.

When she got home, all she wanted to do was go up to her room, go to bed, and try to go to sleep, the only way she could even temporarily get away from the dreadful events of the day. Why ever had she been so foolish as to get involved in this case? Why couldn't she leave well enough alone, stick to being a doctor, and leave the detecting to the detectives?

Fiona and Lisbie were in the entrance hall, looking as if they were waiting for her.

"Mum," said Fiona in a carefully controlled voice, "Dad's coming home."

Jean's hand leapt to her mouth.

"He said he's never going to leave again," said Lisbie, beaming from ear to ear.

Jean was barely able to speak. "When?" she whispered.

"In about ten minutes," said Fiona.

"Oh my goodness, I'd better run upstairs and change!" said Jean, feeling suddenly panicky. "I can't let him see me looking like this."

Don't miss Dr. Jean Montrose's next exciting mystery adventure, *A Fiery Hint of Murder*, coming to you from Signet Books in June 1993.

Chapter One

Visiting parents usually had trouble finding St. Jude's Academy; not that they came in droves, as most of the boys had been sent there by parents who wanted to see as little of their offspring as possible. Seven and one-tenth miles out of Perth, on the Dunkeld road, said the brochure; there was a sign warning of a sharp bend in the road, and just beyond that, on the left, was the narrow side road, unrecorded in AA maps and marked only by a white placard with black letters which read: ST. JUDE'S ACADEMY, and below, in smaller letters, EST. 1978. The road was about a quarter of a mile long, now gray and dusty from the drought, lined on the left by a low drystone dike, crumbling in places, and surmounted by occasional splashes of yellow whin. Beyond the dike was a scruffy wood of mixed pine and spindly silver birch, which thinned out to be replaced by furze and some scattered clumps of heather nearer the gates.

The gates of St. Jude's Academy dated back to the original construction, when the house had the grand-sounding name of Muirs of Strathtay. Their iron tracery was elaborate, but even when fully open there was only a narrow space between the gates, barely wide enough for a small van to pass through. The overall first impression was of a constrictive meanness, well beyond the normal prudent economy that was always well respected in these parts.

The narrow gravel drive up to the front of the house was lined on each side by a two-foot-wide strip of dried brown grass; the tracks of cars and vans left shallow, elongated ruts on the edge of the crumbling drive, now dried out and crazed with the heat and drought, with tire marks emerging from the dried puddles like dinosaur tracks coming out of a mesozoic lake. The drive expanded into a cramped courtyard at the front of the house, leaving barely enough space for a vehicle to turn without backing into the dark, ghostly rhododendrons surrounding the yard. To the right of the house, a few Douglas firs had been cut down to make room for a parking area, and the spaces were jammed together so closely there was barely room to open the car doors.

The finest feature of the house was undoubtedly the facade; built around 1890 by a Dundee industrialist, it incorporated granite turrets, crenelations, and all the useless but impressive embellishments of the full-blown Scottish Baronial style. Inside, however, it was a different story: the house was crammed with a multitude of mean, dark rooms with low ceilings and ancient and unreliable plumbing. It was just the kind of house a man brought up in the slums of Dundee might build, a small mill-owner suddenly made rich by a fortuitous combination of tight-fisted exploitation and economic factors over which he had neither understanding nor control.

It was in every way the ideal place to turn into a private school.

At the back of the building, on the second floor,

Mr. Morgan Stroud was taking a class in interme-
diate physics. Mr. Stroud was only about thirty years
old, but the lines of petulance and failure were already on his face, and self-indulgence was evident
in his corpulent figure. Not that Morgan Stroud
didn't enjoy his work as a teacher; indeed he did,
and he was particularly enjoying himself now.

"Mackay, if you think you could stay awake long
enough to give us the benefit of your wisdom . . ." Mr.
Stroud's eyes flickered over his eight pupils and landed
on Neil Mackay, one of the few day-boys, who had
come to the school only that term. Neil had a stammer
which surfaced only when he was under stress; Morgan
Stroud was well aware of this. ". . . And give us your
definition, and I expect an erudite and thoughtful one,
of the term *energy*, as it applies to physics."

Neil, a tall lanky boy who had difficulty fitting
into the cramped, old-fashioned wooden desks, went
red in the face, not from ignorance, but because of
the effort he would have to make to get his words
out in a coherent form.

"Energy is the capacity to do work," he started,
confidently enough. "There are three kinds, mechanical, chemical, and p-p-p-potential . . ."

"I suppose *p-p-p-potential* would be your favorite," cut in Mr. Stroud with a sneer that looked as
if it had been etched into his face. "If you define
'potential' as 'in the future, with no present sign of
activity.' "

There was a mild giggle from Dick Prothero, the
class sycophant, and Mr. Stroud glanced benignly at
him.

"Well, is that all? Mechanical, chemical and p-p-
p-potential?" He mimicked Neil's stammer and

stared at the boy with an expression of overt disgust before addressing the rest of the class. "Anybody?"

"Thermal?" suggested Billy Wilson, sitting next to Neil, hoping to get Stroud's malignant focus away from his friend.

"Well, finally we have someone who pays attention during my classes," said Stroud, with an expression of bored surprise. "Yes, indeed, thermal energy, the energy of heat and light, including the beneficent radiations from the sun and other warm bodies . . ." He paused for a moment. "We shall ignore for a moment, no doubt to your deep distress, other forms of energy such as electrical, nuclear, etcetera, and concentrate on thermal energy . . ."

"I'd like to concentrate some thermal energy on him," muttered Neil, looking sideways at Billy. Stroud heard him and, quick as a viper, turned, then very deliberately walked down between the two rows of desks and stopped in front of Neil. He paused, his eyes fixed on the boy with a vicious intensity.

"Stand up, scum!" He barked.

Neil, his face white, stood up.

"And what makes you, a day-boy, think you can interrupt my class at will?" he asked. "Is it because your father is so far behind on the payment of your school fees, perhaps?"

Neil stood stone-still, his lower lip quivering in spite of himself.

"Well, aren't you going to answer? Are you proposing to compound insolence with that stubborn impertinence which you have no doubt inherited?"

Billy made a quick move to grab Neil's arm, which he was about to raise, and Morgan Stroud smiled.

"Now then, don't interfere, Wilson," he said, quietly, but with a chilling intensity, not taking his eyes off Neil. "I'll deal with you later. Meanwhile, if Mackay here wishes to strike me . . . Go ahead, boy, go ahead!" He stared at Neil, taunting, daring him. Neil didn't move, but his fingernails dug hard into his palms.

"We hear that your father is having some business problems, is that it?" went on Stroud, relentlessly. "And perhaps he has these problems because he's like you." He still didn't take his eyes off Neil's face; he was positively relishing the boy's humiliation. "Mendel's laws of inheritance, as I'm sure you will agree, have a great deal of validity. Are you aware that stupidity is an inherited factor, recognizable by a low brow and small, ill-shaped head such as yours?"

There was a silence, a painful stillness in the class.

"Sit down, you . . . Darwinian reject! said Stroud finally, and returned to the front of his class. "Now, for those of you provided by nature with adequate neuronal equipment, let us get back to the mysteries of thermal energy . . ."

Stroud felt better now; the venting of his feelings on Neil Mackay had relieved some pent-up tension within him, and the rest of the class went smoothly enough, although he was aware of a simmering hatred emanating from the direction of Neil Mackay.

At this point Stroud had to refer to his notes. Recently he had been having headaches and some difficulty concentrating, and occasionally lost his place or the thread of an argument; he really would have to do something about it.

"Transfer of heat energy," he said, almost talking to himself, then recovered his normal hectoring tone. "You there, in the corner, what's your name, Drummond. How is thermal energy transmitted from one object to another?''

''Conduction?'' asked Terry Drummond, a small, bright boy who blinked frequently behind his round National Health glasses.

''Good. Conduction is transfer of heat by direct contact, right, correct.'' Stroud felt Neil Mackay's smoldering eyes fixed on him, and they were beginning to make him feel uncomfortable. ''And other methods of heat transfer? Anyone? Mackay? You look surprised, as if a thought had somehow inadvertently entered your head . . . No?''

''Radiation,'' said Neil, still looking at Stroud. ''Transfer of heat energy from a distance.''

''Very good!'' said Stroud, oozing sarcasm. ''Can anybody give me an example?''

''The sun,'' said Billy Wilson.

''Wonderful!'' said Stroud, ''Maybe you two boys should form a traveling brains trust, touring Africa, perhaps. Just as long as it was far from these . . .'' he looked around the cramped room with disdain, ''these hallowed halls, whose ancient traditions date back to, when it was, 1978?''

''How about psychic energy?'' asked Neil, suddenly seeming to come to life. His eyes were glowing in a way Stroud had never seen before. ''Can one or more people concentrate enough energy from their minds to heat up an object? Even make it burst into flames? I read in a book that . . .''

''Of course not! Nonsense! Pure rubbish!'' said Stroud, irritated at the intrusion of such an unscientific notion. ''This is a *physics* class we are conducting here, not some kind of . . . supernatural . . . seance!''

''But if it *can* happen, doesn't that bring it into

the world of physics, of reality?'' Neil Mackay was standing up now, and his voice was loud, with a strange, resonant quality to it, and no trace of stammer. Everyone there could feel the power, the energy radiating from him.

At that moment the bell rang for the end of the period, and the boys instantly poised themselves to leave the room, waiting for his word. Stroud looked at them with an expression of undisguised contempt.

''Saint Jude's . . .'' he said slowly, his eyes moving from one boy to the next. ''I can see why your parents would send you to a school named after the patron saint of lost causes.''

He paused, still looking at them. ''Now get out,'' he said. ''You all disgust me more than I can tell you.''

After the boys had gathered their books and left the classroom, Stroud felt suddenly tired, used up. Teaching was an exhausting business. Psychic energy, forsooth! Actually, he thought, I could use some of that myself. He looked at his watch and hesitated. There would be just time to go into Perth and see the doctor before his next class, which started in an hour. If there was a queue at the surgery, he'd ask to be seen first. After all, he had a job to do, unlike the layabouts and smelly women who normally frequented her surgery, with their hordes of dirty, snuffly, disgusting children . . .

Neil Mackay and his friend Billy Wilson walked to their next class and waited with the other dozen or so boys for the teacher to arrive. Billy felt anxious, sensing Neil's boiling rage. ''Don't pay any attention to him,'' he said. ''Everybody knows what a pig he is . . .''

"It doesn't bother me," said Neil, "but it's going to upset my father."

"Then don't tell him," suggested Billy sensibly.

"We have a deal," replied Neil slowly. "We tell each other everything that happens, the good and the bad. We've done that ever since my mother died."

"I'd still not tell him," said Billy. "My God, if it was *me*, my father would come to the school and kill Stroud with is bare hands." Billy was exaggerating; his father, a distinguished actor and the most gentle of men, wouldn't have dreamed of taking direct action of that kind, however severe the provocation. But Neil's father was not gentle, not by any means. He was an exboxer, unsettled by a failing business, and saddled with a very short temper . . .

Two men stood at the window of the teachers' common room on the second floor.

"There goes that bastard Stroud, slipping off early," said the younger one, a muscular, athletic-looking man with carefully styled hair. Without even realizing he was doing it, he cracked the knuckles of his left hand, one after the other. The men were looking down at the portly, prematurely balding figure hurrying across the yard to the car park.

"Now then, George," said the other, a sturdy, middle-aged man. "It's really time you got over your resentment." He puffed a great cloud of smoke from a well-worn cherry-wood pipe. "It's doing *him* no harm, but it's eating you up. Forget it; you're wasting your time and your energies."

"It's easy for you to say, Angus," replied George Elmslie. "He didn't do it to you, and anyway you could leave here today and go and teach anywhere you wanted." George looked over at Angus Townes.

"You know, it really beats me why you ever came to work in a rat-hole like this."

Almost as if he sensed that he was being discussed, Morgan Stroud looked up at the window of the common room and saw the two men. For a moment a strange expression flickered over his face, an ugly combination of dislike and fear, but at that distance, no one could have told at which of the two men the look was directed.

Angus Townes and George Elmslie watched Stroud get into his car and start it, and their eyes followed as his dusty blue Ford Escort negotiated the sharp turn into the drive. The car vanished between the dark rhododendron bushes, one back wheel sliding momentarily off the narrow drive and raising a cloud of yellowish dust. Both men stood there as the dust slowly settled, but neither of them said anything; they were too deeply immersed in their own thoughts.

New from the #1 bestselling author of *Communion*—
a novel of psychological terror and demonic possession. . . .
"A triumph."—Peter Straub

UNHOLY
FIRE
Whitley Strieber

Father John Rafferty is a dedicated priest with only one
temptation—the beautiful young woman he has been coun
seling, and who is found brutally murdered in his Green
wich Village church. He is forced to face his greatest tes
of faith when the NYPD uncovers her sexually twisted
hidden life, and the church becomes the site for increas
ingly violent acts. Father Rafferty knows he must over
come his personal horror to unmask a murderer who
wears an angel's face. This chilling novel will hold you in
thrall as it explores the powerful forces of evil lurking
where we least expect them. "Gyrates with evil energy
. . . fascinating church intrigue."—*Kirkus Reviews*